I saw Aunt En
door. "Birds," sh
"Get in this hou
ease."

"They're not birds," Mom said. She opened the
screen.

Ellen squealed once as the doorway turned white
with wings. When her face reappeared, we could see
the peevishness and fright leaving her.

"They're little people," she said. "Aren't they
lovely?"

We all crowded into the kitchen. It was a busy
place. Across the ceiling wheeled dozens of angels,
darting, touching, staring, trilling. The five of us
stared at each other . . .

—from "A Plethora of Angels" by Robert Sampson

DON'T MISS . . .

HORSES!
Twelve Tales of Fantasy's Most Majestic Animals!
FEATURING URSULA K. LE GUIN, LISA TUTTLE,
HOWARD WALDROP, AND MANY MORE . . .

INVADERS!
Fifteen Fantastic Stories of Aliens on Earth!
FEATURING OCTAVIA E. BUTLER,
FREDERIK POHL, JAMES TIPTREE, JR.,
HOWARD WALDROP, AND MANY MORE . . .

Magic Tales Anthologies
Edited by Jack Dann & Gardner Dozois

UNICORNS!
MAGICATS!
BESTIARY!
MERMAIDS!
SORCERERS!
DEMONS!
DOGTALES!
SEASERPENTS!
DINOSAURS!
LITTLE PEOPLE!
MAGICATS II
UNICORNS II
DRAGONS!
INVADERS!
HORSES!
ANGELS!

Edited by Terri Windling

FAERY!

ANGELS!

EDITED BY
JACK DANN & GARDNER DOZOIS

ACE BOOKS, NEW YORK

This book is an Ace original edition,
and has never been previously published.

ANGELS!

An Ace Book / published by arrangement with
the editors

PRINTING HISTORY
Ace edition / June 1995

ISBN: 0-441-00220-X

ACE®
Ace Books are published by The Berkley Publishing Group,
200 Madison Avenue, New York, NY 10016.
ACE and the "A" design are trademarks
belonging to Charter Communications, Inc.

PRINTED IN THE UNITED STATES OF AMERICA

10 9 8 7 6 5 4 3 2 1

ACKNOWLEDGMENTS

The editors would like to thank the following people for their help and support:

Susan Casper, Janeen Webb, Janet Kagan, Ricky Kagan, George Zebrowski, Peter Nicholls, Kristine Kathryn Rusch, Michael Swanwick, Ellen Datlow, Sheila Williams, Ian Randal Strock, Scott Towner, and special thanks to our own editors, Susan Allison and Ginjer Buchanan.

Contents

BASILEUS
Robert Silverberg 1

ANGELICA
Jane Yolen 21

ANGELS
Bruce McAllister 27

IF ANGELS ATE APPLES (poem)
Geoffrey A. Landis 39

ALFRED
Lisa Goldstein 41

A PLETHORA OF ANGELS
Robert Sampson 57

THE MAN WHO LOVED THE FAIOLI
Roger Zelazny 79

UPON THE DULL EARTH
Philip K. Dick 89

ANGEL
Pat Cadigan 113

CURSE OF THE ANGEL'S WIFE (poem)
Bruce Boston 131

SLEEPERS AWAKE
Jamil Nasir 133

AND THE ANGELS SING
Kate Wilhelm 153

GRAVE ANGELS
Richard Kearns 175

ALL VOWS
Esther M. Friesner 209

ANGELS!

Basileus
by
Robert Silverberg

Robert Silverberg is one of the most famous SF writers of modern times, with dozens of novels, anthologies, and collections to his credit. Silverberg has won five Nebula Awards and four Hugo Awards. His novels include Dying Inside, Lord Valentine's Castle, The Book of Skulls, Downward to the Earth, Tower of Glass, The World Inside, Born with the Dead, Shadrach in the Furnace, Tom O'Bedlam, Star of Gypsies, *and* At Winter's End. *His collections include* Unfamiliar Territory, Capricorn Games, Majipoor Chronicles, The Best of Robert Silverberg, At the Conglomeroid Cocktail Party, *and* Beyond the Safe Zone. *His most recent books are* Nightfall *and* Child of Time, *two novel-length expansions of famous Isaac Asimov stories; the novels* The Face of the Waters *and* Kingdoms of the Wall; *and a massive retrospective collection,* The Collected Stories of Robert Silverberg, Volume One: Secret Sharers. *For many years he edited the prestigious anthology series* New Dimensions, *and has recently, along with his wife, writer Karen Haber, taken over the editing of the* Universe *anthology series. He lives in Oakland, California.*

In Christian lore, demons are literally "fallen angels," angels who have opted against God. The difference between demons and angels is thus a purely doctrinal *difference . . . so that one might fairly say that a demon is just an angel with a bad attitude, one who has declared for evil rather than for good.*

Count them how you will, though, one thing that is certain about angels, fallen or not, is that there are a lot *of them. One rough count, by Kabbalists in the fourteenth century, estimated that there were 301,655,722 angels. That's quite a few angels to keep tabs on, so many that perhaps the best way to keep track of them all would be to use a computer—or perhaps, as the story that follows demonstrates, that would turn out to be a very bad idea indeed . . .*

In the shimmering lemon-yellow October light, Cunningham touches the keys of his terminal and summons angels. An instant to load the program, an instant to bring the file up, and there they are, ready to spout from the screen at his command: Apollyon, Anauel, Uriel, and all the rest. Uriel is the angel of thunder and terror; Apollyon is the Destroyer, the angel of the bottomless pit; Anauel is the angel of bankers and commission brokers. Cunningham is fascinated by the multifarious duties and tasks, both exalted and humble, that are assigned to the angels. "Every visible thing in the world is put under the charge of an angel," said St. Augustine in *The Eight Questions*.

Cunningham has 1,114 angels in his computer now. He adds a few more each night, though he knows that he has a long way to go before he has them all. In the fourteenth century the number of angels was reckoned by the Kabbalists, with some precision, at 301,655,722. Albertus Magnus had earlier calculated that each choir of angels held 6,666 legions, and each legion 6,666 angels; even without knowing the number of choirs, one can see that that produces rather a higher total. And in the Talmud, Rabbi Jochanan proposed that new angels are born "with every utterance that goes forth from the mouth of the Holy One, blessed be He."

If Rabbi Jochanan is correct, the number of angels is infinite. Cunningham's personal computer, though it has extraordinary add-on memory capacity and is capable, if he chooses, of tapping into the huge mainframe machines of the Defense Department, has no very practical way of handling an infinity. But he is doing his best. To have 1,114 angels on line already, after only eight months of part-time programming, is no small achievement.

One of his favorites of the moment is Harahel, the angel of archives, libraries, and rare cabinets. Cunningham has designated Harahel also the angel of computers: it seems appropriate. He invokes Harahel often, to discuss the evolving niceties of data processing with him. But he has many other favorites, and his tastes run somewhat to the sinister: Azrael, the angel of death, for example, and Arioch, the angel of vengeance, and Zebuleon, one of the nine angels who will govern at the end of the world. It is Cunningham's job, from eight to four every working day, to devise programs for the interception of incoming Soviet nuclear warheads, and that, perhaps, has inclined him toward the more apocalyptic members of the angelic host.

He invokes Harahel now. He has bad news for him. The invocation that he uses is a standard one that he found in Arthur Edward Waite's *The Lemegeton, or The Lesser Key of Solomon*, and he has dedicated one of his function keys to its text, so that a single keystroke suffices to load it. "I do invocate, conjure, and command thee, O thou Spirit N, to appear and to show thyself visibly unto me before this Circle in fair and comely shape," is the way it begins, and it proceeds to utilize various secret and potent names of God in the summoning of Spirit N—such names as Zabaoth and Elion and, of course, Adonai—and it concludes, "I do potently exorcise thee that thou appearest here to fulfill my will in all things which seem good unto me. Wherefore, come thou, visibly, peaceably, and affably, now, without delay to manifest that which I desire, speaking with a clear and perfect voice, intelligibly, and to mine understanding." All that takes but a microsecond, and another moment to read in the name of Harahel as Spirit N, and there the angel is on the screen.

"I am here at your summons," he announces expectantly.

Cunningham works with his angels from five to seven every evening. Then he has dinner. He lives alone, in a neat little flat a few blocks west of the Bayshore Freeway, and does not spend much of his time socializing. He thinks of himself as a pleasant man, a sociable man, and he may very well be right about that, but the pattern of his life has been a solitary one. He is thirty-seven years old, five feet eleven, with red hair, pale blue eyes, and a light dusting of freckles on his cheeks. He did his undergraduate work at Cal Tech, his postgraduate studies at Stanford, and for the last nine years he has been involved in ultrasensitive military-computer projects in northern California. He has never married. Sometimes he works with his angels again after dinner, from eight to ten, but hardly ever any later than that. At ten he goes to bed. He is a very methodical person.

He has given Harahel the physical form of his own first computer, a little Radio Shack TRS-80, with wings flanking the screen. He had thought originally to make the appearance of his angels more abstract—showing Harahel as a sheaf of kilobytes, for example—but like many of Cunningham's best and most austere ideas, it had turned out impractical in the execution, since abstract concepts did not translate well into graphics for him.

"I want to notify you," Cunningham says, "of a shift in jurisdiction." He speaks English with his angels. He has it on good, though apocryphal, authority that the primary language of the angels is Hebrew, but his computer's audio algorithms have no Hebrew capacity, nor does Cunningham. But they speak English readily enough with him: they have no choice. "From now on," Cunningham tells Harahel, "your domain is limited to hardware only."

Angry green lines rapidly cross and recross Harahel's screen, "By whose authority do you—"

"It isn't a question of authority," Cunningham replies smoothly. "It's a question of precision. I've just read Vretil into the data base, and I have to code his functions. He's the recording angel, after all. So, to some degree, then, he overlaps your territory."

"Ah," says Harahel, sounding melancholy. "I was hoping you wouldn't bother about him."

"How can I overlook such an important angel? 'Scribe of the knowledge of the Most High,' according to the Book of Enoch. 'Keeper of the heavenly books and records.' 'Quicker in wisdom than the other archangels.'"

"If he's so quick," says Harahel sullenly, "give *him* the hardware. That's what governs the response time, you know."

"I understand. But he maintains the lists. That's data base."

"And where does the data base live? The hardware!"

"Listen, this isn't easy for me," Cunningham says. "But I have to be fair. I know you'll agree that some division of responsibilities is in order. And I'm giving him all data bases and related software. You keep the rest."

"Screens. Terminals. CPUs. Big deal."

"But without you, he's nothing, Harahel. Anyway, you've always been in charge of cabinets, haven't you?"

"And archives and libraries," the angel says. "Don't forget that."

"I'm not. But what's a library? Is it the books and shelves and stacks, or the words on the pages? We have to distinguish the container from the thing contained."

"A grammarian," Harahel sighs. "A hairsplitter. A casuist."

"Look, Vretil wants the hardware, too. But he's willing to compromise. Are you?"

"You start to sound less and less like our programmer and more and more like the Almighty every day," says Harahel

"Don't blaspheme," Cunningham tells him. "Please. Is it agreed? Hardware only?"

"You win," says the angel. "But you always do, naturally."

Naturally. Cunningham is the one with his hands on the keyboard, controlling things. The angels, though they are eloquent enough and have distinct and passionate personalities, are mere magnetic impulses deep within. In any contest with Cunningham they don't stand a chance. Cunningham, though he tries always to play the game by the rules, knows that, and so do they.

It makes him uncomfortable to think about it, but the role he plays is definitely godlike in all essential ways. He puts the angels into the computer; he gives them their tasks, their personalities, and their physical appearances; he summons them or leaves them uncalled, as he wishes.

A godlike role, yes. But Cunningham resists confronting that notion. He does not believe he is trying to be God; he does not even want to think about God. His family had been on comfortable terms with God—Uncle Tim was a priest, there was an archbishop somewhere back a few generations, his parents and sisters moved cozily within the divine presence as within a warm bath—but he himself, unable to quantify the Godhead, preferred to sidestep any thought of it. There were other, more immediate matters to engage his concern. His mother had wanted him to go into the priesthood, of all things, but Cunningham had averted that by demonstrating so visible and virtuosic a skill at mathematics that even she could see he was destined for science. Then she had prayed for a Nobel Prize in physics for him; but he had preferred computer technology. "Well," she said, "a Nobel in computers. I ask the Virgin daily."

"There's no Nobel in computers, Mom," he told her. But he suspects she still offers novenas for it.

The angel project had begun as a lark, but had escalated swiftly into an obsession. He was reading Gustav Davidson's old *Dictionary of Angels,* and when he came upon the description of the angel Adramelech, who had rebelled with Satan and had been cast from heaven, Cunningham thought it might be amusing to build a computer simulation and talk with him. Davidson said that Adramelech was sometimes shown as a winged and bearded lion, and sometimes as a mule with feathers, and sometimes as a peacock, and that one poet had described him as "the enemy of God, greater in malice, guile, ambition, and mischief than Satan, a fiend more curst, a deeper hypocrite." That was appealing. Well, why not build him? The graphics were easy—Cunningham chose the winged-lion form—but getting the personality constructed involved a month of intense labor and some consultations with the artificial-intelligence people over at Kestrel Institute. But finally Adramelech was on line, suave and diabolical, talking amiably of his days as an Assyrian god and his conversations with Beelzebub, who had named him Chancellor of the Order of the Fly (Grand Cross).

Next, Cunningham did Asmodeus, another fallen angel, said to be the inventor of dancing, gambling, music, drama, French fashions, and other frivolities. Cunningham made him look like a very dashing Beverly Hills Iranian, with a pair of tiny wings at his collar. It was Asmodeus who suggested that Cunningham continue the project; so he brought Gabriel and Raphael on line to provide some balance between good and evil, and then Forcas, the angel who renders people invisible, restores lost property, and teaches logic and rhetoric in Hell; and by that time Cunningham was hooked.

He surrounded himself with arcane lore: M. R. James's editions of the Apocrypha, Waite's *Book of Ceremonial Magic* and *Holy Kabbalah*, the *Mystical Theology and Celestial Hierarchies* of Dionysius the Areopagite, and dozens of related works that he called up from the Stanford data base in a kind of manic fervor. As he codified his systems, he became able to put in five, eight, a dozen angels a night; one June evening, staying up well past his usual time, he managed thirty-seven. As the population grew, it took on weight and substance, for one angel cross-filed another, and they behaved now as though they held long conversations with one another even when Cunningham was occupied elsewhere.

The question of actual *belief* in angels, like that of belief in God Himself, never arose in him. His project was purely a technical challenge, not a theological exploration. Once, at lunch, he told a co-worker what he was doing, and got a chilly blank stare. "Angels? *Angels?* Flying around with big flapping wings, passing miracles? You aren't seriously telling me that you believe in angels, are you, Dan?"

To which Cunningham replied, "You don't have to believe in angels to make use of them. I'm not always sure I believe in electrons and protons. I know I've never seen any. But I make use of them."

"And what use do you make of angels?"

But Cunningham had lost interest in the discussion.

He divides his evenings between calling up his angels for conversations and programming additional ones into his pantheon. That requires continuous intensive research, for the literature of angels is extraordinarily large, and he is thorough in everything he does. The research is time-consuming, for he wants his angels to meet every scholarly test of authenticity. He pores constantly over such works as Ginzberg's seven-volume *Legends of the Jews,* Clement of Alexandria's *Prophetic Eclogues,* Blavatsky's *The Secret Doctrine.*

It is the early part of the evening. He brings up Hagith, ruler of the planet Venus and commander of 4,000 legions of spirits, and asks him details of the transmutation of metals, which is Hagith's specialty. He summons Hadranel, who in Kabbalistic lore is a porter at the second gate of Heaven, and whose voice, when he proclaims the will of the Lord, penetrates through 200,000 universes; he questions the angel about his meeting with Moses, who uttered the Supreme Name at him and made him tremble. And then Cunningham sends for Israfel the four-winged, whose feet are under the seventh earth and whose head reaches to the pillars of the divine throne. It will be Israfel's task to blow the trumpet that announces, the arrival of the Day of Judgment. Cunningham asks him to take a few trial riffs now—"just for practice," he says, but Israfel declines, saying he cannot touch his instrument until he receives the signal, and the command sequence for that, says the angel, is nowhere to be found in the software Cunningham has thus far constructed.

When he wearies of talking with the angels, Cunningham begins the evening's programming. By now the algorithms are second nature and he can enter angels into the computer in a matter of minutes; once he has done the research. This evening he inserts nine more. Then he opens a beer, sits back, and lets the day wind down to its close.

He thinks he understands why he has become so intensely involved with this enterprise. It is because he must contend each day in his daily work with matters of terrifying apocalyptic import: nothing less, indeed, than the impending destruction of the world. Cunningham works routinely with megadeath simulation. For six hours a day he sets up hypothetical situations in which Country A goes into alert mode, expecting an attack from Country B, which thereupon begins to suspect a preemptive strike and commences a defensive response, which leads Country A to escalate its own readiness, and so on until the bombs are in the air. He is aware, as are many thoughtful people both in Country A and Country B, that the possibility of computer-generated misinformation leading to a nuclear holocaust increases each year, as the time-window for correcting a malfunction diminishes. Cunningham also knows something that very few others do, or perhaps no one else at all: that it is now possible to send a signal to the giant computers—to Theirs or Ours, it makes no difference—that will be indistinguishable from the impulses that an actual flight of airborne warhead-bearing missiles would generate. If such a signal is permitted to enter the system, a minimum of eleven minutes, at the present time, will be needed to carry out fail-safe determination of its authenticity. That, at the present time, is too long to wait to decide whether the incoming missiles are real; a much swifter response is required.

Cunningham, when he designed his missile-simulating signal, thought at once of erasing his work. But he could not bring himself to do that: the program was too elegant, too perfect. On the other hand, he was afraid to tell anyone about it, for fear that it would be taken beyond his level of classification at once, and sealed away from him. He does not want that, for he dreams of finding an antidote for it, some sort of resonating inquiry mode that will distinguish all true alarms from false. When he has it, if he ever does, he will present both modes, in a single package, to Defense. Meanwhile, he bears the burden of suppressing a concept of overwhelming strategic importance. He had never done anything like that before. And he does not delude himself into thinking his mind is unique: if he could devise something like this, someone else probably could do it also, perhaps someone on the other side. True, it is a useless, suicidal program. But it would not be the first suicidal program to be devised in the interests of military security.

He knows he must take his simulator to his superiors before much more time goes by. And under the strain of that knowledge, he is beginning to show distinct signs of erosion. He mingles less and less with other people, he has unpleasant dreams and occasional periods of insomnia; he has lost his appetite and looks gaunt and haggard. The angel project is his only useful diversion, his chief distraction, his one avenue of escape.

For all his scrupulous scholarship, Cunningham has not hesitated to invent a few angels of his own. Uraniel is one of his: the angel of radioactive decay, with a face of whirling electron shells. And he has coined Dimitrion, too: the angel of Russian literature, whose wings are sleighs, and whose head is a snow-covered samovar. Cunningham feels no guilt over such whimsies. It is his computer, after all, and his program. And he knows he is not the first to concoct angels. Blake engendered platoons of them in his poems: Urizen and Orc and Enitharmon and more. Milton, he suspects, populated *Paradise Lost* with dozens of sprites of his own invention. Gurdjieff and Aleister Crowley and even Pope Gregory the Great had their turns at amplifying the angelic roster: why then not also Dan Cunningham of Palo Alto, California? So from time to time he works one up on his own. His most recent is the dread high lord Basileus, to whom Cunningham has given the title of Emperor of the Angels. Basileus is still incomplete: Cunningham has not arrived at his physical appearance, nor his specific functions, other than to make him the chief administrator of the angelic horde. But there is something unsatisfactory about imagining a new archangel, when Gabriel, Raphael, and Michael already constitute the high command. Basileus needs more work. Cunningham puts him aside, and begins to key in Duma, the angel of silence and of the stillness of death, thousand-eyed, armed with a fiery rod. His style in angels is getting darker and darker.

On a misty, rainy night in late October, a woman from San Francisco whom he knows in a distant, occasional way, phones to invite him to a party. Her name is Joanna; she is in her mid-thirties, a biologist working for one of the little gene-splicing outfits in Berkeley; Cunningham had had a brief and vague affair with her five or six years back, when she was at Stanford, and since then they have kept fitfully in touch, with long intervals elapsing between meetings. He has not seen her or heard from her in over a year. "It's going to be an interesting bunch," she tells him. "A futurologist from New York, Thomson the sociobiology man, a couple of video poets, and someone from the chimpanzee-language outfit, and I forget the rest, but they all sounded first rate."

Cunningham hates parties. They bore and jangle him. No matter how first rate the people are, he thinks, real interchange of ideas is impossible in a large random group, and the best one can hope for is some pleasant low-level chatter. He would rather be alone with his angels than waste an evening that way.

On the other hand, it has been so long since he has done

anything of a social nature that he has trouble remembering what the last gathering was. As he had been telling himself all his life, he needs to get out more often. He likes Joanna and it's about time they got together, he thinks, and he fears that if he turns her down, she may not call again for years. And the gentle patter of the rain, coming on this mild evening after the long dry months of summer, has left him feeling uncharacteristically relaxed, open, accessible.

"All right," he says. "I'll be glad to go."

The party is in San Mateo, on Saturday night. He takes down the address. They arrange to meet there. Perhaps she'll come home with him afterward, he thinks: San Mateo is only fifteen minutes from his house, and she'll have a much longer drive back up to San Francisco. The thought surprises him. He had supposed he had lost all interest in her that way; he had supposed he had lost all interest in anyone that way, as a matter of fact.

Three days before the party, he decides to call Joanna and cancel. The idea of milling about in a roomful of strangers appalls him. He can't imagine, now, why he ever agreed to go. Better to stay home alone and pass a long rainy night designing angels and conversing with Uriel, Ithuriel, Raphael, Gabriel.

But as he goes toward the telephone, that renewed hunger for solitude vanishes as swiftly as it came. He *does* want to go to the party. He *does* want to see Joanna: very much, indeed. It startles him to realize that he positively yearns for some change in his rigid routine, some escape from his little apartment, its elaborate computer hookup, even its angels.

Cunningham imagines himself at the party, in some brightly lit room in a handsome redwood-and-glass house perched in the hills above San Mateo. He stands with his back to the vast-sparkling wraparound window, a drink in his hand and he is holding forth, dominating the conversation, sharing his rich stock of angel lore with a fascinated audience.

"Yes. 300 million of them," he is saying, "and each with his fixed-function. Angels don't have free will, you know. It's Church doctrine that they're created with it, but at the moment of their birth, they're given the choice of opting for God or against Him, and the choice is irrevocable. Once they've made it, they're unalterably fixed, for good or for evil. Oh, and angels are born circumcised, too. At least the Angels of Sanctification and the Angels of Glory are, and maybe the seventy Angels of the Presence."

"Does that mean that all angels are male?" asks a slender dark-haired woman.

"Strictly speaking, they're bodiless and therefore without sex," Cunningham tells her. "But in fact, the religions that believe in angels are mainly patriarchal ones, and when the angels are visualized, they tend to be portrayed as men. Although some of them, apparently, can change sex at will. Milton tells us that in *Paradise Lost:* 'Spirits when they please can either sex assume, or both; so soft and uncompounded is their essence pure.' And some angels seem to be envisioned as female in the first place. There's the Shekinah, for instance, 'the bride of God,' the manifestation of His glory indwelling in human beings. There's Sophia, the angel of wisdom. And Lilith, Adam's first wife, the demon of lust—"

"Are demons considered angels, then?" a tall professorial-looking man wants to know.

"Of course. They're the angels who opted away from God. But they're angels nevertheless, even if we mortals perceive their aspects as demonic or diabolical."

He goes on and on. They all listen as though he is God's own messenger. He speaks of the hierachies of angels—the seraphim, cherubim, thrones, dominations, principalities, powers, virtues, archangels, and angels—and he tells them of the various lists of the seven great angels which differ so greatly once one gets beyond Michael, Gabriel, and Raphael, and he speaks of the 90,000 angels of destruction and the 300 angels of light; he conjures up the seven angels with seven trumpets from the Book of Revelation; he tells them which angels rule the seven days of the week and which the hours of the days and nights; he pours forth the wondrous angelic names, Zadkiel, Hashmal, Orphaniel, Jehudiel, Phaleg, Zagzagel. There is no end to it. He is in his glory. He is a fount of arcana. Then the manic mood passes. He is alone in his room; there is no eager audience. Once again he thinks he will skip the party. No. No. He will go. He wants to see Joanna.

He goes to his terminal and calls up two final angels before bedtime: Leviathan and Behemoth. Behemoth is the great hippopotamus-angel, the vast beast of darkness, the angel of chaos. Leviathan is his mate, the mighty she-whale, the splendid sea serpent. They dance for him on the screen. Behemoth's huge mouth yawns wide. Leviathan gapes even more awesomely. "We are getting hungry," they tell him. "When is feeding time?" In rabbinical lore, these two will swallow all the damned souls at the end of days. Cunningham tosses them some electronic sardines and sends them away. As he closes his eyes he invokes Poteh, the angel of oblivion, and falls into a black dreamless sleep.

At his desk the next morning, he is at work on a standard item, a glitch-clearing program for the third-quadrant surveillance satellites, when he finds himself unaccountably trembling. That has never happened to him before. His fingernails look almost white, his wrists are rigid, his hands are quivering. He feels chilled. It is as though he has not slept for days. In the washroom he clings to the sink and stares at his pallid, sweaty face. Someone comes up behind him and says, "You all right, Dan?"

"Yeah. Just a little attack of the damn queasies."

"All that wild living in the middle of the week wears a man down," the other says, and moves along. The social necessities have been observed: a question, a noncommittal answer, a quip, goodbye. He could have been having a stroke here and they would have played it the same way. Cunningham has no close friends at the office. He knows that they regard him as eccentric—eccentric in the wrong way, not lively and quirky but just a peculiar kind of hermit—and getting worse all the time. I could destroy the world, he thinks. I could go into the Big Room and type for fifteen seconds, and we'd be on all-out alert a minute later and the bombs would be coming down from orbit six minutes later. I could give that signal. I could really do it. I could do it right now.

Waves of nausea sweep him and he grips the edge of the sink until the last racking spasm is over. Then he cleans his face, and calmer now, returns to his desk to stare at the little green symbols on the screen.

That evening, still trying to find a function for Basileus, Cunningham discovers himself thinking of demons, and of one demon not in the classical demonology—Maxwell's Demon, the one that the physicist James Clerk Maxwell postulated to send fast-moving molecules in one direction and slow ones in another, thereby providing an ultra-efficient method for heating and refrigeration. Perhaps some sort of filtering role could be devised for Basileus. Last week a few of the loftier angels had been complaining about the proximity to them of certain fallen angels within the computer. "There's a smell of brimstone on this disk that I don't like," Gabriel had said. Cunningham wonders if he could make Basileus a kind of traffic manager within the program: let him sit in there and ship the celestial angels into one sector of a disk, the fallen ones to another.

The idea appeals to him for about thirty seconds. Then he sees how fundamentally trivial it is. He doesn't need an angel for a job like that; a little simple software could do it. Cunningham's corollary to Kant's categorical imperative: *Never use an angel as mere software.* He smiles, possibly for the first time all week. Why, he doesn't even need software. He can handle it himself, simply by assigning princes of Heaven to one file and demons to a different one. It hadn't seemed necessary to segregate his angels that way, or he would have done it from the start. But since now they were complaining—

He begins to flange up a sorting program to separate the files. It should have taken him a few minutes, but he finds himself working in a rambling, muddled way, doing an untypically sloppy job. With a quick swipe, he erases what he has done. Gabriel would have to put up with the reek of brimstone a little longer, he thinks.

There is a dull throbbing pain just behind his eyes. His throat is dry, his lips feel parched. Basileus would have to wait a little longer, too. Cunningham keys up another angel, allowing his fingers to choose for him, and finds himself looking at a blankfaced angel with a gleaming metal skin. One of the early ones, Cunningham realizes. "I don't remember your name," he says. "Who are you?"

"I am Anaphaxeton."

"And your function?"

"When my name is pronounced aloud, I will cause the angels to summon the entire universe before the bar of justice on Judgment Day."

"Oh, Jesus," Cunningham says. "I don't want you tonight."

He sends Anaphaxeton away and finds himself with the dark angel Apollyon, fish scales, dragon wings, bear feet, breathing fire and smoke, holding the key to the Abyss. "No," Cunningham says, and brings up Michael, standing with drawn sword over Jerusalem, and sends him away only to find on the screen an angel with 70,000 feet and 4,000 wings, who is Azrael, the angel of death. "No," says Cunningham again. "Not you. Oh, Christ!" A vengeful army crowds his computer. On his screen there passes a flurrying regiment of wings and eyes and beaks. He shivers and shuts the system down for the night. Jesus, he thinks. Jesus, Jesus, Jesus. All night long, suns explode in his brain.

On Friday his supervisor, Ned Harris, saunters to his desk in an unusually folksy way and asks if he's going to be doing anything interesting this weekend. Cunningham shrugs. "A party Saturday night, that's about all. Why?"

"Thought you might be going off on a fishing trip, or something. Looks like the last nice weekend before the rainy season sets in, wouldn't you say?"

"I'm not a fisherman, Ned."

"Take some kind of trip. Drive down to Monterey, maybe. Or up into the wine country."

"What are you getting at?"

"You look like you could use a little change of pace," Harris says amiably. "A couple of days off. You've been crunching numbers so hard, they're starting to crunch you, is my guess."

"It's that obvious?"

Harris nods. "You're tired, Dan. It shows. We're a little like air traffic controllers around here, you know, working so hard we start to dream about blips on the screen. That's no good. Get the hell out of town, fellow. The Defense Department can operate without you for a while. Okay? Take Monday off. Tuesday, even. I can't afford to have a fine mind like yours going goofy from fatigue, Dan."

"All right, Ned. Sure. Thanks."

His hands are shaking again. His fingernails are colorless.

"And get a good early start on the weekend, too. No need for you to hang around here today until four."

"If that's okay—"

"Go on. Shoo!"

Cunningham closes down his desk and makes his way uncertainly out of the building. The security guards wave at him. Everyone seems to know he's being sent home early. Is this what it's like to crack up on the job? He wanders about the parking lot for a little while, not sure where he has left his car. At last he finds it, and drives home at thirty miles an hour, with horns honking at him all the way as he wanders up the freeway.

He settles wearily in front of his computer and brings the system on line, calling for Harahel. Surely the angel of computers will not plague him with such apocalyptic matters.

Harahel says, "Well, we've worked out your Basileus problem for you."

"You have?"

"Uriel had the basic idea, building on your Maxwell's Demon notion. Israfel and Azrael developed it some. What's needed is an angel embodying God's justice and God's mercy. A kind of evaluator, a filtering angel. He weighs deeds in the balance, and arrives at a verdict."

"What's new about that?" Cunningham asks. "Something like that's built into every mythology from Sumer and Egypt on. There's always a mechanism for evaluating the souls of the dead—this one goes to Paradise, this one goes to Hell—"

"Wait," Harahel says. "I wasn't finished. I'm not talking about the evaluation of individual souls."

"What then?"

"Worlds," the angel replies. "Basileus will be the judge of worlds. He holds an entire planet up to scrutiny and decides whether it's time to call for the last trump."

"Part of the machinery of Judgment, you mean?"

"Exactly. He's the one who presents the evidence to God and helps Him make his decision. And then he's the one who tells Israfel to blow the trumpet, and he's the one who calls out the name of Anaphaxeton to bring everyone before the bar. He's the prime apocalyptic angel, the destroyer of worlds. And we thought you might make him look like—"

"Ah," Cunningham says. "Not now. Let's talk about that some other time."

He shuts the system down, pours himself a drink, sits staring out the window at the big eucalyptus tree in the front yard. After a while it begins to rain. Not such a good weekend for a drive into the country after all, he thinks. He does not turn the computer on again that evening.

Despite everything, Cunningham goes to the party. Joanna is not there. She has phoned to cancel, late Saturday afternoon, pleading a bad cold. He detects no sound of a cold in her voice, but perhaps she is telling the truth. Or possibly she has found something better to do on Saturday night. But he is already geared for party going, and he is so tired, so eroded, that it is more effort to change his internal program than it is to follow through on the original schedule. So about eight that evening he drives up to San Mateo, through a light drizzle.

The party turns out not to be in the glamorous hills west of town, but in a small cramped condominium, close to the heart of the city, furnished with what looks like somebody's college-era chairs and couches and bookshelves. A cheap stereo is playing the pop music of a dozen years ago, and a sputtering screen provides a crude computer-generated light show. The host is some sort of marketing exec for a large video-games company in San Jose, and most of the guests look vaguely corporate, too. The futurologist from New York has sent his regrets; the famous sociobiologist has also failed to arrive; the video poets are two San Francisco gays who will talk only to each other, and stray not very far from the bar; the expert on teaching chimpanzees to speak is in the red-faced-and-sweaty-stage of being drunk, and is working hard at seducing a plump woman festooned with astrological jewelry. Cunningham, numb, drifts through the party as though he is made of ectoplasm. He speaks to no one; no one speaks to him. Some jugs of red wine are open on a table by the window, and he pours himself a glassful. There he stands, immobile, imprisoned by inertia. He imagines himself suddenly making a speech about angels, telling everyone how Ithuriel touched Satan with his spear in the Garden of Eden as the Fiend crouched next to Eve, and how the hierarch Ataphiel keeps Heaven aloft by balancing it on three fingers. But he says nothing. After a time he find himself approached by a lean, leathery-looking woman with glittering eyes, who says, "And what do you do?"

"I'm a programmer," Cunningham says. "Mainly I talk to angels. But I also do national security stuff."

"Angels?" she says, and laughs in a brittle, tinkling way. "You talk to angels? I've never heard anyone say that before." She pours herself a drink and moves quickly elsewhere.

"Angels?" says the astrological woman. "Did someone say angels?"

Cunningham smiles and shrugs and looks out the window. It is raining harder. I should go home, he thinks. There is absolutely no point in being here. He fills his glass again. The chimpanzee man is still working on the astrologer, but she seems to be trying to get free of him and come over to Cunningham. To discuss angels with him? She is heavy-breasted, a little walleyed, sloppy-looking. He does not want to discuss angels with her. He does not want to discuss angels with anyone. He hold his place at the window until it definitely does appear that the astrologer is heading his way; then he drifts toward the door. She says, "I heard you say you were interested in angels. Angels are a special field of mine, you know. I've studied with—"

"Angles," Cunningham says. "I play the angles. That's what I said. I'm a professional gambler."

"Wait," she says, but he moves past her and out into the night. It takes him a long while to find his key and get his car unlocked, and the rain soaks him to the skin, but that does not bother him. He is home a little before midnight.

He brings Raphael on line. The great archangel radiates a beautiful golden glow.

"You will be Basileus," Raphael tells him. "We've decided it by a vote, hierarchy by hierarchy. Everyone agrees."

"I can't be an angel. I'm human," Cunningham replies.

"There's ample precedent. Enoch was carried off to Heaven and became an angel. So was Elijah. St. John the Baptist was actually an angel. You will become Basileus. We've already done the program for you. It's on the disk: just call him up and you'll see. Your own face, looking out at you."

"No," Cunningham says.

"How can you refuse?"

"Are you really Raphael? You sound like someone from the other side. A tempter. Asmodeus. Astaroth. Belphegor."

"I am Raphael. And you are Basileus."

Cunningham considers it. He is so very tired that he can barely think.

An angel. Why not? A rainy Saturday night, a lousy party, a splitting headache: come home and find out you've been made an angel, and given a high place in the hierarchy. Why not? Why the hell not?

"All right," he says. "I'm Basileus."

He puts his hands on the keys and taps out a simple formulation that goes straight down the pipe into the Defense Department's big northern California system. With an alteration of two keystrokes, he sends the same message to the Soviets. Why not? Redundancy is the soul of security. The world now has about six minutes left. Cunningham has always been good with computers. He knows their secret language as few people before him have.

Then he brings Raphael on the screen again.

"You should see yourself as Basileus while there's still time," the archangel says.

"Yes. Of course. What's the access key?"

Raphael tells him. Cunningham begins to set it up.

Come now, Basileus! We are one!

Cunningham stares at the screen with growing wonder and delight, while the clock continues to tick.

Angelica
by
Jane Yolen

One of the most distinguished of modern fantasists, Jane Yolen has been compared to writers such as Oscar Wilde and Charles Perrault, and has been called "the Hans Christian Andersen of the twentieth century." Primarily known for her work for children and young adults, Yolen has produced more than sixty books, including novels, collections of short stories, poetry collections, picture books, biographies, and a book of essays on folklore and fairy tales. She has received the Golden Kite Award and the World Fantasy Award, and has been a finalist for the National Book Award. In recent years she has also been writing more adult-oriented fantasy, work which has appeared in collections such as Tales of Wonder, Neptune Rising: Songs and Tales of the Undersea Folk, Dragonfield and Other Stories, *and* Merlin's Booke, *and in novels such as* Cards of Grief, Sister Light, Sister Dark, *and* White Jenna. *She lives with her family in Massachusetts.*

In the subtle little story that follows, she shows us that sometimes even angels must do, not what they want *to do, but what they* have *to do.*

*　　*　　*

Linz, Austria, 1898

The boy could not sleep. It was hot and he had been sick for so long. All night his head had throbbed. Finally he sat up and managed to get out of bed. He went down the stairs without stumbling.

Elated at his progress, he slipped from the house without waking either his mother or father. His goal was the river bank. He had not been there in a month.

He had always considered the river bank his own. No one else in the family ever went there. He liked to set his feet in the damp

21

ground and make patterns. It was like a picture, and the artist in him appreciated the primitive beauty.

Heat lightning jetted across the sky. He sat down on a fallen log and picked at the bark as he would a scab. He could feel the log imprint itself on his backside through the thin cotton pajamas. He wished—not for the first time—that he could be allowed to sleep without his clothes.

The silence and the heat enveloped him. He closed his eyes and dreamed of sleep, but his head still throbbed. He had never been out at night by himself before. The slight touch of fear was both pleasure and pain.

He thought about that fear, probing it like a loose tooth, now to feel the ache and now to feel the sweetness, when the faint came upon him and he tumbled slowly from the log. There was nothing but river bank before him, nothing to slow his descent, and he rolled down the slight hill and into the river, not waking till the shock of the water hit him.

It was cold and unpleasantly muddy. He thrashed about. The sour water got in his mouth and made him gag.

Suddenly someone took his arm and pulled him up onto the bank, dragged him up the slight incline.

He opened his eyes and shook his head to get the lank, wet hair from his face. He was surprised to find that his rescuer was a girl, about his size, in a white cotton shift. She was not muddied at all from her efforts. His one thought before she heaved him over the top of the bank and helped him back onto the log was that she must be quite marvelously strong.

"Thank you," he said, when he was seated again, and then did not know where to go from there.

"You are welcome." Her voice was low, her speech precise, almost old-fashioned in its carefulness. He realized that she was not a girl but a small woman.

"You fell in," she said.

"Yes."

She sat down beside him and looked into his eyes, smiling. He wondered how he could see so well when the moon was behind her. She seemed to light up from within like some kind of lamp.

Her outline was a golden glow and her blond hair fell in straight lengths to her shoulder.

"You may call me Angelica," she said.

"Is that your name?"

She laughed. "No. No, it's not. And how perceptive of you to guess."

"It is an alias?" He knew about such things. His father was a customs official and told the family stories at the table about his work.

"It is the name I . . ." She hesitated for a moment and looked behind her. Then she turned and laughed again. "It is the name I travel under."

"Oh."

"You could not pronounce my real name," she said.

"Could I try?"

"*Pistias Sophia!*" said the woman and she stood as she named herself. She seemed to shimmer and grow at her own words, but the boy thought that might be the fever in his head, though he hadn't a headache anymore.

"Pissta . . ." He could not stumble around the name. There seemed to be something blocking his tongue. "I guess I better call you Angelica for now," he said.

"For now," she agreed.

He smiled shyly at her. "My name is Addie," he said.

"I know."

"How do you know? Do I look like an Addie? It means . . ."

"Noble hero," she finished for him.

"How do you know *that*?"

"I am very wise," she said. "And names are important to me. To all of us. Destiny is in names." She smiled, but her smile was not so pleasant any longer. She started to reach for his hand, but he drew back.

"You shouldn't boast," he said. "About being wise. It's not nice."

"I am not boasting." She found his hand and held it in hers. Her touch was cool and infinitely soothing. She reached over with the other hand and put it first palm, then back to his forehead. She made a "tch" against her teeth and scowled. "Your guardian should be Flung Over. I shall have to speak to Uriel about this. Letting you out with such a fever."

"Nobody *let* me out," said the boy. "I let myself out. No one knows I am here—except you."

"Well, there is one who *should* know where you are. And he shall certainly hear from me about this." She stood up and was suddenly much taller than the boy. "Come. Back to the house with you. You should be in bed." She reached down the front of her white shift and brought up a silver bottle on a chain. "You must take a sip of this now. It will help you sleep."

"Will you come back with me?" the boy asked after taking a drink.

"Just a little way." She held his hand as they went.

He looked behind once to see his footprints in the rain-soft earth. They marched in an orderly line behind him. He could not see hers at all.

"Do you believe, little Addie?" Her voice seemed to come from a long way off, farther even than the hills.

"Believe in what?"

"In God. Do you believe that he directs all our movements?"

"I sing in the church choir," he said, hoping it was the proof she wanted.

"That will do for now," she said.

There was a fierceness in her voice that made him turn in the muddy furrow and look at her. She towered above all, all white and gold and glowing. The moon haloed her head, and behind her, close to her shoulders, he saw something like wings, feathery and waving. He was suddenly desperately afraid.

"What are you?" he whispered.

"What do you think I am?" she asked, and her face looked carved in stone, so white her skin and black the features.

"Are you . . . the angel of death?" he asked and then looked down before she answered. He could not bear to watch her talk.

"For you, I am an angel of life," she said. "Did I not save you?"

"What kind of angel are you?" he whispered, falling to his knees before her.

She lifted him up and cradled him in her arms. She sang him a lullaby in a language he did not know. "I told you in the beginning who I am," she murmured to the sleeping boy. "I am Pistias Sophia, angel of wisdom and faith. The one who put the serpent into the garden, little Adolf. But I was only following orders."

Her wings unfurled behind her. She pumped them once, twice, and then the great wind that commanded lifted her into the air. She flew without a sound to the Hitler house and left the boy sleeping, feverless, in his bed.

Angels
by
Bruce McAllister

Bruce McAllister published his first story in 1963, when he was seventeen (it was written at the tender age of fifteen). Since then, with only a handful of stories and a few novels, he has nevertheless managed to establish himself as one of the most respected writers in the business. His short fiction has appeared in Omni, Asimov's Science Fiction, The Magazine of Fantasy and Science Fiction, In the Field of Fire, Alien Sex, *and elsewhere. His first novel,* Humanity Prime, *was part of the original Ace Specials series. His most recent novel is the critically acclaimed* Dream Baby, *and he is at work on several other novel projects. McAllister lives in Redlands, California, where he is the director of the writing program at the University of Redlands.*

In the powerful and unsettling story that follows, he unveils the compelling story of a woman who, no matter what the cost, is determined to create Heaven-on-Earth—or one of its inhabitants, anyway . . .

* * *

The creature she'd had them make cost her the last piece of forest outside Siena. The one with the little medieval chapel in it, the tall umbrella pines shading a forest floor no tourist had ever walked upon.

It cost her the two rocky islands just south of Elba, and the lead mines at Piombino, which she had never cared about, and the villa on Lake Garda, which she had, because, so small and intimate, it had been one of her father's favorites.

When she ordered the doctors from Milan to alter the creature's spine and shoulder blades to accept the remarkable wings, it cost her the thirty-meter ketch as well—the one with the artificial brain that trimmed the sails perfectly—the one she had used only once, forty years ago, and had never really wanted anyway. And when the wings did not take, when the doctors needed to try again, it

27

cost her the two altar paintings of angels by Giotto from her father's hunting lodge outside Siena, where she had spent her childhood with her brother and sisters, and which her father had loved. She had not wanted to sell the paintings, but selling them had helped her to remember him—to see him standing in the long hallway of the lodge, on the green Carrara marble floor, looking down at her and smiling in the gray suit he always wore. He seemed to be laughing, to be saying: *Yes, you may sell them!*

It was the wings, she realized—the sale of the ketch through an electronic brokerage in Nice—that had alerted her older brother, who found her one day in her apartment in Lucca and in his rage shouted: "What are you *doing*, Pupa? What do you imagine you are *doing*?" She knew he meant: *You are doing this to hurt us. We know you are.*

She had taken a room in the old walled city of Lucca, near the ancient university there, above a store that still sold wood-pulp books, but Giancarlo found her nevertheless and shouted at her, as always. As did her sister Olivia the very next week, while Francesca, the youngest at ninety-three, sent a letter instead. "How can you be doing this?" they all asked her, when they actually meant to say: *How can you be doing this to us, Pupa? How?*

They did not know she knew what they had done to her children, and this gave them the courage to ask, she told herself.

They were afraid, of course, that she would continue to sell her possessions until everything their father had left her was gone. They were so afraid, in fact, that they were arranging, even now, for doctors from Rome and Turin to testify about her "illness," this madness of hers, in court. These doctors had not interviewed her in person, no, but that did not matter. What she was doing, her lawyers said, was enough—enough for doctors with reputations like theirs to testify against her. "This thing you are having made for you, *Egregia Signora*, is quite enough," they'd told her.

At these words the world felt a little darker, and she had to remind herself that this was why she was so willing to leave it.

• • •

The first time she was allowed to see him, she found she could not look at him for long. He wasn't yet finished; that was all. A woman of childbearing age, chosen by the doctors from a list, had carried the fertilized ovum for her. At one month they'd removed it. It was not like a fetus, the way an infant grew. There were ways to make it grow quickly outside a woman. It would take six months, they'd said.

He was already the size of a man, yet the skin was like scar tissue, covered with a dozen layers of gauze as he lay in a room-sized tent whose material she could barely see through now. The room smelled of chemicals. The light was too bright. His face was covered, too—with a mask that made the eyes bulge like an insect's, which frightened her. It should not have, she knew. It was simply the way he was being grown, she told herself again.

But it did frighten her, and she had to turn away.

When he was at last finished and the gauze was removed, though not the tent, he appeared to be sleeping. Blood substitutes rich in glucose and oxygen were flowing through his veins, the doctors informed her, but from where she stood outside his tent she could not see tubing. There should be tubing, shouldn't there? She could see only the jaundice color of his arms on the bed, his legs parted akimbo under the sheet, like a child's. For weeks she had imagined that he would be able to say something to her at this moment, but that was silly, she knew. It had been a daydream only, week after week, in her little room in Lucca; nothing more. It was not something the doctors had ever promised. Even if he had been awake, he could not have spoken, she knew. He knew no words to speak.

The eyes did not open for days.

When they allowed her into his tent for the first time, they made her bathe first, dried her with gusts of hot air, then gave her a thin garment to wear. As she approached his bed, she saw that his eyes were open at last, that they were watching her, although now and then they rolled back into his head like white marbles and his mouth fell slack. She looked at the doctor beside her, questioning, but the woman nodded, as if saying: *Do not worry, Signora. He is doing fine*.

She was afraid—more afraid than she could ever remember being—but she leaned over nevertheless and touched her lips to his forehead, the way she had done so long ago to three children . . . her own . . . or someone's. She could not remember. No. That wasn't true. She could remember. She'd had three children—a gangly, dark-haired son when she was very young, and then, when she was nearly sixty, two daughters as well. She'd touched her lips to their three foreheads in this same way.

She put her lips to his forehead again and felt his eyes roll away. But he did not pull away from her or hit at her, and these, she realized, were the only things she'd really been afraid of.

One afternoon in August, when the tent was gone and she was standing over his bed, she asked the doctors and nurses to leave them alone. The bed was only a bed. It was the kind any human being could sleep in comfortably. A father, a mother. A child. She could not remember a bed like it from the long century of her life, but it was somehow familiar—a bed a father might sleep in, one a child might climb into in the morning while he slept. A dream, a wish. Nothing more.

His body was blond, just like hers. As she'd told them it should be. It was long and heavy-boned, too, like hers, but the curls on his head were those of a marble god—Athenian, not Spartan—as she'd requested. It had not been difficult, they'd told her. The generic material was there, they'd said; the alterations, where necessary, would be easy. It was only that no one had ever asked for something like this to be done, or had had the money to pay for it.

The wings had been another matter entirely. Caravaggio's sweeping feathers, the glory of Leda's swan, not the puny things a Giotto might paint. Grown separately—not a part of him at all—and perhaps that had been the problem.

Later, as she sat in a small room that smelled faintly of jasmine, she would remember how on this very August afternoon, when the doctors had left them alone at last, when the first pair of wings were doing their best to take, and the osteomyelitis had not yet set in, there had still been hope. The shoulders looked massive; and they would need to be, whether he ever really moved the wings or not, whether the shoulders did nothing more than keep them away from the naked back, so that the stiff quills would not rub the skin raw. He would never fly, of course. No amount of wealth could buy that and this she had known all along. She had simply wanted him to have wings because they were beautiful, because she could remember seeing paintings of beautiful wings somewhere.

The organ between his legs was beautiful too. Pale, golden and rosy—and perfect. It hung like David's, like the white marble under its new dome in Florence, where tourists could walk by it each day. Just as she'd told the doctors it should be. She'd told them: *Make it so that even when it is soft, even when he is sleeping, or spent, it is beautiful. Make it so that women will want to touch it even in death.*

She had offered them the director of archives at the Pitti Palace, the man who could provide them with drawings by Michelangelo, or arrange for holograms of the statue itself to be delivered if they were needed. But the doctors had said *No.* There were equations for the arc and symmetry of such things, they'd told her, and they would use these.

His arms were covered with hair the color of sunlight, a golden down, and this had been easy, too. Her father had been German, her mother Northern Italian; the blond hair was there to work with. The doctors had seen it in the genetic mapping. It would cost little. Growing the fetus outside a womb would be the costly thing.

He was awake and staring at her now, the wings bound tightly with gauze behind him and supported by a pillow, the sheet gathered to one side of his naked body. He was not embarrassed, she saw. Embarrassment would be one of the things he would have to learn, of course.

One arm was across his stomach, the other by his side. The wings, even with the feathers bound, did not seem to bother him. He looked relaxed and the legs, as always, lay akimbo. They would always lie that way—for as long as he should live, she told herself. These were the habits a body was born with. She could see clearly how each of her own three children had slept—a boy, two girls—each lying a bit differently, like paintings in a hallway somewhere, like holograms inseparable from their souls.

She could not help herself. She tried, but she could not. She imagined what it would be like to make love to him, to feel that perfect organ inside her, her own arms strong once more, her hands on his shoulders perhaps, or her palms on his chest, his curls bright in the sunlight of the garden at Assisi or the topiary garden at Parma, the wings moving as if with a life of their own, his naked back reddening under the sun, arching even as her own back arched, then falling slowly like a sigh from the roses and snapdragons around them.

On that August afternoon, when the doctors left them, she imagined what it might be like to make love with him before words and deeds would change him forever.

When they had boosted his immune system with antigens and the engineered leukocytes, and felt it was safe for him to leave the room, she took him to the beach at Viareggio—three weeks before the floats were ready for *la festa*, three weeks before the crowds would parade themselves down the shadowy King's Highway with their rubber clubs and strange masks. The city was dead as winter now. She'd had her people clean the beach around the pines for two hundred meters in all directions, testing it for salmonella, typhus, any of the things the beach had become famous for in the past thirty years: all the microbes that might hurt him.

Her bodyguards remained in the shadows of the trees, like shadows themselves.

She laid out an old blanket of Yugoslavian cotton embroidered with silver—the one her first husband had given her when they'd begun a life together in the floating city of Taranto, right before the turn of the millennium. The young man could walk now, though unsteadily, the weeks of antibiotic treatments and hydration leaving him weak but happy, his head turning to look at everything, just like a child's. The scars on his shoulder blades were as pink as the bottoms of *putti* in a Tiepolo fresco, as the soles of the feet of the babies she could remember a little more clearly now, and no longer seemed to bother him. The eyes were alive with a feeling she could remember feeling, and as she watched him she felt it too.

They sat down together on the blanket and she gave him an orange, the small red kind they grew in Jaffa. He took it from her but waited, wanting to do it exactly the way she did. So she did it slowly, peeling it carefully, keeping her eyes on him and smiling with each bite, until his movements had lost their nervousness and he was calm again.

She looked at the trees. Later, sitting in the little room, she would remember looking at the trees, seeing the shadows there, and for a moment feeling they were something else . . . a darkness moving closer and closer to her. She laughed. It wouldn't come now, the darkness, unless she asked it to. It was hers to invite. It wouldn't come until she wanted it to.

And it was not the same darkness as before, she knew. The one she had felt in Pisa long ago. . . .

She thought of her father, who had left all four of them many things, but who had left her so much more, and how this had driven her brother and sisters to do many many things.

The shadows remained where they were.

When she turned back to him, he was sleepy again, his eyelids heavy, his left elbow barely holding him up. He would not, she knew, lie down unless she lay down with him. The blanket was big—colorless now in the glare of the sun—and warm, and she lay down with him, making sure that their arms touched.

She watched him as he dreamed. He made a whining noise, the kind she had heard a child make long ago. Then he frowned, his eyes still closed, and the dream gone. His face was quiet again.

The chemical they had put on his skin to protect it from the sun glistened like ocean waves. She let her own eyes close.

Even in this darkness, she was not afraid. The shadows under the trees did not move. Nothing moved toward her that she would not have welcomed.

• • •

When he was again rested, she took him by helicopter one evening—in the one infrared Pirelli that remained to her—to the town of Assisi, where they slept together in the largest canopy bed of her villa. He tossed and moaned all night. He hit her four times with his elbow and lay against her quietly only once, for a few minutes. She thought at first that it might be the wings. But that was wrong, wasn't it. The wings were gone. Even the scars could not be bothering him now, could they? Why had she thought he still had wings?

In the morning, her guards escorting them like priests, she took him by the hand down the stone path to the courtyard of the church, to the hologram of Saint Francis that had been there ever since she could remember. The tourists had left. They had been asked to leave. Those who'd objected had been paid handsomely.

The hologram was much larger than life, a full three meters, and the grainy texture of the ruby light made the saint look almost ill. They sat together on one of the benches. The tape played on.

The young man at her side, dressed in summer linen while she wore silk, looked at the grass, at the bees and the bright *farfalle* on the flowers near them, and did not listen. The tape was made of words, she realized suddenly. He did not yet know these words. He did not even know what words were, perhaps.

The red arms of the hologram moved as if in prayer, moving again in exactly the same way, while the voice said:

Laudato si, mi signore, per frate vento et per aere et nubilo et sereno et onne tempo, per le quale a le tue creature dai sustentamento.

It said:

"Praised be my Lord for our brother the wind, for air and cloud by which Thou upholdest life in every creature."

The voice then repeated the words in French, in German, in four other languages, but she wasn't listening. She was watching the ground, too. She was watching what he was watching there: the green lizard making its way in fits and starts across the stone path, the insects moving through the grass so near their shoes, and the white butterfly that wanted to land, but never did.

"Praised be my Lord for our brother fire, through whom Thou givest us light in the darkness," the voice was saying somewhere. "Praised be my Lord for our sister, the death of our body, from which no man or woman may escape."

An angry voice made her look up suddenly. Two of the guards were arguing with a man, a tourist who wore a single heavy holo-camera around his neck. She recognized the camera. Her father's factory in Rimini had made it. She got up quickly, took the young man's hand in hers and pulled him with her, his eyes never leaving the ground.

That night in bed, she took his hand again and thought she might teach him, that it might be possible, that he might enjoy it, but when he looked at her in the dim light of the room and cocked his head like a child, she knew she could not.

They tried to kill him the very next week. They were afraid that she would find new ways to spend, on this thing she'd had the doctors make for her, the very wealth they believed was theirs, the wealth their many lawyers had assured them would indeed be theirs, because ·at her passing—the one they knew she was planning (an injection in the vein of one arm? a perfumed gas in a little perfumed room?)—it would pass to them. There was no one else—no children, no other siblings, no organization whose rights could not be successfully contested—to whom her wealth should go. Their lawyers could not assure them, however, that she would not put a new skin, another pair of wings, a scaly tail, a second hand on this creature, and so it needed to be killed, didn't it?

They tried at Lake Como during the height of the tourist season, while she was sleeping on the deck of the biggest villa, tired out by the sun. The young man was standing on the dock just below her, looking down into the dark waters as he always did, and only a movement by the quickest guard was able to save him. The hydrofoil removed the first ten meters of the dock, somehow avoided the retaining wall, and moved down the lake without stopping. Shaking, naked, she stood in the sunlight and *knew*.

To the guard, a middle-aged Tuscan by the name of Cichinelli, she gave one of the new apartment buildings in the Ligurian castle-town of Pozzuoli, smiling as she presented him with the papers the next day. To the other guards, who would certainly have done the same had they been able, she presented new Alfa Stellanovas. Someone back at the lodge would report it all, of course. Even the smile, she knew.

When they tried again, at Assisi, in the garden there, while she sat with him quietly on a bench watching the lizards move on the walls, and the bullets from the assassin's rifle shattered the marble corner, she had him moved back to Siena, to within the grounds of her father's hunting lodge. It would cost her two of the gambling barges in Trieste to establish the newest security technology on the grounds. It would cost her half of her interest in the cablecar network on Anacapri—the one her father had given her when she was twelve—to establish the same for the building in Lucca, which she no longer used. All of this would be reported to her brother and her sisters, she knew.

Being with him each day, holding his hand, helped her to *remember*. Was this perhaps why she'd had him made? She saw it clearly the day she led him through the hallways of the hunting lodge to show him all of the paintings of wings—the very kind she had once hoped he might have. Caravaggio's "Angeli di Dio." Fra Angelico's "Il Sogno del Cielo." The dancing angels of Turacco, the long wings of Pagano. The paintings had always been there. They lined the oak walls of the hallways, as they always had, but as she watched him look at them, as she watched him turn to her with questions in his eyes—because he had no *words* to ask them—it came to her suddenly.

They had been her father's paintings. He had given them to *her*. He had loved them: he had loved the wings.

How could she have forgotten? How?

They were never going to try the poison, she admitted to herself finally. The cardiotoxin they had used on Piero, her gangly son, sixty years old the day he drove his two sisters, teenagers, from Old Genoa down the *galleria* highway to the birthday party for her in Pisa—the gradual poison in his veins, the Alfa Romeo D'Oro tumbling to the rocks at Cinque Terre, the bodies floating in the bay, like pale ghosts, for three whole hours. For some reason they were not going to try it this time and she was sorry. Perhaps they knew; perhaps they did not. The doctors had made alterations and it would not have worked this time.

It had cost her half of what her father had left her to have the creature made. The other half remained, and this was what her brother and sisters wanted—more than anything in the world.

Love is sometimes a terrible thing, she would remember thinking, sitting in a little room.

In September he began to make sounds with his throat at last. He tried to make her understand what he wanted by them, and she did her best to understand. But she did not try to teach him a language. It would have taken too long, she knew. Others would have the time. For now she wanted him to herself, before words could change him.

She could remember it now. Lying on the beach at Viareggio as a child, her father, his beard, the crow's feet at the corners of his eyes, his eyes bluer than any Italian should have had. His hands were in his pockets, his legs only a few steps away in the warm sand. The sunlight seemed to go forever. A poet had died there, she knew. Even as a child she had known this. It had bothered her even then—that a poet could have drowned in such a beautiful sea, the Ligurian Sea, near where her own mother had been born, and where she, even now in memory, was a child playing in the sand, her father, his beard, his legs so near her in a sunlight that went forever.

She could remember it now. She could remember him standing in the sand, day after day, saying: *Tu sei mi'angelo, Pupa.*

You are my angel. You will always be my angel, Pupa.

It was the last thing she would need to remember, she knew, sitting in a room that smelled of jasmine, breathing it in at last.

The young man sat in the corner of another room and tried his best to think. It was difficult. The men and women around him were telling him—in words, ones he had only recently learned to understand—how many things in the world were now his, how these things could never be taken from him, and how this was all that the woman had really wanted.

If Angels Ate Apples
by
Geoffrey A. Landis

Geoffrey A. Landis won the Hugo Award for his story "A Walk in the Sun," and a Nebula Award for his story "Ripples in the Dirac Sea." His most recent book is a collection, Myths, Legends, and True History. *When not writing, he works as a physicist, and is engaged in solar cell research.*

* * *

If angels ate apples, potatoes and pears
they'd grow to be chubby and cheerful as bears
nibbling knishes and other such things,
tickling your face with the tips of their wings

If seraphim shouted and whistled at girls,
drank drafts from thimbles, all friends with the world
drained the best ale and chased it with rye,
then fluttered in circles while trying to fly

Angels on tables! (Watch out for your glass!)
Slipping on puddles, right plop on their ass!
Laughing at music that only they hear,
then tweaking the barmaids a pinch on the rear.

Fuzzy fat angels, that's something to see,
as they dance to the jukebox at quarter to three,
and ace out the pinball, a marvelous feat,
the lights and bells flashing (though sometimes they cheat).

If angels made merry, would that be so odd?
Must they always be solemn, to stay friends with God?
It's a pity that Heaven is so far away
angels hardly ever come down and just *play*.

Alfred

by
Lisa Goldstein

*Lisa Goldstein is a Bay Area writer who won the American Book
Award for her first novel,* The Red Magician, *and who has
subsequently gone on to become one of the most critically
acclaimed novelists of her day with books such as* Tourists, The
Dream Years, *and* A Mask for the General. *Her most recent book
is the novel* Strange Devices of the Sun and Moon, *and forthcoming
is a novel,* Summer King, Winter Fool, *and a collection of her
short fiction,* Travelers in Magic.

*She is less prolific at shorter lengths, although her stories have
appeared in* Asimov's Science Fiction, Interzone, Pulphouse, Full
Spectrum, Snow White, Blood Red, The Magazine of Fantasy and
Science Fiction, *and elsewhere, and are well worth waiting
for—as is true of the poignant story that follows, a finalist for the
World Fantasy Award last year, a bittersweet study of the
continuity of love.*

*   *   *

Alison walked slowly through the park near school. Usually she
went to Laura's house after school let out, but on Fridays Laura
had a Girl Scout meeting. She passed a few older boys playing
basketball, two women pushing baby strollers. Bells from the
distant clock-tower rang out across the park: five o'clock, still too
early to go home.

A leaf fell noiselessly to the path in front of her. The sun broke
through the dark edge of the clouds and illuminated a spider web
on one of the trees, making it shine like a gate of jewels. A spotted
dog, loping alone down the path, looked back and grinned at her
as if urging her on. She followed after it.

An old man sat on a bench ahead of her, his eyes closed and his
face turned toward the sun.

If Laura had been here they'd be whispering together about
everyone, laughing over their made-up stories. The two women

would have had their babies switched at the hospital, and they would pass each other without ever knowing how close they were to their true children. The old man was a spy, of course.

As Alison walked by the man she saw that his face and hands were pale, almost transparent. At that moment he opened his eyes and said, "I wonder—Could you please tell me the time?"

He had a slight accent, like her parents. Her guess had been right after all—he *was* a spy. "Five o'clock," she said.

"Ah. And the year?"

This was much too weird; the man had to be crazy. Alison glanced around, acting casual but at the same time looking for someone to run to if things got out of hand. You weren't supposed to talk to strangers, she knew that. Her mother told her so all the time.

But what could this man do to her here, in front of all these people? And she had to admit that his question intrigued her—most adults asked you if you liked school and didn't seem to know where to go from there. "It's 1967," she said. Somehow this strange question made it all right to ask him one in return. "Why do you want to know?"

"Oh, you know how it is. We old people, we can never remember anything."

She tried to study him without being obvious. She'd been right about his accent: it sounded German, like her parents'. He had a narrow face and high forehead, with thinning black hair brushed back from his face. He wore glasses with John Lennon wire frames—very cool, Alison thought.

But other than the glasses, which he'd probably had forever, there wasn't anything fashionable about him. He had on a thin black tie and his coat was nearly worn through in places.

He pushed back his sleeves. Nothing up my sleeves, Alison thought. Then she saw the numbers tattooed on his arm, and she looked away. Her parents had numbers like that.

"What is your name?" he asked.

She shook her head; she wasn't going to fall for that one. "My mother told me never to talk to strangers," she said.

"Your mother is a very smart woman. My mother never told me anything like that. My name is Alfred."

"Aren't you supposed to offer me candy now?" Alison said.

"Candy? Why?"

"That's the other thing my mother said. Strangers would try to give me candy."

He rummaged in his pockets as if searching for something. Alison saw with relief that his coat sleeves had fallen back over his arms, covering the tattoo. "I don't have any candy. All I have here is a pocket-watch. What would your mother say to that?"

He brought out a round gold watch. The letter "A" was engraved on it, the ends of the letter looping and curling around each other. Her initial, his initial. She reached for the watch but he moved it away from her and pressed the knob on top to open it. It had stopped hours ago.

"Aren't you going to wind it?" she asked.

"It's broken," he said. "I can tell you an interesting story about this watch, if you want to hear it."

She hesitated. She didn't want to hear about concentration camps; people—adults—got too strange when they talked about their experiences. It made her uncomfortable. Terrible things weren't supposed to happen to your parents; your parents were supposed to protect you.

On the other hand, she didn't want to go home just yet. "Okay," she said. She was almost certain now that he was harmless, but just to be safe she wouldn't sit on the bench next to him. She could probably outrun him anyway.

"My parents gave this watch to me a long time ago," he said. "I used to carry it with me wherever I went, and bring it out and look at it." He pried open the back and showed her a photograph of a dark-eyed boy and girl who looked a little like her and her brother Joey. But this back opened as well, revealing a small world of gears and springs and levers, all placed one over the other in careful layers, all unaccountably stopped.

"I took the watch down to the river once. I had my own place there where no one could find me, where I would sit and think and dream. That day I was dreaming that someday I would learn how to make a watch like this. Someday I would find out its secrets."

He fell silent. The sun glinted over the watch in his hand. "And did you?" she asked, to bring him back from wherever he had gone.

He didn't seem to hear her. "And then the angel came," he said. "Do you know, I had thought angels were courteous, kind. This one had a force of some sort, a terrifying energy I could feel even from where I sat. His eyes were fierce as stars. I thought he asked me a question, asked me if I desired anything, anything in the world, but in that confused instant I could not think of a thing I wanted. I was completely content. And so he left me.

"I looked down at the watch, which I still held in my hand, but it had stopped. And no one in the world has ever been able to make it start again."

He looked at her as if expecting a reply. But all she could think of was that her first thought had been correct; he was crazy after all. No one in her family believed in angels. Still, what if—what if his story were true?

"But I think the angel granted my desire," he said. He nodded slowly. "Do you know, I think he did."

The shadows of the trees had grown longer while he'd talked to her; it was later than she'd thought. "I've got to go now," she said reluctantly. "My parents are expecting me."

"Come again," he said. "I'm in the park nearly every day."

The bus was just pulling out when she got to the bus stop; she had to wait for the next one and got home just as her father and Joey were sitting down to dinner. Her mother carried plates filled with chicken and potatoes into the dining room. She frowned as Alison came in; it was a family rule that everyone had to be on time for dinner.

Her mother sat and her parents began to eat. Joey looked from one parent to the other uncertainly. Finally he said, "What happens to planes when they crash?"

Alison could see that he was trying to be casual, but he had obviously been worrying about the question all day. "What do you mean?" Alison's father said.

"Well, like when they fall. Where do they land?"

Her mother sighed. Joey was six, and afraid of everything. He refused to get on an elevator because he thought the cable would break. When they went walking he tried to stay with their parents at all times, and would grow anxious if he couldn't see them. Sometimes at night Alison heard screams coming from his room, his nightmares waking him up.

"I mean, could they land on the house?" he said. "Could they come through my bedroom?"

"No, of course not," Alison's father said. "The pilots try to land where there aren't any people."

"Well, but it could happen, couldn't it? What if—if they just fall?"

"Look," Alison's father said. "Let's say that this piece of chicken is the plane. Okay? And your plate here is where the plane comes down." Speaking carefully, his accent only noticeable as a slight gentleness on the "r" and "th" sounds, he took his son through a pretended plane crash. "Past where all the people live, see?" he said.

Joey nodded, but Alison saw that the answer didn't satisfy him. Their father was a psychologist, and Alison knew that it frustrated him not to be able to cure Joey's nightmares. He had told her once that he had studied to become a rabbi before the war, but that after he had been through the camps he had lost his faith in God and turned to psychology. It had made her uncomfortable to hear that her father didn't believe in God.

"He had another nightmare last night," her mother said softly.

"I don't know what it is," her father said. "We try to make a safe place here for the kids. They're in no danger here. I don't understand why he's so frightened all the time."

"Eat your dinner before it gets cold, Alison," her mother said, noticing for the first time that Alison had not touched her food. "There was a time when I would have given anything to have just one bite of what you're turning down now."

The next day, Saturday, Alison called Laura and told her about the old man in the park. She wanted to go back and talk to him again, but Laura said she was crazy. "He's some kind of pervert or something, I bet," Laura said. "Didn't your parents tell you not to talk to strangers?"

"He's not—"

"Why don't you come over here instead?"

Alison liked going to Laura's house, liked her parents and the rest of the family. They were Jewish, the same as her family, but Laura's grandfather had come to America before the war. To Alison that made them exotic, different. They seemed to laugh more, for one thing. "Okay," she said.

The minute Alison stepped into the house Laura's mother called Laura to the phone, then disappeared on some errand of her own. No one had invited Alison farther in than the living room. She looked around her, hoping the call wouldn't last long. In the next room Laura laughed and said something about the Girl Scout meeting.

The furniture in the living room was massive and overstuffed: a couch, two easy chairs, a coffee table and several end tables. A grandfather clock ticked noisily in the corner of the room, and opposite it stood a clunky old-fashioned television that Alison knew to be black and white.

For the first time she noticed the profusion of photographs, what looked like hundreds of them, spread out over the mantelpiece and several end tables. All of them had heavy, ornate frames, and doilies to protect the surfaces under them. Curious, she went over to the mantelpiece to get a closer look.

Most were black and white, groups of children bunched around a stern-looking mother and father. Everyone stared straight ahead, unsmiling. The fathers wore fancy evening clothes Alison had never seen outside of movies, and sometimes a top hat and even a walking cane. The mothers wore dresses covering them from head to foot, yards and yards of flowing, shiny material. In one of the pictures the children were all dressed alike, the girls in dark dresses and bows and the boys in coats and shorts.

A trembling hand came over her shoulder and pointed to a small boy in the front row. She turned quickly. Laura's grandfather stood there, leaning on his cane, his eyes watery behind thick glasses.

"That's me," he said. Alison looked back at the photograph,

trying to see this ancient man in the picture of the young boy. The shaking finger moved to another kid in the same picture. "And that's my brother Moishe."

He looked down at her, uncertain. His face was flushed now, suffused with blood, a waxy yellow mixed with red. His eyes were vacant; something had gone out of them.

The clock sounded loud in the room. Finally he said, "Which one are you?"

"What?"

"Which one of these are you? You're one of the cousins, aren't you?"

"No, I'm—I'm Alison—"

"Alice? I don't know an Alice. That's me in that picture there, and that's my brother Moishe. Or did I already tell you that?"

Should she tell him? She was unused to dealing with old people; all her grandparents had died in the war. But just then he seemed to pull himself together, to concentrate; she could see the man he used to be before he got old.

"Moishe played the trombone—it was a way of getting out of the army in Russia. If you played an instrument you could be in the marching band. He played for anyone, Moishe did, any army in the world. He didn't care. The only army he ever quit was the White Russians. You know why?"

Alison shook her head.

"Because they made their band march in front of them in the war," the old man said. He laughed loudly.

Alison laughed too. "What happened to him?"

The old man started to cough.

"Hi, Alison," Laura said. Alison turned; she hadn't heard Laura come in. "Let's go to my room. I got a new record yesterday."

As they walked up the stairs Laura said, "God, he's embarrassing. Sometimes he calls my mother by her maiden name—he thinks she's still a kid. My dad wants to put him in a nursing home but she won't let him. I hope he didn't bother you too much."

"No," Alison said. She felt something she couldn't name, a feeling like longing. "He's okay."

• • •

She didn't get a chance to go back to the park for another week, until Friday. Laura had remained firm about not wanting to meet Alfred. But when she finally got there she couldn't see him anywhere. Her heart sank. Why had she listened to Laura? Why hadn't she insisted?

No wait—there he was, sitting on the same bench, his head tilted back toward the sun. He looked thin, frail, even more transparent than the first time she'd seen him. She hurried toward him.

He opened his eyes and smiled. "Here she is—the child without a name," he said. "I was afraid you would not come again. I thought your mother might have told you not to talk to me."

"She doesn't know," Alison said.

"Ah. You should not keep secrets from your mother, you know that. But if you do, you should make sure that they are good ones."

Alison laughed. "Got any candy?"

"No, no candy." He looked around him, seeming to realize only then where he was. "Do you want to take a walk?"

"Sure."

He stood and they went down a shaded path. Alison shuffled through the fallen leaves; she wondered how Alfred managed to walk so quietly. Ahead of them, where the path came out into the sun, she saw a man with an ice cream cart, and she thought for a moment that Alfred might have intended to buy her a sweet after all. But they passed the cart without stopping, and she realized, ashamed, that he probably didn't have much money. "Do you want some ice cream?" she asked.

He laughed. "Thank you, no. I eat very little these days."

The path fell back into shade again. At the end of the path stood the old broken carousel, with a chain-link fence around it so that children could not play on it. Alfred stood and looked at it for a long time. "I made something like this once," he said.

"Really? Carousel animals?"

"No, not the animals. The—what do you call it? The mechanism that makes the thing go around." He moved his hand in a slow circle to demonstrate.

"Could you fix this?"

"Could I?" He looked at a carousel for a long time, studying the tilting floor, the cracked and leaning animals, the proud horse on which someone had carved "Freddy & Janet." Dirt and cobwebs had dulled the animals' paint. "How long has it been broken?"

"I don't know. It's been like this since I started coming to the park."

"I think I can fix it, yeah," he said. He pronounced it "Yah," just like her parents. "Yah, probably I could. Mostly I made large figures that moved. A king and a queen who came out like this"—he moved his hands together—"and kissed. And a magician who opened a box, and there was nothing inside it, and then he closed it, and opened it again, and there was a dove that flew away. I made that one for the Kaiser. Do you know who the Kaiser was?"

She shook her head.

"He was the king. The king of Germany."

"Did you have any kids?" she asked, thinking how great it would be to have a father like this man, and remembering the photograph of the two children in his watch. But almost immediately she wished she hadn't said anything. What if his children had died in the war, like so many of her parents' relatives?

"I did, yah," he said. "A boy and a girl. I wanted them to take over the business when I retired. It was a funny thing, though—they didn't want to."

"They were nuts," Alison said. "I would have done it in a minute."

"Ah, but you would have had to understand electricity, and how the mechanisms work, and mathematics. . . . Both my children were terrible at mathematics."

She was terrible at mathematics, too. But she thought that if she had been given a chance at the kind of work Alfred did she would have studied until she understood everything there was to know.

She could almost see his workshop in front of her, the gears and chains and hinges, the tall wooden cabinets filled with hands and silver hair, tin stars, carved dogs, and trumpets. The king and queen lay on their sides like fallen wooden angels, wearing robes

of silk and gauze, and wooden crowns with gaudy paste jewels.
The bird hung from the ceiling, waiting for its place inside the
magician's box. All around Alfred apprentices were cutting into
wood, or doing something incomprehensible with pieces of
machinery. She thought that she could even smell the wood; it had
the elusive scent of great trees, like a forest from a childhood fairy
tale.

She turned back to Alfred. What had happened? The day had
grown cold; she saw the sun set through the trees, dazzling her
vision. "I've got to go home," she said. "I'll be late for dinner."

"Oh. I hope I have not bored you terribly. I don't get much of
a chance to talk."

"No," she said. "Oh, no."

She hurried down the path, shivering in the first real cold of the
year. Once she looked back but Alfred had vanished among the
shadows of the trees and the carousel.

Her parents and Joey were already eating dinner when she got
home. "Where do you go on Fridays?" her mother said as she sat
down. "Doesn't Laura have her Girl Scout meeting today?"

"I don't go anywhere," Alison said.

"You know you're not supposed to be late for dinner. And what
about your homework?"

"Come on, Mom—it's Friday."

"That's right, it's Friday. Remember how long it took you to do
your math homework last week? If you start now you'll have it
done on time."

"We didn't get very much. I can do the whole thing on Sunday."

"Can you? I want to see it after dinner."

Her father looked at her mother. Sometimes Alison thought her
father might be on her side in the frequent arguments she had with
her mother, but that he didn't feel he had the right to interrupt.
Now he laughed and said to her mother, "What would you know
about math homework? You told me you didn't understand
anything past addition and subtraction."

"Well, then, you look at it," her mother said. "I want to make
sure she gets it done this time. And maybe you can ask her where
she goes after school. I don't think she's telling me the truth."

Alison looked down at her plate. What did her mother know? Sometimes she made shrewd guesses based on no evidence at all. She said nothing.

"Mrs. Smith says she saw you talking to an old man in the park," her mother said.

Alison didn't look up. Didn't Mrs. Smith have anything better to do than spy on everyone in the neighborhood?

"When I was your age I knew enough not to talk to strangers," her mother said. "The Gestapo came after my father—did I ever tell you that?"

Alison nodded miserably. She didn't want to hear the story again.

"They came to our house in Germany and asked for my father," her mother said. "I was twelve or thirteen then, just about your age. This was before they started sending Jews to the camps without a reason, and someone had overheard my father say something treasonous about Hitler. My mother said my father wasn't home.

"But he was home—he was up in the attic, hiding. What do you think would have happened if I'd talked to the Gestapo the way you talk to this man in the park? If I'd said, 'Oh, yes, Officer, he's up in the attic'? I was only twelve and I knew enough not to say anything. You kids are so stupid, so pampered, living here."

It wasn't the same thing, Alison thought, realizing it for the first time. Germany and the United States weren't the same countries. And Alfred had been in the camps too; he and her mother were on the same side. But she felt the weight of her mother's experience and couldn't say anything. Her mother had seen so much more than she had, after all.

"We escaped to Holland, stayed with relatives," her mother said. "And eight years later the Nazis invaded Holland and took us to concentration camps. My father worked for a while as an electrician, but finally he died of typhus. All of that, and he died anyway."

Her mother's voice held the bitterness Alison had heard all her life. Now she sighed and shook her head. Alison wanted to do something for her, to make everything all right. But what could she do, after all? She was only twelve.

She took the bus back to the park the next day. Alfred sat on his usual bench, his eyes closed and turned toward the sun. She dropped down on the bench next to him.

"Tell me a story," she said.

He opened his eyes slowly, as if uncertain where he was. Then he smiled. "You look sad," he said. "Did something happen?"

"Yeah. My mother doesn't want me to talk to you anymore."

"Why not?"

This was tricky. She couldn't say that her mother had compared him to the Gestapo. She couldn't talk about the camps at all with him; she never wanted to hear that note of bitterness and defeat come into his voice. Alfred was hers, her escape from the fears and sadness she had lived with all her life. He had nothing to do with what went on between Alison and her mother.

He was looking at her with curiosity and concern now, expecting her to say something. "It's not you. She doesn't trust most people," Alison said.

"Do you know why?"

"Yeah." His eyes were deep brown, she noticed, like hers, like her mother's. Why not tell him, after all? "She—she has a number on her arm. Like yours."

He nodded.

"And she—well, she went through a bad time, I guess." It felt strange to think of her mother as a kid. "She said the Gestapo came after her father when she was my age. She said he had to hide in the attic."

To her surprise Alfred started to nod. "I bet it was crowded in that attic too. Boxes and boxes of junk—I bet they never threw anything away. Probably hot too. But then who knew that someday someone would have to hide in it?"

At first his words made no sense whatsoever. Then she said, slowly, "You're him, aren't you? You're her father. My—my grandfather." The unfamiliar word felt strange on her tongue.

"What?" He seemed to rouse himself. "Your grandfather? I'm a crazy old man you met in the park."

"She said he died. You died. You're a ghost." She was whispering now. Chills kept coming up her spine, wave after wave of them. The sun looked cold and very far away.

He laughed. "A ghost? Is that what you think I am?"

She nodded reluctantly, not at all certain now.

"Listen to me," he said. "You're right about your mother—she went through a bad time. And it's hard for her to understand you, to understand what you're going through. Sometimes she's jealous of you."

"Jealous?"

"Sure, jealous. You never had to distrust people, or hide from them. You never went hungry, or saw anyone you loved killed. She thinks it's easy for you—she doesn't understand that you have problems too."

"She called me stupid. She said I would have talked to the Gestapo, would have told them where my father was. But I never would have done that."

"No. It was unfair of her to say that. She wants you to think of the world the way she does, as an unsafe place. But you have to make up your own mind about what the world is like."

She was nodding even before he had finished. "Yeah. Yeah, that's what I thought, only I couldn't say it. Because she's been through so much more than I have, so everything she thinks seems so important. I couldn't tell her that what happens to me is important too."

"No, and you might never be able to tell her. But you'll know it, and I'll know it too."

"What was your father's name?" Alison asked her mother that night at dinner. Joey stopped eating and gave her a pleading look; he was old enough to know that she was taking the conversation in a dangerous direction.

"Alfred," her mother said. "Why do you ask?"

There were probably a lot of old men named Alfred running around. Did she only think he was her grandfather because she wanted what Laura had, wanted someone to tell her family stories, to connect her with her past?

"Oh, I don't know," she said, trying to keep her voice casual. "I was wondering about him, that's all. Do you have a picture of him?"

"What do you think—we were allowed to take photographs with us to the camps?" The bitterness was back in her mother's voice. "We lost everything."

"Well, what did he look like?"

"He was—I don't know. A thin man, with black hair. He brushed it back, I remember that."

"Did he wear glasses?"

Her mother looked up at that. "Yah, he did. How did you know?"

"Oh, you know," Alison said quickly. "Laura's grandfather has glasses, so I thought . . . What did he do?"

"I named you after him," her mother said. "I wanted a name that started with A." To Alison's great astonishment, she began to laugh. "He told that story about the attic all the time, when we lived in Holland. How crowded it was. He said my mother never threw anything away." She took a deep breath and wiped her eyes. "He made it sound like the funniest thing that ever happened to him."

Alison walked slowly through the park. It was Sunday and dozens of families had come out for the last warmth of the year, throwing frisbees, barbecuing hamburgers in the fire pits. Joey held her hand tightly, afraid to let go.

She began to hurry, pushing her way through the crowds. Had she scared Alfred off by guessing his secret? She knew what he was now. He had drifted the way Laura's grandfather sometimes drifted, had forgotten his own time and had slipped somehow into hers. Or maybe this was the one wish the angel had granted him, the wish he hadn't known he wanted. However it had happened he had come to her, singled her out. She had a grandfather after all.

But what if she was wrong? What if he was just a lonely old man who needed someone to talk to?

There he was, up ahead. She ran toward him. "Hey," Joey said anxiously. "Hey, wait a minute."

"Hi," Alison said to the old man, a little breathless. "I've decided to tell you my name. My name's Alison, and I was named after my grandfather Alfred. And this is my brother, Joey. Joey's afraid of things. I thought you might talk to him."

A Plethora of Angels
by
Robert Sampson

The late Robert Sampson was a veteran pulp-era author who had sold to Planet Stories *and* Weird Tales, *and who, toward the end of his life, retired from NASA's Marshall Space Flight Center and began to revitalize his career with a number of sales to some of the top short fiction markets in both the science fiction and mystery fields. In mystery, he won the Edgar Award for the best mystery story of 1986. In the science fiction genre, his stories appeared in* Full Spectrum, Strange Plasma, Asimov's Science Fiction, *and elsewhere. His most recent book was* Dangerous Horizons, *a study of famous series characters of the pulp-magazine era. He lived for many years in Huntsville, Alabama, and died in 1993 at the age of sixty-five.*

The story that follows shows that yes, you can *have too much of anything—even angels . . .*

* * *

No one agrees why the angels came to Twin Tree. Some claim they were sent and find confirmation in Genesis or Revelation. Others, younger and infected by science, speak of an accidental opening rubbed between alternate worlds. Myself, sometimes I believe the angels were an expedition that went wrong. Sometimes I think that.

But what do I know? I'm guessing like everyone else. And I have an advantage: I was there at the beginning, watching the angels spill from that shimmery place near the cliff face.

Not from a hole. It was nothing like that. It was more a dim indentation of air close to the rock. That's a vague description, I grant you. How else could it be? When those angels poured out, all those hundreds of angels rustling like blown canvas, I never thought to look at their doorway.

Neither did Dad nor Uncle Win. We all stood unbelieving in that muddy road.

"A million butterflies," Uncle Win yelped.

"They're little women," Dad cried. He sounded shocked to his bones.

Both were wrong. The angels weren't either. To tell the truth, I don't know what they were. We called them angels, and they might have been. But at first, I thought they were doves.

Until one fluttered down not two feet from my eyes. Its wings pulsed air against my face. It peered at me with golden eyes. Its face was the size of my thumbnail, even-featured, with a minute round mouth. Clearly not a bird, or a woman, either.

This happened in Twin Tree, Alabama, my hometown, an undistinguished little place just south of the Tennessee line.

If it hadn't been for a week-long rain, I don't suppose Twin Tree would have come closer to angels than Christmas decorations.

For one solid week, cold gray water sheeted down. The creek shoved into our back fields, tumbling and rough, growling to itself. Trees slumped black and leafless and gloomy. When you went outside between rain spasms, ground water rose around your shoes.

This was a few years ago. Back then I was fresh out of the Army and inclined to spend my separation money on jeans and beer and seeing if the girls were still cute. Only I felt shaky about going back to college. I'd spent two years in Germany, defending the Free World against the Evil Empire. That was great for the Free World. But I wasn't sure the Army had left anything in my head except brown fuzz.

The university waited for me a month away, glowing with menace like a red-hot block. That scared me. I decided to hole up at home to get reacquainted with calculus.

Dad said only a wimp would get free of the military and start reading calculus. Probably he was right. Anyhow, I settled in with the book, the sky curdled, the rain roared down.

You might think that weather was perfect for studying. But I wasn't alone in the house. Mom and Dad were cooped in with me. Also Aunt Ellen and Uncle Win.

That's too many people in too few rooms, listening to the rain pouncing at the roof, and the air so wet you stuck to what you touched. After a week of it, we could barely stand to look at each other.

Finally, on Wednesday afternoon, the storm blew out. Dad tossed his cards down on the table and ducked outside. Said he wanted to check things. About an hour later, he came tramping into the barn, where I was shoveling out the horse stalls. I should have been at calculus, but stalls were easier.

His pants hung black with water. Looking soaked and cheerful, he said: "That rock face down by the creek, it's got a crack in it big as the Mayor's mouth. Think we ought to take some dynamite to it."

That dig was at Mayor Stevens of Twin Tree. When Dad and his old friend, Sheriff Hock, get together over a weekend, they keep mentioning the Mayor. He is a crooked, rancid liar with the brains of a tick, according to Dad, who doesn't often exaggerate.

I was tired of books and stalls, so I followed Dad to the outbuilding where he keeps gas and dynamite and such excitable stuff.

"Those rocks let go," Dad remarked, "they'll cripple up some of those pet horses of yours. It's right by where they water."

I knew that the cliff face is usually thirty feet uphill from the creek. Any horse wanting to get hit by falling rock would have to hike for the pleasure. Since Dad sounded defensive, I figured he really wanted to hear the bang. That's more entertaining than watching the trees drip.

While he was fingering through the sawdust in the dynamite box for those yellow-brown sticks, I saw Uncle Win picking his way toward us. He moved through the wet grass as cautiously as a cat meeting company.

Sticking his head into the doorway, he said in his thin voice: "By God, Sam, you take care now."

I saw Dad go a little tight around the mouth. Over the past week, he'd heard a lot of advice from Uncle Win.

I said: "Dad's going to knock down some loose rock, Win. Want to go watch?"

"Well, I was thinking of doing something else," Win said. "But I guess I better go along. He might make some fool mistake."

That was not the smartest thing to let out of his mouth. That's why we slopped down to the creek in a haze of bad feelings, the two of them biting off short sentences at each other.

The fields stopped at a line of thin trees, tangled and black. Beyond them bare rock angled down to a cut roaring with water. Along the upper cliff ran a two-inch crack, deep and ugly, looking ready to drop by itself. I doubted that we needed dynamite. But this was entertainment, not business.

"Now," Dad said to me, "let's see if the Army learned you anything."

We fixed a couple of sticks with detonators and fuse. Dad eased them down into the crack, and I packed them good with mud and rock.

Win cleared his throat and edged toward the road. "Sam, you cut that fuse mighty short."

"Long enough," Dad growled. "No need to stand in the wet all day."

He bent to fire the fuse. As it spurted smoke, we stepped off down the road, Win well ahead of us. Dad ambled slowly behind, demonstrating that he knew exactly how long to cut a fuse.

We stopped in an angle of the road that gave a clear view of the cliff face. After a longish wait, there came a dull little thud, sounding like a sack of cement dropped off the tailgate. Vague gray mist hazed up. A section of rock shrugged loose and slumped leisurely into the creek, slapping up brown foam.

As the stonefall lolled into the water, a bray of thunder hit us. It was just one peal but violent enough to jar us good.

Uncle Win yelped like he'd been scalded. Bits of white swirled against the gray rock. A cloud of white spurted up, expanding, whirling, becoming huge, fluttering like confetti in the wind. White billowed and tumbled out over the creek, swelled above the trees. It sprayed all around us.

Heard Dad's breath suck in his mouth.

Wings shone all around us. I heard liquid chattering, musical and soft. The air smelled faintly of sunny flower beds.

"Look out!" yelled Uncle Win, throwing up his hands. "They'll bite!"

Out of the crazy whirl dropped an angel. It hung before me, balanced on slowly pulsing wings. It was a tiny lustrous thing, perhaps a foot between wing tips. The feathers were lovely soft white, edged by faint blue and transparent yellow. Gliding shades of white flowed like liquid across the inside of the wings.

Between the wings canted a slender body, long as your hand, the color of rich milk. It had golden eyes. Silver-white fuzz, like dandelion fluff, covered its head. It was completely beautiful.

Not that it was anything like a woman. It had no sex. Just a smooth, neat, dainty body. It smiled at me and uttered a single silver-tone.

The world around me became peculiar and far off. Only the angel seemed real. It was solid as crystal. Every detail of feathers, arms, face, shone clear and bright. Myself, I felt like a ghost shaking in the wind.

As if it understood my feelings, the angel cooed softly. Next thing I knew, it was perched on my shoulder, pressing up against my cheek.

The minute it touched me, I felt better. The shock faded out of me. The angel couldn't have weighed over a couple of ounces and it felt resilient and warm. It felt completely right sitting there.

"Comfortable?" I asked, turning my head.

Murmuring dainty sounds floated from it. One little hand touched my face. It didn't say words, then or later. The angels got along on musical sounds. And touches. Their touch explained more than words.

Dad was standing in the road, face an absolute blank. On each shoulder rode an angel. All around Win, angels wheeled, patting his bald head and trilling.

"Why, ain't these cute!" he yelled, reached out a hand. An angel swooped down on his fingers and let its bright wings trail.

By then, hundreds of angels swirled around us, reached out to touch, their golden eyes wide, as if we were something they had always heard about but never expected to see. Their wings made the sound of crushing tissue paper.

Sometime later, surrounded by angels, we splashed back to the house.

Mom was outside, pouring pellets into the dog dish. When she saw us, her mouth came open. She dropped the sack and grabbed for the door.

"Sam Williamson," she shouted, "don't you bring those things in here!"

Two or three angels swooped to pat her face and hair, and marvel at the way she talked, and cuddle on her shoulders.

"Why, aren't they dear?" she said. "Ellen! Ellen, come out here and look."

I saw Aunt Ellen glaring from inside the screen door. "Birds," she cried, her voice sharp with disgust. "Get in this house, Virginia Ann. They carry disease."

"They're not birds," Mom said. She opened the screen.

Ellen squealed once as the doorway turned white with wings. When her face reappeared, we could see the peevishness and fright leaving her.

"They're little people," she said. "Aren't they lovely?"

We all crowded into the kitchen. It was a busy place. Across the ceiling wheeled dozens of angels, darting, touching, staring, trilling. The five of us stared at each other.

"Where did these come from, Sam?" Mom asked.

So Dad had to tell about the rock wall and the dynamite.

By the look on Mom's face, she had strong feelings about dynamite and was inclined to talk about them. Before she got started, an angel pressed its minute fingers against her mouth.

Wide-eyed amazement caught Mom's face. Instead of scolding, she looked gently concerned, said: "Sam, you know that's dangerous."

"Now, honey," Dad said. "I didn't want to worry you."

They fell to hugging each other in a surprising way for mid-morning.

Uncle Win glanced sideways at them and cleared his throat. He said: "Lemme get the mop. I'll just clean me some mud off this floor."

I saw we'd brought a lot of field into the kitchen. So I slipped off my shoes, and collected Dad's and Win's, intending to scrape them off outside. I was at the door, when angels began bobbing and chiming, all excited, around the kitchen table. Their white arms waved toward the cards scattered there. They might have been pointing out snakes.

Dad stared from cards to angels. Finally he gave a big sigh. "Well, I guess . . ."

He tossed the cards into the wastebasket. That pleased the angels. They flocked all over him, cooing and flapping, caressing his hair.

I went outside and cleaned shoes. When I stepped back into the kitchen, Uncle Win had finished mopping the floor. Dad was at the sink washing dishes, which I'd heard him swear he'd never do, no, sir, not ever in this life.

In the living room, Mom was on the telephone. Half a dozen angels sang at her. More glided around inspecting the room.

Mom said: "Reverend James. This is Mrs. Williamson. I want you to come right over. It's the most wonderful thing. . . ."

Aunt Ellen caught at my arm. "Now would you look at this," she said.

A wall of angels fluttered between us and the television. Their backs were to the tube; their little hands gestured us away. They made a nervous chittering sound, like hens watching a hawk.

"They don't like TV," Aunt Ellen said. "It's the *Spin for a Million* show, too."

"Change channels," I suggested.

"I did. They don't like anything."

She fretted, working her mouth. Finally she reached among the vibrating wings to punch the screen off. "I wouldn't want to upset the poor things."

The angels seemed delighted. After the menace of television ended, a swirl of them spun around her, making a sugary murmur. Others floated about the room, fingering the curtains and probing the ceiling corners. On the coffee table, a pair rustled through the magazines, shoving all the hunting issues onto the floor.

Along the wall, half a dozen angels inspected Mom's collection of family photographs. After a while, they broke into an indignant belling. Two of them got hold of Aunt Fay's photograph—the one where she looks so blond and racy—and twisted it to face the wall.

Aunt Ellen looked at me. "You know," she said, "I always wondered about Fay."

I thought we might get awful tired of angels in judgment. But I said: "Guess I might go try the calculus again."

"You just do that," Ellen said. She sounded vaguely elated. "Believe I'll just sew up some potholders for the church."

That overjoyed the angels. As they chirped around Ellen, I went in back and opened the book. Angels clustered around to see if they could help. After the second problem, they gave it up and sat around purring sympathetically.

Before I worked half a page, a car door slammed out front. Looking out the window, I saw the Reverend James of the United Holiness Congregation hurrying toward the house.

The Reverend was short and heavy. Fighting sin had dragged down the corners of his mouth and eyes and bent his head. He moved like a man carrying too many rocks.

His full voice said: "Sister Williamson, it's a joy and a blessing to see you—"

At the way his voice cut off, I judged he'd got a good look at the angels.

"What on earth?" he barked.

Mom said: "They're just angels, Reverend. You come right in."

I closed up the calculus and drifted out to the kitchen. It wasn't every day I could see a minister face to face with the stuff of sermons.

He stood in the kitchen, looking as edgy as a man with a snake in his pocket. "But they're tiny!" he boomed.

"I guess an angel can be any size it wants," Mom told him.

"Can't be angels." He jerked off his hat and waved it at them. That amused the angels. They flittered around his head, making tiny joyous sounds.

"The Holy Scriptures say—" he began, trying to shake himself and talk at the same time.

Whatever the Holy Scriptures had to say, it was lost as the

angels' touch took effect. His face lightened and some of his deeper wrinkles smoothed out.

"God's mercy," he gasped. "It's a miracle."

"Aren't they sweet?" Mom asked.

"Under the circumstances," he said, "I think we might join together in prayer."

I caught an un-Christian flash in Dad's eyes. Reverend James' prayers were more like novels than short stories, and they tended to get louder as they got longer.

I grinned to myself. And the Reverend prayed.

All the angels settled down to listen, their wings folded respectfully, their little hands closed. Now and then a wing jerked to a more comfortable position. Their bare feet rubbed together.

The Reverend started with our family and he prayed for each of us until you wondered when we'd had time to get that sinful. Then he discussed the angels, the solar system, the mystery of the universe, and the Inscrutable Will. He didn't leave much out. Before he finished, I noticed a lot of wing folding and foot twisting. The angels seemed used to less comprehensive prayers.

When he finally thundered, "Amen!" angels shot into the air to whirl crazily around the kitchen, belling and chiming, making a golden racket.

"Dare I hope," the Reverend said to Mom, "dare I hope that they will join us in church in demonstration of the Infinite Glory of God?"

"I should think so," she said.

As he drove off, a cloud of angels traveled with him, floating above his automobile. Even after he was out of sight, we could track the car by the flock dipping and wheeling and moving slowly off through the trees.

Dad laughed. "Gonna be some surprised people come Sunday."

As it worked out, some people were amazed before then.

Long before supper time, Mom got to worrying about what she could feed the angels.

"They eat manna," I said.

She said thoughtfully: "I should have asked Reverend James. I'm not that sure about manna."

"It looks like goldfish food," I said. "White and sort of thin and sweet."

"Maybe I can make some little cakes," she said, sidestepping as Dad slouched into the kitchen.

He was smiling as if a tooth hurt. One hand clutched his pipe and tobacco. On his shoulders rode a pair of angels, hiding their faces and making a dismal low moaning.

In a forced voice, he said, "Guess I think I'll give up smoking."

He banged open a drawer, slammed in pipe and tobacco, and whacked the drawer shut.

"I'm proud of you," Mom said. "You should of quit years ago."

"I suppose so," Dad said glumly. The angels took their faces out of their hands to make sparkling little sounds.

Mom said to me: "Jack, you better go down to the store. I need some good flour."

"I'll see if they got any manna," I said.

"Get me some chewing gum," Dad growled.

Which is why I walked into Doc Steeger's One Stop at five-thirty, wearing an angel on each shoulder.

To tell the truth, I wasn't that eager to walk in decorated with angels. It was sure to draw lip from Buddy, Doc's son. Buddy is a red-faced lump of fat with curly black hair and a mouth that never quits.

I figured that when I couldn't stand his cracks anymore, I'd lean over and quick bump him with my fist before the angels made me love him. But that wasn't necessary. Angels had arrived at the One Stop before me.

A swarm of them floated around that big old store, playing tag with the four-bladed ceiling fan. More fluttered along the top shelves, inspecting cereal boxes. In the hardware section, wings flashed among the churns and tin tubs.

Doc himself was busy taping a sheet of butcher paper across the beer coolers. On the paper he'd printed SECTION CLOSED. When he saw me, he called: "Don't sell beer no more, Jack," as if I never came in for anything else.

I told him no beer was needed and moved to the counter. Buddy slouched there, as greasy and sulky as ever. Angels loaded him down.

"You, too?" he asked, looking at my angels.

"Uh-huh."

"Well, I tell you this, Williamson," he snapped. He stopped, swallowed, glowered, said: "You and me, we've had our differences. But I want to tell you, I forgive you. I don't hold no hard feelings and hope you feel the same."

His eyes said he'd like to bend my neck.

I grinned into his fat face. "That's mighty Christian, Buddy. I'm glad you've quit being such a worthless, no-good pain—"

Three angels dropped between us, lamenting and fluttering pitifully. The angel on my left shoulder placed an arm over my mouth. It made a fading, weeping sound.

"Oh, shoot," I said. "I guess I feel the same way."

"It's no use," Buddy said. "I've tried. They don't let you be natural."

I decided not to tell him that when he was natural, he was disgusting. Instead I gave him Mom's order. He waddled off, accompanied by a covey of angels, fluttering up and down the shelves. Their wings blew out an astonishing amount of dust.

While I was sitting on the counter, keeping quiet, the Mayor's wife, Amelia Stevens, trotted in. As usual, she wore a pound of powder and a ton of Indian jewelry. She was enjoying her share of angels, too.

Marching up to Doc, she asked: "You got any Bibles, Mr. Steeger?"

"Well, no," he said, coming away from the beer cooler. "I'm ordering a gross tomorrow."

"I need one tonight," she said. "It's for the Mayor."

I saw Doc's eyebrows reach for his hair. "The Mayor?"

"I guess we've misplaced our Bible," she said, looking as if she had borrowed someone else's smile. "The Mayor wants to read about angels."

I thought it more likely he wanted to check the description of Hell. But I had enough sense to keep quiet. I slipped off home with the groceries and told Dad that the Mayor couldn't find his Bible.

"Burn the fingers off him to touch it," Dad said.

That remark set the angels lamenting and looking sad. Dad swallowed and put on an unreal smile. "I tell you, Jack," he sighed, "this living a blameless life is hard."

He was right. Over the next few days, the effort to live blamelessly took a lot out of us. Some of us gave up beer. All of us gave up second helpings at dinner. The angels didn't eat that much, being content with five or six crumbs from Mom's cakes. I thought small flying creatures ate their own weight every day; but not these.

Since television upset the angels, we spent evenings sitting around in clean clothes, telling each other how good we felt, how glad we were to live in a state of grace.

The cards stayed in the wastebasket and the tobacco in the kitchen drawer. Uncle Win and Dad chewed about eleven packs of gum between them. I read calculus till I almost believed it. It was Sunday all week.

Now and then, when the silence grew terrible, the angels sang in chorus. They never sang anything that I knew. They favored slow chants, soft and remote, sounding like gold and silver sheets shimmering through each other. Bursts of trills fell across that sound like dashes of rain. It was delicate, very lovely. But by the time you went to bed, you felt you'd spent the whole night crying.

"You figure this is all they do in Heaven?" Uncle Win asked. He had been slouched down in the chair for an hour, staring at the backs of his hands.

I said: "I've been thinking about that. You know, when it comes down to it, they don't have to be from Heaven. They don't even have to be angels."

Dad rolled his eyes toward the kitchen. "Your mother hear that, she'd set you straight in a hurry."

"I read something once," I said. "About parallel universes. If there gets to be a hole between them, you could cross right over. See the angels could be from another dimension. Maybe another star."

Dad sniffed. "You've been reading those magazines. They make you think funny."

"Besides," I added, "the angels don't even understand English. They just react to voice tones."

Uncle Win looked as blank as if he'd been erased and Dad snorted and grinned. "Well, look here," I said, picking up an angel. After making sure that Aunt Ellen and Mom were in the kitchen, I addressed the angel in a loving, respectful voice, using some of the words I'd learned while defending the Free World. Given the right tone, they were exactly the right words for describing officers or removing scale from metal.

"Merciful salvation," Dad said sharply. "Sounds like you were brought up behind a mule."

The angel, which had been playing contentedly with my fingers, went stiff at the sound of his voice. It wailed dolefully.

"Good grief," he said.

"See," I told him, "It's all in the voice."

"Well, I'll be damned," Uncle Win said, gentle-voiced. When the angel didn't respond to that, Win grinned all over. Lifting out of his chair, he hurried off to practice his art on other angels.

Dad shook his head. "I don't want to hear such talk. I brought you up better than that. Angels probably don't speak English in Heaven. Old Testament, likely."

I was feeling ashamed that I had deceived the angel, so I stroked its back with a finger, making it arc its wings in pleasure. I said: "They may look like angels. But I bet they're extraterrestrials."

"You let the women hear you," Dad said, "and there'll be war."

But I noticed elation in his eyes. I suspect he was thinking more about his pipe than angelic origins.

The next morning, Saturday, Dad rose from the breakfast table and said: "I'm going to Twin Tree. Want to see about a fan belt."

"I'll come along and help," I said.

Fifteen or twenty angels seemed interested in fan belts, too. No sooner did they get outside, away from the choral society, than they exploded straight up into the sky. We stood watching them roll and tumble and spread their arms to plunge headlong through the sunlight. They were winged creatures, after all. And wings like to fly. Not sit in a narrow house, harmonizing in five sharps and two intervals.

"Happy," I said, squinting up at them.

"So'm I," Dad said.

I realized then that, for the first time in days, neither one of us had an angel perched on him.

"We get back home," Dad said, "I'm going to open me a beer, angels or not. Being good's dry work."

"We can get us a couple in town," I said.

If I were paid for predicting, I wouldn't have made a cent. The two taverns in town were shut tight, blinds drawn, lights out. On Saturday morning, yet.

The one place in town doing big business was the United Holiness Congregational church. Cars and trucks, all bright with polish, jammed the parking lot. From the open doors surged singing. It wasn't as sweet as angel music, but it was enthusiastic.

Dad listened without unusual excitement. "I always sort of liked Willie Nelson," he remarked. And didn't say a thing more till we parked at Blackwort's Transportation City.

Blackwort's huge sign that usually flashed CRAZY DEALS in three colors was dark. Dad vanished through the open door. I stayed outside, enjoying the sun.

The air smelled softly sweet, like washed leaves. The sky glowed transparent blue, smooth and rich as glaze. I felt light and mildly foolish. Off over the center of town, a flock of angels drifted in a sleepy shifting spiral.

As I sprawled against the truck, enjoying the feel of warm metal, an angel glided over Blackwort's roof and curved lazily toward me.

I jerked erect, scowling at it, wondering what would happen if I ducked when it tried to sit on me. But that I never found out. The angel paid no attention to me.

As it curved by, not ten feet away, I saw that it peered eagerly back toward Blackwort's roof. Its wings glowed bright pink in the sunshine. It was the first angel I'd seen with colored wings.

As it floated overhead, I got the second shock of the day.

It was a little woman, all right. No question about it. Firm little breasts rose from the smooth white chest. Her lips shone bright red.

As she angled smoothly away, another angel streaked past. He was a he, too. No mistake. Blue-tinted wings twitched just a fraction, flicking him above the truck.

Over the middle of the road, he caught up with pink wing. They linked arms. Silver sound spilled out of the air, like tiny laughing. They curved up past the telephone lines, out of sight.

When Dad came out, carrying his fan belt, I was still squinting open-mouthed at the sky.

He said: "That Blackwort's gone slap crazy. Know what he's about? He's in there writing refund checks. Said the angels made him realize how bad he's been overcharging his customers. Wants to make it up to them."

"Know what I just saw?" I cried, all excited.

"He's worked back through 1984," Dad said. "Now he's starting on 1983. What's the matter with you?"

I told him what I'd seen. He laughed till he dropped the fan belt. "Why, they've been around people too much," he yelled. "Stands to reason. Little women. Now I heard it all."

He leaned against the truck, ha-ha-ing till I got disgusted and offered to drive.

By rights we should have headed home. But I was curious to see more angels holding hands. So I drove toward the center of town.

It was quiet as the Intensive Care ward. Nobody was on the streets. Half the stores were closed. Nothing moved except a dozen angels whizzing among the trees. One of them, the color of new grass, chased one a light lemon shade. I saw at least a dozen reds and blues, and single gaudy purple fellow.

"Pull over there by the jail," Dad said. His eyes were swollen from laughing. "I'll just stop in and tell the Sheriff to do something about that undressed lady."

I trailed him into the jail, which was also the post office, police station, and court. It was a low brick building that had been painted gray before it was painted white. Both colors were flaking off. Inside it smelled like wax and old cigarettes.

Dad pushed open the door to the Sheriff's office. We stepped into a narrow room packed with desks and filing cabinets heaped with papers. A tall, thin lady, with a cigarette hanging out of her mouth, tapped at a computer keyboard. At her elbow sat an ashtray mounded with cigarette butts. Beside it sprawled an angel, head propped on one arm, watching her. The angel had blue wings and looked as if he needed a shave.

"Hey, Dottie," Dad said, looking sideways at the angel. "Where's the Sheriff?"

"In the jail," she said, not looking up.

"Good place for him," Dad said. "I want to see him."

"Can't," she said. "Not visiting hours."

She spurted smoke down over the angel. Instead of leaping to her shoulder and looking unhappy, he tipped back his head to suck in a long breath. It was a he and could have done with a pair of pants.

"What's visiting hours got to do with it?" Dad asked.

"You can't see prisoners except at visiting hours." Her voice would have curdled lemon juice.

"Sheriff Hock!"

"Put himself in jail yesterday. Said he was in with bootleggers and should be locked up." She snorted. "I think he's gone crazy. Been listening to too many angels. I'm the only one here and I don't have time to—"

The phone rang. She scooped it up and, in a voice like cut glass, said: "Sheriff's office." A pause. "OK, Mildred. I dunno what we can do. But I'll send somebody around."

Whacking down the phone, she punched the intercom. "Johnny. You there, Johnny? Damn that fool, he's never there when— Hello, Johnny. Listen, Mildred Panatokis just called. Said there's a bunch of angels acting dirty outside her house. Run over and calm her down, will you?"

She slapped off the intercom and attacked the computer again. Dad cleared his throat loudly. "About the Sheriff . . ."

"Got the cell right next to the Mayor's," she said irritably. "Give me a break, Sam. I got to get this report out by twelve."

"What did the Mayor do?"

"Turned himself in," she snarled. "I had to listen to him confess half the night. If we arrested everybody he named, we'd put wire around the town and call it Twin Tree Concentration Camp."

The angel rolled over on his stomach and sniggered.

"What's all that color on his wings?" I asked.

She transferred her glare from Dad to me. "It's that dry pigment. Mix it with water and you get poster paint. It's a big fad with the angels. Now, please, for God's sake, close the door on your way out."

As I closed the door, the angel lifted a butt from the ash tray and took a long sniff.

I stamped to the truck, mad to my bones.

"What's the matter?" Dad asked.

"Nothing."

A purple feather drifted down the windshield and blew across the hood. Overhead, two angels, pink and purple, rolled over and over across the sky, tightly clenched.

Squinting up at them, Dad remarked: "They sure learned quick."

"I liked them better when they were white." My own violence surprised me. "They were pretty, white."

"Things change," he said after a while.

We drove home silently. Not an angel returned with us. All the way back, I felt waves of anger beating in me. I felt sorry for the angels, embarrassed for them. Every time I thought of the purple and pink angels clinging to each other, I got mad all over again.

This week, gaudy feathers. Bright lips. Sex characteristics. Next week, they'd be swilling beer and shortchanging friends.

We hadn't meant to contaminate them. It was completely accidental. That's what burned me. For some reason or the other, they came rushing into this world. Unwary, friendly, impressionable, vulnerable to our casual bad habits. I felt ashamed for the human race.

If I'd come across Buddy Steeger just them, I'd have smacked his fat face sideways.

As we drove up to our house, Aunt Ellen came scampering to

meet us. She oozed happy malice. "Those angels are hugging each other," she called. "I call that scandalous."

Scandalous was the word. While we had been gone, there had been an influx of decadence. Pairs of brightly colored angels threshed along the ceiling, piping and exuberant. Little legs kicked. A feather tumbled down.

"It was just half an hour ago," Aunt Ellen said. "Came flying in here like they'd gone crazy. Now look." She waved fiercely at an intertwined couple at the top of the curtains. "Stop that! Shoo!"

On the coffee table sat an angel, wings rigidly outstretched. Two others brushed pink powder onto her feathers. A dozen others watched, jingling musically among themselves. Some wore lipstick and sat swelling out their tiny breasts.

Mom eyed us grimly. "I'm going to have to pass out nightgowns," she said. "I don't hold with all this nakedness."

"All over Twin Trees the same way," I said, ashamed to look at the angels.

Cool air puffed in the side door, bringing faint thunder.

A cluster of white angels huddled on a bookcase watched the proceedings with amazed golden eyes. They looked fascinated and scared. I stalked over to them, said:

"Do something. They're your friends, aren't they? Settle them down. Don't just sit there."

"They don't understand the language, Jack," Dad drawled.

They understood my tone, though. They wouldn't look at me. They pressed close together, gripping hands, all humped up and looking sick. Even their feathers looked miserable.

Hot flecks of anger swam in me. Turning on my heel, I said to the angel on the coffee table. "Now stop that. Stop messing yourself up. You look terrible. You look like a prize from the midway."

Pink wings fluttered, throwing off a faint cloud of powder. The angel tipped back her head, impertinence in every line. She spilled out crystal teasing tones and darted to the top of a window. She began to posture and prance.

Thunder muttered in the distance. At the sound, the white angels bobbed and twittered. They sounded like hysterical chickens.

"Comin' up rain," Dad said, cocking his head. "I do admit, Jack, they don't act like they came from Heaven."

"They're heavenly creatures," Mom said grimly. "Or they used to be."

"They should have better sense," he said.

"We're heavenly creatures," Mom said, "and look at us."

In the kitchen, a dozen angels pressed against the screen door, peering toward the thunder. I opened the door for them. One by one, they soared out, skimming across the grass, flashing up suddenly to curve smoothly away above the trees.

The sky was clear but that dull thunder pulsed to my left.

Dad came to stand beside me. "It thundered when they came," he said.

Wings flashed and a velvet touch crossed my hand. A white angel hovered near my face. It uttered a single melancholy syllable. As I reached out, the angel pressed its face against my finger. Then it rustled away through the open door.

That seemed so much like a goodbye that I stepped outside to watch its flight. It was gone. High across the cloudless sky hurried a disorderly stream of angels. Uneven lines of them undulated overhead, white and blue and red, like bits of a shattered rainbow.

Dad shaded his eyes. "They're coming down at the creek."

"Let's run down there and watch," I said.

Uncle Win joined us in the yard. He looked bright-eyed and tickled. "You should of seen that pink angel dance," he said. "Say, when I was in Philadelphia—I guess it was in 1943—I paid three dollars to watch a worse dance than that."

Another rush of angels pushed from the kitchen. Crying in their sweet voices, they sailed past, wings rattling as they angled into the air. Among them, I glimpsed the pink-winged angel. She spiraled above my head, laughing down, making a teasing face.

"Best we get moving," Dad said.

Thunder growled.

Above the creek, the air churned with angels, thousands of them. They angled in clusters from the sky, flocking over the fields, swirling among the trees. They spun like merging galaxies, suns flashing among suns. The air shivered with the beat of wings.

I felt the hard pulse of my heart; my breath came short.

Over the creek, the whirling fed into a thick stream of angels that rushed steeply toward the gray rock wall. No thunder now. Only the sound of wings, and a softer sighing sound, like shaken silk. As the angels plunged into the stream, their wings folded; arms and legs extended like divers, they swept straight toward the rock.

To vanish a few inches from the wall. Even then, I never thought to look hard at their doorway.

I felt stifled. Images swarmed through my head and twisting bits of words. I thought of angry gods and other worlds, punishment, wings. My brains had melted to soup.

High above us, at the edge of the stream, sun glowed on pink wings. I saw a little arm wave jauntily toward us. Pink Wing seemed merrily unconcerned. No shadow of retribution marred that airy gesture.

She plunged smoothly into the stream and was gone.

I saw with a shock that the stream of angels had thinned. A few stragglers shot past, minnows fleeing for shelter. Thunder growled over the creek. The sound of wings stopped.

That was all. No angels. No depression in the air. All gone. Leaving behind only the liquid purling of the creek, a sound coarse after the delicate crying of the angels. A sore emptiness opened in me.

"Well, that's done," Dad said.

We moved slowly to the lip of the rock wall, peering down at the rocks below and the creek sliding past. A few straggling redbuds grew at the edge. Behind them, a long ugly hole had opened in the soil, as if a groundhog tunnel had collapsed there.

Uncle Win knelt at the edge and stared over. "What I want to know is where those angels got to? Stands to reason, they must of gone someplace."

He sniffed sharply. "Stinks here. You can still smell the dynamite."

Faint breeze rattled limbs. I saw shadows twitch across Win's back and slip across his neck.

I took a quick step back. Just for a second, I seemed to see movement down in that hole. Movement and a transient glitter like mica bits, bright as tiny eyes.

The breeze died and the shadows stopped moving and, for the life of me, I couldn't decide whether one had flowed down inside Win's collar or not.

"Uncle Win," I said. "That sure looks like a snake hole."

"Snakes," he yelped, bouncing up away from the hole. "Lord, I purely hate snakes."

I saw Dad staring hard at the hole. A startled expression was smoothing from his face. "We best get back," he said loudly.

"Lord, yes," Win said. "I tell you what I want right now. It just come over me that I need a bottle of beer and a good game of stud."

I whispered to Dad: "Did you see it too? In the hole?"

"Didn't see a thing," he told me. "Not a thing."

He may have been right at that. Still I wasn't sure. It seems reasonable to me that if you can have angels, you can also have whatever things are opposite to angels.

So after dark, I borrowed some dynamite and eased off down to the creek. I used plenty of fuse. I was sitting at the kitchen table, having a beer and watching the card game, when that distant thud finally came.

Dad looked up from his cards. His eyes jerked around to mine. But he didn't say anything. No need to explain. He knew that sound. And I saw by his expression that he'd been thinking about the hole near the redbuds.

There's just no point taking chances. Not when dynamite is so cheap.

The Man Who Loved the Faioli
by
Roger Zelazny

*Like a number of other writers, Roger Zelazny began publishing in
1962 in the pages of Cele Goldsmith's* Amazing. *Many writers in
this so-called "Class of '62" would eventually achieve promi-
nence, but Zelazny's subsequent career would be one of the most
meteoric in the history of SF. By the end of that decade, he had
won two Nebula Awards and two Hugo Awards and was widely
regarded as one of the most important American SF writers of the
sixties. Since then, he has won several more awards, and his series
of novels about the enchanted land of Amber has made him one of
the best-selling SF and fantasy writers of our time. His books
include* This Immortal, The Dream Master, Lord of Light, Isle of
the Dead, *and the collection* The Doors of His Face, the Lamps of
His Mouth and Other Stories. *His most recent novel is* Sign of
Chaos.

In the evocative romance that follows, he shows us that you can
*have your heart's desire—but that sometimes you're allowed to
change your mind, too . . .*

* * *

It is the story of John Auden and the Faioli, and no one knows it
better than I. Listen—

It happened on that evening, as he strolled (for there was no
reason not to stroll) in his favorite places in the whole world, that
he saw the Faioli near the Canyon of the Dead, seated on a rock,
her wings of light flickering, flickering, flickering and then gone,
until it appeared that a human girl was sitting there, dressed all in
white and weeping, with long black tresses coiled about her waist.

He approached her through the terrible light from the dying,
half-dead sun, in which human eyes could not distinguish distances nor grasp perspectives properly (though his could), and he
laid his right hand upon her shoulder and spoke a word of greeting
and of comfort.

It was as if he did not exist, however. She continued to weep, streaking with silver her cheeks the color of snow or a bone. Her almond eyes looked forward as though they saw through him, and her long fingernails dug into the flesh of her palms, though no blood was drawn.

Then he knew that it was true, the things that are said of the Faioli—that they see only the living and never the dead, and that they are formed into the loveliest women in the entire universe. Being dead himself, John Auden debated the consequences of becoming a living man once again, for a time.

The Faioli were known to come to a man the month before his death—those rare men who still died—and to live with such a man for that final month of his existence, rendering to him every pleasure that it is possible for a human being to know, so that on the day when the kiss of death is delivered, which sucks the remaining life from his body, that man accepts it—no, seeks it—with desire and with grace, for such is the power of the Faioli among all creatures that there is nothing more to be desired after such knowledge.

John Auden considered his life and his death, the conditions of the world upon which he stood, the nature of his stewardship and his curse and the Faioli—who was the loveliest creature he had seen in all of his four hundred thousand days of existence—and he touched the place beneath his left armpit which activated the necessary mechanism to make him live again.

The creature stiffened beneath his touch, for suddenly it was flesh, his touch, and flesh, warm and woman-filled, that he was touching, now that the sensations of life had returned to him. He knew that his touch had become the touch of a man once more.

"I said 'hello, and don't cry,'" he said, and her voice was like the breezes he had forgotten through all the trees that he had forgotten, with their moisture and their odors and their colors all brought back to him thus. "From where do you come, man? You were not here a moment ago."

"From the Canyon of the Dead," he said.

"Let me touch your face," and he did, and she did.

"It is strange that I did not feel you approach."

"This is a strange world," he replied.

"That is true," she said. "You are the only living thing upon it."

And he said, "What is your name?"

She said, "Call me Sythia," and he did.

"My name is John," he told her, "John Auden."

"I have come to be with you, to give you comfort and pleasure," she said, and he knew that the ritual was beginning.

"Why were you weeping when I found you?" he asked.

"Because I thought there was nothing upon this world, and I was so tired from my travels," she told him. "Do you live near here?"

"Not far away," he answered. "Not far away at all."

"Will you take me there? To the place where you live?"

"Yes."

And she rose and followed him into the Canyon of the Dead, where he made his home.

They descended and they descended, and all about them were the remains of people who once had lived. She did not seem to see these things, however, but kept her eyes fixed upon John's face and her hand upon his arm.

"Why do you call this place the Canyon of the Dead?" she asked him.

"Because they are all about us here, the dead," he replied.

"I feel nothing."

"I know."

They crossed through the Valley of the Bones, where millions of the dead from many races and worlds lay stacked all about them, and she did not see these things. She had come to the graveyard of all the worlds, but she did not realize this thing. She had encountered its tender, its keeper, and she did not know what he was, he who staggered beside her like a man drunken.

John Auden took her to his home—not really the place where he lived, but it would be now—and there he activated ancient circuits within the building within the mountain, and in response light leaped forth from the walls, light he had never needed before but now required.

The door slid shut behind them and the temperature built up to a normal warmth. Fresh air circulated and he took it into his lungs and expelled it, glorying in the forgotten sensation. His heart beat within his breast, a red warm thing that reminded him of the pain and of the pleasure. For the first time in ages, he prepared a meal and fetched a bottle of wine from one of the deep, sealed lockers. How many others could have borne what he had borne?

None, perhaps.

She dined with him, toying with the food, sampling a bit of everything, eating very little. He, on the other hand, glutted himself fantastically, and they drank of the wine and were happy.

"This place is so strange," she said. "Where do you sleep?"

"I used to sleep in there," he told her, indicating a room he had almost forgotten; and they entered and he showed it to her, and she beckoned him toward the bed and the pleasures of her body.

That night he loved her, many times, with a desperation that burnt away the alcohol and pushed all of his life forward with something like a hunger, but more.

The following day, when the dying sun had splashed the Valley of the Bones with its pale, moonlike light, he awakened and she drew his head to her breast, not having slept herself, and she asked him, "What is the thing that moves you, John Auden? You are not like one of the men who live and who die, but you take life almost like one of the Faioli, squeezing from it everything that you can and pacing it at a tempo that bespeaks a sense of time no man should know. What are you?"

"I am one who knows," he said. "I am one who knows that the days of a man are numbered and one who covets their dispositions as he feels them draw to a close."

"You are strange," said Sythia. "Have I pleased you?"

"More than anything else I have ever known," he said.

And she sighed, and he found her lips once again.

They breakfasted, and that day they walked in the Valley of the Bones. He could not distinguish distances nor grasp perspectives properly, and she could not see anything that had been living and now was dead. So, of course, as they sat there on a shelf of stone, his arm about her shoulders, he pointed out to her the rocket which had just come down from out of the sky, and she squinted after his gesture. He indicated the robots, which had begun unloading the remains of the dead of many worlds from the hold of the ship, and she cocked her head to one side and stared ahead, but she did not really see what he was talking about.

Even when one of the robots lumbered up to him and held out the board containing the receipt and the stylus, and as he signed the receipt for the bodies received, she did not see or understand what it was that was occurring.

In the days that followed, his life took upon it a dreamlike quality, filled with the pleasure of Sythia and shot through with certain inevitable steaks of pain. Often, she saw him wince, and she asked him concerning his expressions.

And always he would laugh and say, "Pleasure and pain are near to one another," or some thing such as that.

And as the days wore on, she came to prepare the meals and to rub his shoulders and mix his drinks and to recite to him certain pieces of poetry he had somehow once come to love.

A month. A month, he knew, and it would come to an end. The Faioli, whatever they were, paid for the life that they took with the pleasures of the flesh. They always knew when a man's death was near at hand. And in this sense, they always gave more than they received. The life was fleeing anyway, and they enhanced it before they took it away with them, to nourish themselves most likely, price of the things that they'd given.

John Auden knew that no Faioli in the entire universe had ever met a man such as himself.

Sythia was mother-of-pearl, and her body was alternately cold and warm to his caresses, and her mouth was a tiny flame, igniting wherever it touched, with its teeth like needles and its tongue like the heart of a flower. And so he came to know the thing called love for the Faioli called Sythia.

Nothing much really happened beyond the loving. He knew that she wanted him, to use him ultimately, and he was perhaps the only man in the universe able to gull one of her kind. His was the perfect defense against life and against death. Now that he was human and alive, he often wept when he considered it.

He had more than a month to live.

He had maybe three or four.

This month, therefore, was a price he'd willingly pay for what it was that the Faioli offered.

Sythia racked his body and drained from it every drop of pleasure contained within his tired nerve cells. She turned him into a flame, an iceberg, a little boy, an old man. When they were together, his feelings were such that he considered the *consolamentum* as a thing he might really accept at the end of the month, which was drawing near. Why not? He knew she had filled his mind with her presence, on purpose. But what more did existence hold for him? This creature from beyond the stars had brought him every single thing a man could desire. She had baptized him with passion and confirmed him with the quietude which follows after. Perhaps the final oblivion of her final kiss was best after all.

He seized her and drew her to him. She did not understand him, but she responded.

He loved her for it, and this was almost his end.

There is a thing called disease that battens upon all living things, and he had known it beyond the scope of all living men. She could not understand, woman-thing who had known only life.

So he never tried to tell her, though with each day the taste of her kisses grew stronger and saltier and each seemed to him a strengthening shadow, darker and darker, stronger and heavier, of that one thing which he now knew he desired most.

And the day would come. And come it did.

He held her and caressed her, and the calendars of all his days fell about them.

He knew, as he abandoned himself to her ploys and the glories of her mouth, her breasts, that he had been ensnared, as had all men who had known them, by the power of the Faioli. Their strength was their weakness. They were the ultimate in Woman. By their frailty they begat the desire to please. He wanted to merge himself with the pale landscape of her body, to pass within the circles of her eyes and never depart.

He had lost, he knew. For as the days had vanished about him, he had weakened. He was barely able to scrawl his name upon the receipt proffered him by the robot who had lumbered toward him, crushing rib cages and cracking skulls with each terrific step. Briefly, he envied the thing. Sexless, passionless, totally devoted to duty. Before he dismissed it, he asked it, "What would you do if you had desire and you met with a thing that gave you all things you wished for in the world?"

"I would—try to—keep it," it said, red lights blinking about its dome, before it turned and lumbered off, across the Great Graveyard.

"Yes," said John Auden aloud, "but this thing cannot be done."

Sythia did not understand him, and on that thirty-first day they returned to that place where he had lived for a month and he felt the fear of death, strong, so strong, come upon him.

She was more exquisite than ever before, but he feared this final encounter.

"I love you," he said finally, for it was a thing he had never said before, and she stroked his brow and kissed it.

"I know," she told him, "and your time is almost at hand, to love me completely. Before the final act of love, my John Auden, tell me a thing: What is it that sets you apart? Why is it that you know so much more of things-that-are-not-life than mortal man should know? How was it that you approached me on that first night without my knowing it?"

"It is because I am already dead," he told her. "Can't you see it when you look into my eyes? Do you not feel it, as a certain special chill, whenever I touch you? I came here rather than sleep the cold sleep, which would have me to be in a thing like death anyhow, an oblivion wherein I would not even know I was waiting, waiting for the cure which might never happen, the cure for one of the very last fatal diseases remaining in the universe, the disease which now leaves me only small time of life."

"I do not understand," she said.

"Kiss me and forget it," he told her. "It is better this way. There will doubtless never be a cure, for some things remain always dark, and I have surely been forgotten. You must have sensed the death upon me, when I restored my humanity, for such is the nature of your kind. I did it to enjoy you, knowing you to be of the Faioli. So have your pleasure of me now, and know that I share it.

I welcome thee. I have courted thee all the days of my life, unknowing."

But she was curious and asked him (using the familiar for the first time), "How then dost thou achieve this balance between life and that-which-is-not-life, this thing which keeps thee conscious yet unalive?"

"There are controls set within this body I happen, unfortunately, to occupy. To touch this place beneath my armpit will cause my lungs to cease their breathing and my heart to stop its beating. It will set into effect an installed electrochemical system, like those my robots (invisible to you, I know) possess. This is my life within death. I asked for it because I feared oblivion. I volunteered to be gravekeeper to the universe, because in this place there are none to look upon me and be repelled by my deathlike appearance. This is why I am what I am. Kiss me and end it."

But having taken the form of woman, or perhaps being woman all along, the Faioli who was called Sythia was curious, and she said, "This place?" and she touched the spot beneath his left armpit.

With this he vanished from her sight, and with this also, he knew once again the icy logic that stood apart from emotion. Because of this, he did not touch upon the critical spot once again.

Instead, he watched her as she sought for him about the place where he once had lived.

She checked into every closet and adytum, and when she could not discover a living man, she sobbed once, horribly, as she had on that night when first he had seen her. Then the wings flickered, flickered, weakly flickered, back into existence upon her back, and her face dissolved and her body slowly melted. The tower of sparks that stood before him then vanished, and later on that crazy night during which he could distinguish distances and grasp perspectives once again he began looking for her.

And that is the story of John Auden, the only man who ever loved a Faioli and lived (if you could call it that) to tell of it. No one knows it better than I.

No cure has ever been found. And I know that he walks the Canyon of the Dead and considers the bones, sometimes stops by the rock where he met her, blinks after the moist things that are not there, wonders at the judgment that he gave.

It is that way, and the moral may be that life (and perhaps love also) is stronger than that which it contains, but never that which contains it. But only a Faioli could tell you for sure, and they never come here any more.

Upon the Dull Earth
by
Philip K. Dick

A dedicated investigator of the elusive nature of reality, an intrepid explorer of alternate states of consciousness, a wickedly effective and acidulous satirist, the late Philip K. Dick wrote some of the most brilliant novels and short stories in the history of the SF genre, and is now widely recognized as one of the major authors of the late twentieth century, in any genre. He won a Hugo Award for his novel The Man in the High Castle, *and his many other novels include* Ubik, Martian Time-Slip, The Three Stigmata of Palmer Eldrich, Time Out of Joint, *and* Do Androids Dream of Electric Sheep?, *which was somewhat disappointingly filmed as* Blade Runner. *His most recent books, published posthumously, include* The Transmigration of Timothy Archer, Radio Free Albemuth, Puttering About in a Small Land, The Man Whose Teeth Were All Exactly Alike, *and the massive five-volume set* The Collected Stories of Philip K. Dick.*

In the hair-raising tale that follows, one of Dick's least-known stories, he shows us that there may be some very good reasons why the dead are traditionally kept separate from the living . . .

* * *

Silvia ran laughing through the night brightness, between the roses and cosmos and Shasta daisies, down the gravel paths and beyond the heaps of sweet-tasting grass swept from the lawns. Stars, caught in pools of water, glittered everywhere, as she brushed through them to the slope beyond the brick wall. Cedars supported the sky and ignored the slim shape squeezing past, her brown hair flying, her eyes flashing.

"Wait for me," Rick complained, as he cautiously threaded his way after her, along the half familiar path. Silvia danced on without stopping. "Slow down!" he shouted angrily.

"Can't—we're late." Without warning, Silvia appeared in front of him, blocking the path. "Empty your pockets," she gasped, her gray eyes sparkling. "Throw away all metal. You know they can't stand metal."

Rick searched his pockets. In his overcoat were two dimes and a fifty-cent piece. "Do these count?"

"Yes!" Silvia snatched the coins and threw them into the dark heaps of calla lilies. The bits of metal hissed into the moist depths and were gone. "Anything else?" She caught hold of his arm anxiously. "They're already on their way. Anything else, Rick?"

"Just my watch." Rick pulled his wrist away as Silvia's wild fingers snatched for the watch. *"That's* not going in the bushes."

"Then lay it on the sundial—or the wall. Or in a hollow tree." Silvia raced off again. Her excited, rapturous voice danced back to him. "Throw away your cigarette case. And your keys, your belt buckle—everything metal. You know how they hate metal. Hurry, we're late!"

Rick followed sullenly after her. "All right, *witch.*"

Silvia snapped at him furiously from the darkness. "Don't *say* that! It isn't true. You've been listening to my sisters and my mother and—"

Her words were drowned out by the sound. Distant flapping, a long way off, like vast leaves rustling in a winter storm. The night sky was alive with the frantic poundings; they were coming very quickly this time. They were too greedy, too desperately eager to wait. Flickers of fear touched the man and he ran to catch up with Silvia.

Silvia was a tiny column of green skirt and blouse in the center of the thrashing mass. She was pushing them away with one arm and trying to manage the faucet with the other. The churning activity of wings and bodies twisted her like a reed. For a time she was lost from sight.

"Rick!" she called faintly. "Come here and help!" She pushed them away and struggled up. "They're suffocating me!"

Rick fought his way through the wall of flashing white to the edge of the trough. They were drinking greedily at the blood that spilled from the wooden faucet. He pulled Silvia close against him; she was terrified and trembling. He held her tight until some of the violence and fury around them had died down.

"They're hungry," Silvia gasped feebly.

"You're a little cretin for coming ahead. They can sear you to ash!"

"I know. They can do anything." She shuddered, excited and frightened. "Look at them," she whispered, her voice husky with awe. "Look at the size of them—their wing-spread. And they're *white*, Rick. Spotless—perfect. There's nothing in our world as spotless as that. Great and clean and wonderful."

"They certainly wanted the lamb's blood."

Silvia's soft hair blew against his face as the wings fluttered on all sides. They were leaving now, roaring up into the sky. Not up, really—away. Back to their own world whence they had scented the blood. But it was not only the blood—they had come because of Silvia. *She* had attracted them.

The girl's gray eyes were wide. She reached up towards the rising white creatures. One of them swooped close. Grass and flowers sizzled as blinding white flames roared in a brief fountain. Rick scrambled away. The flaming figure hovered momentarily over Silvia and then there was a hollow *pop*. The last of the white-winged giants was gone. The air, the ground, gradually cooled into darkness and silence.

"I'm sorry," Silvia whispered.

"Don't do it again," Rick managed. He was numb with shock. "It isn't safe."

"Sometimes I forget. I'm sorry, Rick. I didn't mean to draw them so close." She tried to smile. "I haven't been that careless in months. Not since the other time, when I first brought you out here." The avid, wild look slid across her face. "Did you *see* him? Power and flames! And he didn't even touch us. He just—looked at us. That was all. And everything's burned up, all around."

Rick grabbed hold of her. "Listen," he grated. "You mustn't call them again. It's wrong. This isn't their world."

"It's not wrong—it's beautiful."

"It's not safe!" His fingers dug into her flesh until she gasped. "Stop tempting them down here!"

Silvia laughed hysterically. She pulled away from him, out into the blasted circle that the horde of angels had seared behind them as they rose into the sky. "I can't *help* it," she cried. "I belong with them. They're my family, my people. Generations of them, back into the past."

"What do you mean?"

"They're my ancestors. And some day I'll join them."

"You are a little witch!" Rick shouted furiously.

"No," Silvia answered. "Not a witch, Rick. Don't you see? I'm a saint."

The kitchen was warm and bright. Silvia plugged in the Silex and got a big red can of coffee down from the cupboards over the sink. "You mustn't listen to them," she said, as she set out plates and cups and got cream from the refrigerator. "You know they don't understand. Look at them in there."

Silvia's mother and her sisters, Betty Lou and Jean, stood huddled together in the living-room, fearful and alert, watching the young couple in the kitchen. Walter Everett was standing by the fireplace, his face blank, remote.

"Listen to *me*," Rick said. "You have this power to attract them. You mean you're not—isn't Walter your real father?"

"Oh, yes—of course he is. I'm completely human. Don't I look human?"

"But you're the only one who has the power."

"I'm not physically different," Silvia said thoughtfully. "I have the ability to see, that's all. Others have had it before me—saints, martyrs. When I was a child, my mother read to me about Saint Bernadette. Remember where her cave was? Near a hospital. They were hovering there and she saw one of them."

"But the blood! It's grotesque. There never was anything like that."

"Oh, yes. The blood draws them, lamb's blood especially. They hover over battlefields. Valkyries—carrying off the dead to Valhalla. That's why saints and martyrs cut and mutilate themselves. You know where I got the idea?"

Silvia fastened a little apron around her waist and filled the Silex with coffee. "When I was nine years old, I read of it in Homer, in the Odyssey. Ulysses dug a trench in the ground and filled it with blood to attract the spirits. The shades from the nether world."

"That's right," Rick admitted reluctantly. "I remember."

"The ghosts of people who died. They had lived once. Everybody lives here, then dies and goes there." Her face glowed. "We're all going to have wings! We're all going to fly. We'll all be filled with fire and power. We won't be worms any more."

"Worms! That's what you always call me."

"Of course you're a worm. We're all worms—grubby worms creeping over the crust of the Earth, through dust and dirt."

"Why should blood bring them?"

"Because it's life and they're attracted by life. Blood is *uisge beatha*—the water of life."

"Blood means death! A trough of spilled blood . . ."

"It's *not* death. When you see a caterpillar crawl into its cocoon, do you think it's dying?"

Walter Everett was standing in the doorway. He stood listening to his daughter, his face dark. "One day," he said hoarsely, "they're going to grab her and carry her off. She wants to go with them. She's waiting for that day."

"You see?" Silvia said to Rick. "He doesn't understand either." She shut off the Silex and poured coffee. "Coffee for you?" she asked her father.

"No," Everett said.

"Silvia," Rick said, as if speaking to a child, "if you went away with them, you know you couldn't come back to us."

"We all have to cross sooner or later. It's all part of our life."

"But you're only nineteen," Rick pleaded. "You're young and healthy and beautiful. And our marriage—what about our marriage?" He half rose from the table. "Silvia, you've got to stop this!"

"I *can't* stop it. I was seven when I saw them first." Silvia stood by the sink, gripping the Silex, a faraway look in her eyes. "Remember, Daddy? We were living back in Chicago. It was winter. I fell, walking home from school." She held up a slim arm. "See the scar? I fell and cut myself on the gravel and slush. I came home crying—it was sleeting and the wind was howling around me. My arm was bleeding and my mitten was soaked with blood. And then I looked up and saw them."

There was silence.

"They want you," Everett said wretchedly. "They're flies— bluebottles, hovering around, waiting for you. Calling you to come along with them."

"Why not?" Silvia's gray eyes were shining and her cheeks radiated joy and anticipation. "You've seen them, Daddy. You know what it means. Transfiguration—from clay into gods!"

Rick left the kitchen. In the living-room, the two sisters stood together, curious and uneasy. Mrs. Everett stood by herself, her face granite-hard, eyes bleak behind her steel-rimmed glasses. She turned away as Rick passed them.

"What happened out there?" Betty Lou asked him in a taut whisper. She was fifteen, skinny and plain, hollow cheeked, with mousy, sand-colored hair. "Silvia never lets us come out with her."

"Nothing happened," Rick answered.

Anger stirred the girl's barren face. "That's not true. You were both out in the garden, in the dark, and—"

"Don't talk to him!" her mother snapped. She yanked the two girls away and shot Rick a glare of hatred and misery. Then she turned quickly from him.

Rick opened the door to the basement and switched on the light. He descended slowly into the cold, damp room of concrete and dirt, with its unwinking yellow light hanging from dust-covered wires overhead.

In one corner loomed the big floor furnace with its mammoth hot air pipes. Beside it stood the water heater and discarded bundles, boxes of books, newspapers and old furniture, thick with dust, encrusted with strings of spider webs.

At the far end were the washing machine and spin dryer. And Silvia's pump and refrigeration system.

From the work bench Rick selected a hammer and two heavy pipe wrenches. He was moving towards the elaborate tanks and pipes when Silvia appeared abruptly at the top of the stairs, her coffee cup in one hand.

She hurried quickly down to him. "What are you doing down here?" she asked, studying him intently. "Why that hammer and those two wrenches?"

Rick dropped the tools back onto the bench. "I thought maybe this could be solved on the spot."

Silvia moved between him and the tanks. "I thought you understood. They've always been a part of my life. When I brought you with me the first time, you seemed to see what—"

"I don't want to lose you," Rick said harshly, "to anybody or anything—in this world or any other. *I'm not going to give you up.*"

"It's not giving me up!" Her eyes narrowed. "You came down here to destroy and break everything. The moment I'm not looking you'll smash all this, won't you?"

"That's right."

Fear replaced anger on the girl's face. "Do you want me to be chained here? I have to go on—I'm through with this part of the journey. I've stayed here long enough."

"Can't you wait?" Rick demanded furiously. He couldn't keep the ragged edge of despair out of his voice. "Doesn't it come soon enough anyhow?"

Silvia shrugged and turned away, her arms folded, her red lips tight together. "You want to be a worm always. A fuzzy, little creeping caterpillar."

"I want *you.*"

"You can't *have* me!" She whirled angrily. "I don't have any time to waste with this."

"You have higher things in mind," Rick said savagely.

"Of course." She softened a little. "I'm sorry, Rick. Remember Icarus? You want to fly, too. I know it."

"In my time."

"Why not now? Why wait? You're afraid." She slid lithely away from him, cunning twisting her red lips. "Rick, I want to show you something. Promise me first—you won't tell anybody."

"What is it?"

"Promise?" She put her hand to his mouth. "I have to be careful.

It cost a lot of money. Nobody knows about it. It's what they do in China—everything goes towards it."

"I'm curious," Rick said. Uneasiness flicked at him. "Show it to me."

Trembling with excitement, Silvia disappeared behind the huge lumbering refrigerator, back into the darkness behind the web of frost-hard freezing coils. He could hear her tugging and pulling at something. Scraping sounds, sounds of something large being dragged out.

"See?" Silvia gasped. "Give me a hand, Rick. It's heavy. Hardwood and brass—and metal lined. It's hand-stained and polished. And the carving—see the carving! Isn't it beautiful?"

"What is it?" Rick demanded huskily.

"It's my cocoon," Silvia said simply. She settled down in a contented heap on the floor, and rested her head happily against the polished oak coffin.

Rick grabbed her by the arm and dragged her to her feet. "You can't sit with that coffin, down here in the basement with—" He broke off. "What's the matter?"

Silvia's face was twisting with pain. She backed away from him and put her finger quickly to her mouth. "I cut myself—when you pulled me up—on a nail or something." A thin trickle of blood oozed down her fingers. She groped in her pocket for a handkerchief.

"Let me see it." He moved towards her, but she avoided him. "Is it bad?" he demanded.

"Stay away from me," Silvia whispered.

"What's wrong? Let me see it!"

"Rick," Silvia said in a low intense voice, "get some water and adhesive tape. As quickly as possible." She was trying to keep down her rising terror. "I have to stop the bleeding."

"Upstairs?" He moved awkwardly away. "It doesn't look too bad. Why don't you . . ."

"Hurry." The girl's voice was suddenly bleak with fear. "Rick, *hurry!*"

Confused, he ran a few steps.

Silvia's terror poured after him. "No, it's too late," she called thinly. "Don't come back—keep away from me. It's my own fault. I trained them to come. *Keep away!* I'm sorry, Rick. *Oh*—" Her voice was lost to him, as the wall of the basement burst and shattered. A cloud of luminous white forced its way through and blazed out into the basement.

It was Silvia they were after. She ran a few hesitant steps towards Rick, halted uncertainly, then the white mass of bodies and wings settled around her. She shrieked once. Then a violent explosion blasted the basement into a shimmering dance of furnace heat.

He was thrown to the floor. The cement was hot and dry—the whole basement crackled with heat. Windows shattered as pulsing white shapes pushed out again. Smoke and flames licked up the walls. The ceiling sagged and rained plaster down.

Rick struggled to his feet. The furious activity was dying away. The basement was a littered chaos. All surfaces were scorched black, seared and crusted with smoking ash. Splintered wood, torn cloth and broken concrete were strewn everywhere. The furnace and washing machine were in ruins. The elaborate pumping and refrigeration system—now a glittering mass of slag. One whole wall had been twisted aside. Plaster was rubbed over everything.

Silvia was a twisted heap, arms and legs doubled grotesquely. Shriveled, carbonized remains of fire-scorched ash, settling in a vague mound. What had been left behind were charred fragments, a brittle burned-out husk.

It was a dark night, cold and intense. A few stars glittered like ice from above his head. A faint, dank wind stirred through the dripping calla lilies and whipped gravel up in a frigid mist along the path between the black roses.

He crouched for a long time, listening and watching. Behind the cedars, the big house loomed against the sky. At the bottom of the slope a few cars slithered along the highway. Otherwise, there was no sound. Ahead of him jutted the squat outline of the porcelain trough and the pipe that had carried blood from the refrigerator in the basement. The trough was empty and dry, except for a few leaves that had fallen in it.

Rick took a deep breath of thin night air and held it. Then he got stiffly to his feet. He scanned the sky, but saw no movement. They were there, though, watching and waiting—dim shadows, echoing into the legendary past, a line of god-figures.

He picked up the heavy gallon drums, dragged them to the trough and poured blood from a New Jersey abattoir, cheap-grade steer refuse, thick and clotted. It splashed against his clothes and he backed away nervously. But nothing stirred in the air above. The garden was silent, drenched with night fog and darkness.

He stood beside the trough, waiting and wondering if they were coming. They had come for Silvia, not merely for the blood. Without her there was no attraction but the raw food. He carried the empty metal cans over to the bushes and kicked them down the slope. He searched his pockets carefully, to make sure there was no metal on him.

Over the years, Silvia had nourished their habit of coming. Now she was on the other side. Did that mean they wouldn't come? Somewhere in the damp bushes something rustled. An animal or a bird?

In the trough the blood glistened, heavy and dull, like old lead. It was their time to come, but nothing stirred the great trees above. He picked out the rows of nodding black roses, the gravel path down which he and Silvia had run—violently he shut out the recent memory of her flashing eyes and deep red lips. The highway beyond the slope—the empty, deserted garden—the silent house in which her family huddled and waited. After a time, there was a dull, swishing sound. He tensed, but it was only a diesel truck lumbering along the highway, headlights blazing.

He stood grimly, his feet apart, his heels dug into the soft black ground. He wasn't leaving. He was staying there until they came. He wanted her back—at any cost.

Overhead, foggy webs of moisture drifted across the moon. The sky was a vast barren plain, without life or warmth. The deathly cold of deep space, away from suns and living things. He gazed up until his neck ached. Cold stars, sliding in and out of the matted layer of fog. Was there anything else? Didn't they want to come, or weren't they interested in him? It had been Silvia who had interested them—now they had her.

Behind him there was a movement without sound. He sensed it and started to turn, but suddenly, on all sides, the trees and undergrowth shifted. Like cardboard props they wavered and ran together, blending dully in the night shadows. Something moved through them, rapidly, silently, then was gone.

They had come. He could feel them. They had shut off their power and flame. Cold, indifferent statues, rising among the trees, dwarfing the cedars—remote from him and his world, attracted by curiosity and mild habit.

"Silvia," he said clearly. "Which are you?"

There was no response. Perhaps she wasn't among them. He felt foolish. A vague flicker of white drifted past the trough, hovered momentarily and then went on without stopping. The air above the trough vibrated, then died into immobility, as another giant inspected briefly and withdrew.

Panic breathed through him. They were leaving again, receding back into their own world. The trough had been rejected; they weren't interested.

"Wait," he muttered thickly.

Some of the white shadows lingered. He approached them slowly, wary of their flickering immensity. If one of them touched him, he would sizzle briefly and puff into a dark heap of ash. A few feet away he halted.

"You know what I want," he said. "I want her back. She shouldn't have been taken yet."

Silence.

"You were too greedy," he said. "You did the wrong thing. She was going to come over to you, eventually. She had it all worked out."

The dark fog rustled. Among the trees the flickering shapes stirred and pulsed, responsive to his voice. *"True,"* came a detached impersonal sound. The sound drifted around him, from tree to tree, without location or direction. It was swept off by the night wind to die into dim echoes.

Relief settled over him. They had paused—they were aware of him—listening to what he had to say.

"You think it's right?" he demanded. "She had a long life here. We were to marry, have children."

There was no answer, but he was conscious of a growing tension. He listened intently, but he couldn't make out anything. Presently he realized a struggle was taking place, a conflict among them. The tension grew—more shapes flickered—the clouds, the icy stars, were obscured by the vast presence swelling around him.

"Rick!" A voice spoke close by. Wavering, drifting back into the dim regions of the trees and dripping plants. He could hardly hear it—the words were gone as soon as they were spoken. "Rick—help me get back."

"Where you are?" He couldn't locate her. "What can I do?"

"I don't know." Her voice was wild with bewilderment and pain. "I don't understand. Something went wrong. They must have thought I—wanted to come right away. I *didn't*!"

"I know," Rick said. "It was an accident."

"They were waiting. The cocoon, the trough—but it was too soon." Her terror came across to him, from the vague distances of another universe. "Rick, I've changed my mind. I want to come back."

"It's not as simple as that."

"I know. Rick, time is different on this side. I've been gone so long—your world seems to creep along. It's been years, hasn't it?"

"One week," Rick said.

"It was their fault. You don't blame me, do you? They know they did the wrong thing. Those who did it have been punished, but that doesn't help me." Misery and panic distorted her voice so he could hardly understand her. "How can I come back?"

"Don't they know?"

"They say it can't be done." Her voice trembled. "They say they destroyed the clay part—it was incinerated. There's nothing for me to go back to."

Rick took a deep breath. "Make them find some other way. It's up to them. Don't they have the power? They took you over too soon—they must send you back. It's *their* responsibility."

The white shapes shifted uneasily. The conflict rose sharply; they couldn't agree. Rick warily moved back a few paces.

"They say it's dangerous." Silvia's voice came from no particular spot. "They say it was attempted once." She tried to control her voice. "The nexus between this world and yours is unstable. There are vast amounts of free-floating energy. The power we—on this side—have isn't really our own. It's universal energy, tapped and controlled."

"Why can't they . . ."

"This is a higher continuum. There's a natural process of energy from lower to higher regions. But the reverse process is risky. The blood—it's a sort of guide to follow—a bright marker."

"Like moths around a light bulb," Rick said bitterly.

"If they send me back and something goes wrong—" She broke off and then continued, "If they make a mistake. I might be lost between the two regions. I might be absorbed by the free energy. It seems to be partly alive. It's not understood. Remember Prometheus and the fire . . ."

"I see," Rick said, as calmly as he could.

"Darling, if they try to send me back, I'll have to find some shape to enter. You see, I don't exactly have a shape any more. There's no real material form on this side. What you see, the wings and the whiteness, are not really there. If I succeeded in making the trip back to your side . . ."

"You'd have to mold something," Rick said.

"I'd have to take something there—something of clay. I'd have to enter it and reshape it. As He did a long time ago, when the original form was put on your world."

"If they did it once, they can do it again."

"The One who did that is gone. He passed on upward." There was unhappy irony in her voice. "There are regions beyond this. The ladder doesn't stop here. Nobody knows where it ends, it just seems to keep on going up and up. World after world."

"Who decides about you?" Rick demanded.

"It's up to me," Silvia said faintly. "They say, if I want to take the chance, they'll try it."

"What do you think you'll do?" he asked.

"I'm afraid. What if something goes wrong? You haven't seen it, the region between. The possibilities there are incredible—they terrify me. He was the only one with enough courage. Everyone else has been afraid."

"It was their fault. They have to take responsibility."

"They know that." Silvia hesitated miserably. "Rick, darling, please tell me what to do."

"Come back!"

Silence. Then her voice, thin and pathetic. "All right, Rick. If you think that's the right thing."

"It is," he said firmly. He forced his mind not to think, not to picture or imagine anything. *He had to have her back.* "Tell them to get started now. Tell them—"

A deafening crack of heat burst in front of him. He was lifted up and tossed into a flaming sea of pure energy. They were leaving and the scalding lake of sheer power bellowed and thundered around him. For a split second he thought he glimpsed Silvia, her hands reaching imploringly towards him.

Then the fire cooled and he lay blinded in dripping, night-moistened darkness. Alone in the silence.

Walter Everett was helping him up. "You damn fool!" he was saying, again and again. "You shouldn't have brought them back. They've got enough from us."

Then he was in the big, warm living-room. Mrs. Everett stood silently in front of him, her face hard and expressionless. The two daughters hovered anxiously around him, fluttering and curious, eyes wide with morbid fascination.

"I'll be all right," Rick muttered. His clothing was charred and blacked. He rubbed black ash from his face. Bits of dried grass stuck to his hair—they had seared a circle around him as they'd ascended. He lay back against the couch and closed his eyes. When he opened them, Betty Lou Everett was forcing a glass of water into his hand.

"Thanks," he muttered.

"You should never have gone out there," Walter Everett repeated. "Why? Why'd you do it? You know what happened to her. You want the same thing to happen to you?"

"I want her back," Rick said quietly.

"Are you mad? You can't get her back. She's gone." His lips twitched convulsively. "You saw her."

Betty Lou was gazing at Rick intently. "What happened out there?" she demanded. "They came again, didn't they?"

Rick got heavily to his feet and left the living-room. In the kitchen he emptied the water in the sink and poured himself a drink. While he was leaning wearily against the sink, Betty Lou appeared in the doorway.

"What do you want?" Rick demanded.

The girl's face was flushed an unhealthy red. "I know something happened out there. You were feeding them, weren't you?" She advanced towards him. "You're trying to get her back?"

"That's right," Rick said.

Betty Lou giggled nervously. "But you can't. She's dead—her body's been cremated—I saw it." Her face worked excitedly. "Daddy always said that something bad would happen to her, and it did." She leaned close to Rick. "She was a witch! She got what she deserved!"

"She's coming back," Rick said.

"*No!*" Panic stirred the girl's drab features. "She *can't* come back. She's dead—like she always said—worm into butterfly— she's a butterfly!"

"Go inside," Rick said.

"You can't order me around," Betty Lou answered. Her voice rose hysterically. "This is *my* house. We don't want you around here any more. Daddy's going to tell you. He doesn't want you and I don't want you and my mother and sister . . ."

The change came without warning. Like a film gone dead. Betty Lou froze, her mouth half open, one arm raised, her words dead on her tongue. She was suspended, an instantly lifeless thing raised off the floor, as if caught between two slides of glass. A vacant insect, without speech or sound, inert and hollow. Not dead, but abruptly thinned back to primordial inanimacy.

Into the captured shell filtered new potency and being. It settled over her, a rainbow of life that poured into place eagerly—like hot fluid—into every part of her. The girl stumbled and moaned; her body jerked violently and pitched against the wall. A china teacup tumbled from an overhead shelf and smashed on the floor. The girl retreated numbly, one hand to her mouth, her eyes wide with pain and shock.

"Oh!" she gasped. "I cut myself." She shook her head and gazed up mutely at him, appealing to him. "On a nail or something."

"Silvia!" He caught hold of her and dragged her to her feet, away from the wall. It was *her* arm he gripped, warm and full and mature. Stunned gray eyes, brown hair, quivering breasts—she was now as she had been those last moments in the basement.

"Let's see it," he said. He tore her hand from her mouth and shakily examined her finger. There was no cut, only a thin white line rapidly dimming. "It's all right, honey. You're all right. There's nothing wrong with you!"

"Rick, I was over *there*." Her voice was husky and faint. "They came and dragged me across with them." She shuddered violently. "Rick, am I actually *back*?"

He crushed her tight. "Completely back."

"It was so long. I was over there a century. Endless ages. I thought—" Suddenly she pulled away. "Rick . . ."

"What is it?"

Silvia's face was wild with fear. "There's something wrong."

"There's nothing wrong. You've come back home and that's all that matters."

Silvia retreated from him. "But they took a living form, didn't they? Not discarded clay. They don't have the power, Rick. They altered His work instead." Her voice rose in panic. "A mistake— they should have known better than to alter the balance. It's unstable and none of them can control the . . ."

Rick blocked the doorway. "Stop talking like that!" he said fiercely. "It's worth it—*anything's* worth it. If they set things out of balance, it's their own fault."

"We can't turn it back!" Her voice rose shrilly, thin and hard, like drawn wire. "We've set it in motion, started the waves lapping out. The balance He set up is *altered*."

"Come on, darling," Rick said. "Let's go and sit in the living-room with your family. You'll feel better. You'll have to try to recover from this."

They approached the three seated figures, two on the couch, one in the straight chair by the fireplace. The figures sat motionless, their faces blank, their bodies limp and waxen, dulled forms that did not respond as the couple entered the room.

Rick halted, uncomprehending. Walter Everett was slumped forward, newspaper in one hand, slippers on his feet; his pipe was still smoking in the deep ashtray on the arm of his chair. Mrs. Everett sat with a lapful of sewing, her face grim and stern, but strangely vague. An unformed face, as if the material were melting and running together. Jean sat huddled in a shapeless heap, a ball of clay wadded up, more formless each moment.

Abruptly Jean collapsed. Her arms fell loose beside her. Her head sagged. Her body, her arms and legs filled out. Her features altered rapidly. Her clothing changed. Colors flowed in her hair, her eyes, her skin. The waxen pallor was gone.

Pressing her fingers to her lips she gazed up at Rick mutely. She blinked and her eyes focused. "Oh," she gasped. Her lips moved awkwardly; the voice was faint and uneven, like a poor sound track. She struggled up jerkily, with uncoordinated movements that propelled her stiffly to her feet and towards him—one awkward step at a time—like a wire dummy.

"Rick, I cut myself," she said. "On a nail or something."

What had been Mrs. Everett stirred. Shapeless and vague, it made dull sounds and flopped grotesquely. Gradually it hardened and shaped itself. "My finger," its voice gasped feebly. Like mirror echoes dimming off into darkness, the third figure in the easy chair took up the words. Soon, they were all of them repeating the phrase, four fingers, their lips moving in unison.

"My finger. I cut myself, Rick."

Parrot reflections, receding mimicries of words and movement. And the settling shapes were familiar in every detail. Again and again, repeated around him, twice on the couch, in the easy chair, close beside him—so close he could hear her breathe and see her trembling lips.

"What is it?" the Silvia beside him asked.

On the couch one Silvia resumed its sewing—she was sewing methodically, absorbed in her work. In the deep chair another took up its newspapers, its pipe and continued reading. One huddled, nervous and afraid. The one beside him followed as he retreated to the door. She was panting with uncertainty, her gray eyes wide, her nostrils flaring.

"Rick . . ."

He pulled the door open and made his way out onto the dark porch. Machine-like, he felt his way down the steps, through the pools of night collected everywhere, towards the driveway. In the yellow square of light behind him, Silvia was outlined, peering unhappily after him. And behind her, the other figures, identical, pure repetitions, nodding over their tasks.

He found his coupe and pulled out onto the road.

Gloomy trees and houses flashed past. He wondered how far it would go. Lapping waves spreading out—a widening circle as the imbalance spread.

He turned onto the main highway; there were soon more cars around him. He tried to see into them, but they moved too swiftly. The car ahead was a red Plymouth. A heavyset man in a blue business suit was driving, laughing merrily with the woman beside him. He pulled his own coupe up close behind the Plymouth and followed it. The man flashed gold teeth, grinned, waved his plump hands. The girl was dark-haired, pretty. She smiled at the man, adjusted her white gloves, smoothed down her hair, then rolled up the window on her side.

He lost the Plymouth. A heavy diesel truck cut in between them. Desperately he swerved around the truck and nosed in beyond the swift-moving red sedan. Presently it passed him and, for a moment, the two occupants were clearly framed. The girl resembled Silvia. The same delicate line of her small chin—the same deep lips, parting slightly when she smiled—the same slender arms and hands. It was Silvia. The Plymouth turned off and there was no other car ahead of him.

He drove for hours through the heavy night darkness. The gas gauge dropped lower and lower. Ahead of him dismal rolling countryside spread out, blank fields between towns and unwinking stars suspended in the bleak sky. Once, a cluster of red and yellow lights gleamed. An intersection—filling stations and a big neon sign. He drove on past it.

At a single-pump stand, he pulled the car off the highway, onto the oil-soaked gravel. He climbed out, his shoes crunching the stone underfoot, as he grabbed the gas hose and unscrewed the cap of his car's tank. He had the tank almost full when the door of the drab station building opened and a slim woman in white overalls and navy shirt, with a little cap lost in her brown curls, stepped out.

"Good evening, Rick," she said quietly.

He put back the gas hose. Then he was driving out onto the highway. Had he screwed the cap back on again? He didn't remember. He gained speed. He had gone over a hundred miles. He was nearing the state line.

At a little roadside café, warm, yellow light glowed in the chill gloom of early morning. He slowed the car down and parked at the edge of the highway in the deserted parking lot. Bleary-eyed he pushed the door open and entered.

Hot, thick smells of cooking ham and black coffee surrounded him, the comfortable sight of people eating. A juke box blared in the corner. He threw himself onto a stool and hunched over, his head in his hands. A thin farmer next to him glanced at him curiously and then returned to his newspaper. Two hard-faced women across from him gazed at him momentarily. A handsome youth in denim jacket and jeans was eating red beans and rice, washing it down with steaming coffee from a heavy mug.

"What'll it be?" the pert blonde waitress asked, a pencil behind her ear, her hair tied back in a tight bun. "Looks like you've got some hangover, mister."

He ordered coffee and vegetable soup. Soon he was eating, his hands working automatically. He found himself devouring a ham and cheese sandwich; had he ordered it? The juke box blared and people came and went. There was a little town sprawled beside the road, set back in some gradual hills. Gray sunlight, cold and sterile, filtered down as morning came. He ate hot apple pie and sat wiping dully at his mouth with a paper napkin.

The café was silent. Outside nothing stirred. An uneasy calm hung over everything. The juke box had ceased. None of the people at the counter stirred or spoke. An occasional truck roared past, damp and lumbering, windows rolled up tight.

When he looked up, Silvia was standing in front of him. Her arms were folded and she gazed vacantly past him. A bright yellow pencil was behind her ear. Her brown hair was tied back in a hard bun. At the corner others were sitting, other Silvias, dishes in front of them, half dozing or eating, some of them reading. Each the same as the next, except for their clothing.

He made his way back to his parked car. In half an hour he had crossed the state line. Cold, bright sunlight sparkled off dew-moist roofs and pavements as he sped through tiny unfamiliar towns.

Along the shiny morning streets he saw them, moving—early risers, on their way to work. In twos and three they walked, their heels echoing in sharp silence. At bus stops he saw groups of them collected together. In the houses, rising from their beds, eating breakfast, bathing, dressing, were more of them—hundreds of them, legions without number. A town of them preparing for the day, resuming their regular tasks, as the circle widened and spread.

He left the town behind. The car slowed under him as his foot slid heavily from the gas pedal. Two of them walked across a level field together. They carried books—children on their way to school. Repetitions, unvarying and identical. A dog circled excitedly after them, unconcerned, his joy untainted.

He drove on. Ahead a city loomed, its stern columns of office buildings sharply outlined against the sky. The streets swarmed with noise and activity as he passed through the main business section. Somewhere, near the center of the city, he overtook the expanding periphery of the circle and emerged beyond. Diversity took the place of the endless figures of Silvia. Gray eyes and brown hair gave way to countless varieties of men and women, children and adults, of all ages and appearances. He increased his speed and raced out on the far side, onto the wide four-lane highway.

He finally slowed down. He was exhausted. He had driven for hours; his body was shaking with fatigue.

Ahead of him a carrot-haired youth was cheerfully thumbing a ride, a thin bean-pole in brown slacks and light camel's-hair sweater. Rick pulled to a halt and opened the front door. "Hop in," he said.

"Thanks, buddy." The youth hurried to the car and climbed in as Rick gathered speed. He slammed the door and settled gratefully back against the seat. "It was getting hot, standing there."

"How far are you going?" Rick demanded.

"All the way to Chicago." The youth grinned shyly. "Of course, I don't expect you to drive me that far. Anything at all is appreciated." He eyed Rick curiously. "Which way you going?"

"Anywhere," Rick said. "I'll drive you to Chicago."

"It's two hundred miles."

"Fine," Rick said. He steered over into the left lane and gained speed. "If you want to go to New York, I'll drive you there."

"You feel all right?" The youth moved away uneasily. "I sure appreciate a lift, but . . ." He hesitated. "I mean, I don't want to take you out of your way."

Rick concentrated on the road ahead, his hands gripping hard around the rim of the wheel. "I'm going fast. I'm not slowing down or stopping."

"You better be careful," the youth warned, in a troubled voice. "I don't want to get in an accident."

"I'll do the worrying."

"But it's dangerous. What if something happens? It's too risky."

"You're wrong," Rick muttered grimly, eyes on the road. "It's worth the risk."

"But if something goes wrong—" The voice broke off uncertainly and then continued, "I might be lost. It would be so easy. It's all so unstable." The voice trembled with worry and fear. "Rick, please . . ."

Rick whirled. "How do you know my name?"

The youth was crouched in a heap against the door. His face had a soft, molten look, as if it were losing its shape and sliding together in an unformed mass. "I want to come back," he was saying, from within himself, "but I'm afraid. You haven't seen it—the region between. It's nothing but energy, Rick. He tapped it a long time ago, but nobody else knows how."

The voice lightened, became clear and treble. The hair faded to a rich brown. Gray, frightened eyes flickered up at Rick. Hands frozen, he hunched over the wheel and forced himself not to move. Gradually he decreased speed and brought the car over into the right-hand lane.

"Are we stopping?" the shape beside him asked. It was Silvia's voice now. Like a new insect, drying in the sun, the shape hardened and locked into firm reality. Silvia struggled up on the seat and peered out. "Where are we? We're between towns."

He jammed on the brakes, reached past her and threw open the door. "Get out!"

Silvia gazed at him uncomprehendingly. "What do you mean?" she faltered. "Rick, what is it? What's wrong?"

"Get out!"

"Rick, I don't understand." She slid over a little. Her toes touched the pavement. "Is there something wrong with the car? I thought everything was all right."

He gently shoved her out and slammed the door. The car leaped ahead, out into the stream of mid-morning traffic. Behind him the small, dazed figure was pulling itself up, bewildered and injured. He forced his eyes from the rear-view mirror and crushed down the gas pedal with all his weight.

The radio buzzed and clicked in vague static when he snapped it briefly on. He turned the dial and, after a time, a big network station came in. A faint, puzzled voice, a woman's voice. For a time he couldn't make out the words. Then he recognized it and, with a pang of panic, switched the thing off.

Her voice. Murmuring plaintively. Where was the station? Chicago. The circle had already spread that far.

He slowed down. There was no point hurrying. It had already passed him by and gone on. Kansas farms—sagging stores in little old Mississippi towns—along the bleak streets of New England manufacturing cities swarms of brown-haired gray-eyed women would be hurrying.

It would cross the ocean. Soon it would take in the whole world. Africa would be strange—kraals of white-skinned young women, all exactly alike, going about the primitive chores of hunting and fruit-gathering, mashing grain, skinning animals. Building fires and weaving cloth and carefully shaping razor-sharp knives.

In China . . . he grinned inanely. She'd look strange there, too. In the austere high-collar suit, the almost monastic robe of the young Communist cadres. Parade marching up the main streets of Peiping. Row after row of slim-legged full-breasted girls, with heavy Russian-made rifles. Carrying spades, picks, shovels. Columns of cloth-booted soldiers. Fast-moving workers with their precious tools. Reviewed by an identical figure on the elaborate stand overlooking the street, one slender arm raised, her gentle, pretty face expressionless and wooden.

He turned off the highway onto a side road. A moment later he was on his way back, driving slowly, listlessly, the way he had come.

At an intersection a traffic cope waded out through traffic to his car. He sat rigid, hands on the wheel, waiting numbly.

"Rick," she whispered pleadingly as she reached the window. "Isn't everything all right?"

"Sure," he answered dully.

She reached in through the open window and touched him imploringly on the arm. Familiar fingers, red nails, the hand he knew so well. "I want to be with you so badly. Aren't we together again? Aren't I back?"

"Sure."

She shook her head miserably. "I don't understand," she repeated. "I thought it was all right again."

Savagely he put the car into motion and hurtled ahead. The intersection was left behind.

It was afternoon. He was exhausted, riddled with fatigue. He guided the car towards his own town automatically. Along the streets she hurried everywhere, on all sides. She was omnipresent. He came to his apartment building and parked.

The janitor greeted him in the empty hall. Rick identified him by the greasy rag clutched in one hand, the big push-broom, the bucket of wood shavings. "Please," she implored, "tell me what it is, Rick. Please tell me."

He pushed past her, but she caught at him desperately. "Rick, *I'm back.* Don't you understand? They took me too soon and then they sent me back again. It was a mistake. I won't ever call them again—that's all in the past." She followed after him, down the hall to the stairs. "I'm never going to call them again."

He climbed the stairs. Silvia hesitated, then settled down on the bottom step in a wretched, unhappy heap, a tiny figure in thick workman's clothing and huge cleated boots.

He unlocked his apartment door and entered.

The late afternoon sky was a deep blue beyond the windows. The roofs of nearby apartment buildings sparkled white in the sun.

His body ached. He wandered clumsily into the bathroom—it seemed alien and unfamiliar, a difficult place to find. He filled the bowl with hot water, rolled up his sleeves and washed his face and hands in the swirling hot steam. Briefly, he glanced up.

It was a terrified reflection that showed out of the mirror above the bowl, a face, tear-stained and frantic. The face was difficult to catch—it seemed to waver and slide. Gray eyes, bright with terror. Trembling red mouth, pulse-fluttering throat, soft brown hair. The face gazed out pathetically—and then the girl at the bowl bent to dry herself.

She turned and moved wearily out of the bathroom into the living-room.

Confused, she hesitated, then threw herself onto a chair and closed her eyes, sick with misery and fatigue.

"Rick," she murmured pleadingly. "Try to help me. I'm back, aren't I?" She shook her head, bewildered. "Please, Rick, I thought everything was all right."

Angel
by
Pat Cadigan

*Pat Cadigan was born in Schenectady, New York, and now lives in
Overland Park, Kansas. She made her first professional sale in
1980, and has subsequently come to be regarded as one of the best
new writers in SF. She was the coeditor of* Shayol, *perhaps the best
of the semiprozines of the late 1970s; it was honored with a World
Fantasy Award in the Special Achievement, Non-Professional
category in 1981. She has also served as Chairman of the Nebula
Award Jury and as a World Fantasy Award Judge. Her story
"Pretty Boy Crossover" has recently appeared on several critics'
lists as among the best science fiction stories of the 1980s, and
her collection* Patterns *has been hailed as one of the landmark
collections of its decade. Her first novel,* Mindplayers, *was released
in 1987 to excellent critical response, and her second novel,*
Synners, *won the prestigious Arthur C. Clarke Award. Her most
recent books are the novel* Fools *and a new collection called* Dirty
Work. *Coming up is a novel tentatively entitled* Parasites.*

"Angel" was a finalist for the Hugo Award, the Nebula Award,*
and *the World Fantasy Award, one of the few stories ever to earn
that rather unusual distinction. In it, she gives us an elegant and
bittersweet lesson in the consequences of trust . . .*

* * *

Stand with me awhile, Angel, I said, and Angel said he'd do that.
Angel was good to me that way, good to have with you on a cold
night and nowhere to go. We stood on the street corner together
and watched the cars going by and the people and all. The streets
were lit up like Christmas, streetlights, store lights, marquees over
the all-night movie houses and bookstores blinking and flashing;
shank of the evening in east midtown. Angel was getting used to
things here and getting used to how I did nights. Standing outside,
because what else are you going to do. He was *my* Angel now, had
been since that other cold night when I'd been going home,

because where are you going to go, and I'd found him and took him with me. It's good to have someone to take with you, someone to look after. Angel knew that. He started looking after me, too.

Like now. We were standing there awhile and I was looking around at nothing and everything, the cars cruising past, some of them stopping now and again for the hookers posing by the curb, and then I saw it, out of the corner of my eye. Stuff coming out of the Angel, shiny like sparks but flowing like liquid. Silver fireworks. I turned and looked all the way at him and it was gone. And he turned and gave a little grin like he was embarrassed I'd seen. Nobody else saw it, though; not the short guy who paused next to the Angel before crossing the street against the light, not the skinny hype looking to sell the boom-box he was carrying on his shoulder, not the homeboy strutting past us with both his girlfriends on his arms, nobody but me.

The Angel said, Hungry?

Sure, I said. I'm hungry.

Angel looked past me. Okay, he said. I looked, too, and here they came, three leather boys, visor caps, belts, boots, keyrings. On the cruise together. Scary stuff, even though you know it's not looking for you.

I said, them? *Them?*

Angel didn't answer. One went by, then the second, and the Angel stopped the third by taking hold of his arm.

Hi.

The guy nodded. His head was shaved. I could see a little grey-black stubble under his cap. No eyebrows, disinterested eyes. The eyes were because of the Angel.

I could use a little money, the Angel said. My friend and I are hungry.

The guy put his hand in his pocket and wiggled out some bills, offering them to the Angel. The Angel selected a twenty and closed the guy's hand around the rest.

This will be enough, thank you.

The guy put his money away and waited.

I hope you have a good night, said the Angel.

The guy nodded and walked on, going across the street to where his two friends were waiting on the next corner. Nobody found anything weird about it.

Angel was grinning at me. Sometimes he was *the* Angel, when he was doing something, sometimes he was Angel, when he was just with me. Now he was Angel again. We went up the street to the luncheonette and got a seat by the front window so we could still watch the street while we ate.

Cheeseburger and fries, I said without bothering to look at the plastic-covered menus lying on top of the napkin holder. The Angel nodded.

Thought so, he said. I'll have the same, then.

The waitress came over with a little tiny pad to take our order. I cleared my throat. It seemed like I hadn't used my voice in a hundred years. "Two cheeseburgers and two fries," I said, "and two cups of—" I looked up at her and froze. She had no face. Like, *nothing*, blank from hairline to chin, soft little dents where the eyes and nose and mouth would have been. Under the table, the Angel kicked me, but gentle.

"And two cups of coffee," I said.

She didn't say anything—how could she?—as she wrote down the order and then walked away again. All shaken up, I looked at the Angel, but he was calm like always.

She's a new arrival, Angel told me and leaned back in his chair. Not enough time to grow a face.

But how can she breathe? I said.

Through her pores. She doesn't need much air yet.

Yah, but what about—like, I mean, don't other people *notice* that she's got nothing there?

No. It's not such an extraordinary condition. The only reason you notice is because you're with me. Certain things have rubbed off on you. But no one else notices. When they look at her, they see whatever face they expect someone like her to have. And eventually, she'll have it.

But you have a face, I said. You've always had a face.

I'm different, said the Angel.

You sure are, I thought, looking at him. Angel had a beautiful face. That wasn't why I took him home that night, just because he had a beautiful face—I left all that behind a long time ago—but it was there, his beauty. The way you think of a man being beautiful, good clean lines, deep-set eyes, ageless. About the only way you could describe him—look away and you'd forget everything except that he was beautiful. But he did have a face. He *did*.

Angel shifted in the chair—these were like somebody's old kitchen chairs, you couldn't get too comfortable in them—and shook his head, because he knew I was thinking troubled thoughts. Sometimes you could think something and it wouldn't be troubled and later you'd think the same thing and it would be troubled. The Angel didn't like me to be troubled about him.

Do you have a cigarette? he asked.

I think so.

I patted my jacket and came up with most of a pack that I handed over to him. The Angel lit up and amused us both by having the smoke come out his ears and trickle out of his eyes like ghostly tears. I felt my own eyes watering for his; I wiped them and there was that *stuff* again, but from me now. I was crying silver fireworks. I flicked them on the table and watched them puff out and vanish.

Does this mean I'm getting to *be* you, now? I asked.

Angel shook his head. Smoke wafted out of his hair. Just things rubbing off on you. Because we've been together and you're—susceptible. But they're different for you.

Then the waitress brought our food and we went on to another sequence, as the Angel would say. She still had no face but I guess she could see well enough because she put all the plates down just where you'd think they were supposed to go and left the tiny little check in the middle of the table.

Is she—I mean, did you know her, from where you—

Angel gave his head a brief little shake. No. She's from somewhere else. Not one of my—people. He pushed the cheese-burger and fries in front of him over to my side of the table. That was the way it was done; I did all the eating and somehow it worked out.

I picked up my cheeseburger and I was bringing it up to my

mouth when my eyes got all funny and I saw it coming up like a whole *series* of cheeseburgers, whoom-whoom-whoom, trick photography, only for real. I closed my eyes and jammed the cheeseburger into my mouth, holding it there, waiting for all the other cheeseburgers to catch up with it.

You'll be okay, said the Angel. Steady, now.

I said with my mouth full, That was—that was *weird*. Will I ever get used to this?

I doubt it. But I'll do what I can to help you.

Yah, well, the Angel *would* know. Stuff rubbing off on me, he could feel it better than I could. He was the one it was rubbing off *from*.

I had put away my cheeseburger and half of Angel's and was working on the french fries for both of us when I noticed he was looking out the window with this hard, tight expression on his face.

Something? I asked him.

Keep eating, he said.

I kept eating, but I kept watching, too. The Angel was staring at a big blue car parked at the curb right outside the diner. It was silvery blue, one of those lots-of-money models and there was a woman kind of leaning across from the driver's side to look out the passenger window. She was beautiful in that lots-of-money way, tawny hair swept back from her face, and even from here I could see she had turquoise eyes. Really beautiful woman. I almost felt like crying. I mean, jeez, how did people get that way and me too harmless to live.

But the Angel wasn't one bit glad to see her. I knew he didn't want me to say anything, but I couldn't help it.

Who is she?

Keep eating, Angel said. We need the protein, what little there is.

I ate and watched the woman and the Angel watch each other and it was getting very—I don't know, very *something* between them, even through the glass. Then a cop car pulled up next to her and I knew they were telling her to move it along. She moved it along.

Angel sagged against the back of his chair and lit another cigarette, smoking it in the regular, unremarkable way.

What are we going to do tonight? I asked the Angel as we left the restaurant.

Keep out of harm's way, Angel said, which was a new answer. Most nights we spent just kind of going around soaking everything up. The Angel soaked it up, mostly. I got some of it along with him, but not the same way he did. It was different for him. Sometimes he would use me like a kind of filter. Other times he took it direct. There'd been the big car accident one night, right at my usual corner, a big old Buick running a red light smack into somebody's nice Lincoln. The Angel had had to take it direct because I couldn't handle that kind of stuff. I didn't know how the Angel could take it, but he could. It carried him for days afterwards, too. I only had to eat for myself.

It's the intensity, little friend, he'd told me, as though that were supposed to explain it.

It's the intensity, not whether it's good or bad. The universe doesn't know good or bad, only less or more. Most of you have a bad time reconciling this. *You* have a bad time with it, little friend, but you get through better than other people. Maybe because of the way you are. You got squeezed out of a lot, you haven't had much of a chance at life. You're as much an exile as I am, only in your own land.

That may have been true, but at least I *belonged* here, so that part was easier for me. But I didn't say that to the Angel. I think he liked to think he could do as well or better than me at living—I mean, I couldn't just look at some leather boy and get him to cough up a twenty dollar bill. Cough up a fist in the face or worse, was more like it.

Tonight, though, he wasn't doing so good, and it was that woman in the car. She'd thrown him out of step, kind of.

Don't think about her, the Angel said, just out of nowhere. Don't think about her any more.

Okay, I said, feeling creepy because it was creepy when the

Angel got a glimpse of my head. And then, of course, I couldn't think about anything else hardly.

Do you want to go home? I asked him.

No. I can't stay in now. We'll do the best we can tonight, but I'll have to be very careful about the tricks. They take so much out of me, and if we're keeping out of harm's way, I might not be able to make up for a lot of it.

It's okay, I said. I ate. I don't need anything else tonight, you don't have to do any more.

Angel got that look on his face, the one where I knew he wanted to give me things, like feelings I couldn't have any more. Generous, the Angel was. But I didn't need those feelings, not like other people seem to. For awhile, it was like the Angel didn't understand that, but he let me be.

Little friend, he said, and almost touched me. The Angel didn't touch a lot. I could touch him and that would be okay, but if *he* touched somebody, he couldn't help *doing* something to them, like the trade that had given us the money. That had been deliberate. If the trade had touched the Angel first, it would have been different, nothing would have happened unless the Angel touched him back. All touch meant something to the Angel that I didn't understand. There was touching without touching, too. Like things rubbing off on me. And sometimes, when I did touch the Angel, I'd get the feeling that it was maybe more his idea than mine, but I didn't mind that. How many people are going their whole lives never being able to touch an Angel?

We walked together and all around us the street was really coming to life. It was getting colder, too. I tried to make my jacket cover more. The Angel wasn't feeling it. Most of the time hot and cold didn't mean much to him. We saw the three rough trade guys again. The one Angel had gotten the money from was getting into a car. The other two watched it drive away and then walked on. I looked over at the Angel.

Because we took his twenty, I said.

Even if we hadn't, Angel said.

So we went along, the Angel and me, and I could feel how different it was tonight than it was all the other nights we'd walked or stood together. The Angel was kind of pulled back into himself and seemed to be keeping a check on me, pushing us closer together. I was getting more of those fireworks out of the corners of my eyes, but when I'd turn my head to look, they'd vanish. It reminded me of the night I'd found the Angel standing on my corner all by himself in pain. The Angel told me later that was real talent, knowing he was in pain. I never thought of myself as any too talented, but the way everyone else had been just ignoring him, I guess I must have had something to see him after all.

The Angel stopped us several feet down from an all-night bookstore. Don't look, he said. Watch the traffic or stare at your feet, but don't look or it won't happen.

There wasn't anything to see right then, but I didn't look anyway. That was the way it was sometimes, the Angel telling me it made a difference whether I was watching something or not, something about the other people being conscious of me being conscious of them. I didn't understand, but I knew Angel was usually right, So I was watching traffic when the guy came out of the bookstore and got his head punched.

I could almost see it out of the corner of my eye. A lot of movement, arms and legs flying and grunty noises. Other people stopped to look but I kept my eyes on the traffic, some of which was slowing up so they could check out the fight. Next to me, the Angel was stiff all over. Taking it in, what he called the expenditure of emotional kinetic energy. No right, no wrong, little friend, he'd told me. Just energy, like the rest of the universe.

So he took it in and I *felt* him taking it in, and while I was feeling it, a kind of silver fog started creeping around my eyeballs and I was in two places at once. I was watching the traffic and I was in the Angel watching the fight and feeling him charge up like a big battery.

It felt like nothing I'd ever felt before. These two guys slugging it out—well, one guy doing all the slugging and the other skittering around trying to get out from under the fists and having his head punched but good, and the Angel drinking it like he was sipping at an empty cup and somehow getting it to have something in it after all. Deep inside him, whatever made the Angel go was getting a little stronger.

I kind of swung back and forth between him and me, or swayed might be more like it was. I wondered about it, because the Angel wasn't touching me. I really was getting to *be* him, I thought; Angel picked that up and put the thought away to answer later. It was like I was traveling by the fog, being one of us and then the other, for a long time, it seemed, and then after awhile I was more me than him again, and some of the fog cleared away.

And there was that car, pointed the other way this time, and the woman was climbing out of it with this big weird smile on her face, as though she'd won something. She waved at the Angel to come to her.

Bang went the connection between us dead and the Angel shot past me, running away from the car. I went after him. I caught a glimpse of her jumping back into the car and yanking at the gear shift.

Angel wasn't much of a runner. Something funny about his knees. We'd gone maybe a hundred feet when he started wobbling and I could hear him pant. He cut across a Park & Lock that was dark and mostly empty. It was back-to-back with some kind of private parking lot and the fences for each one tried to mark off the same narrow strip of lumpy pavement. They were easy to climb but Angel was too panicked. He just *went* through them before he even thought about it; I knew that because if he'd been thinking, he'd have wanted to save what he'd just charged up with for when he really needed it bad enough.

I had to haul myself over the fences in the usual way, and when he heard me rattling on the saggy chainlink, he stopped and looked back.

Go, I told him. Don't wait on me!

He shook his head sadly. Little friend, I'm a fool. I could stand to learn from you a little more.

Don't stand, run! I got over the fences and caught up with him. Let's go! I yanked his sleeve as I slogged past and he followed at a clumsy trot.

Have to hide somewhere, he said, camouflage ourselves with people.

I shook my head, thinking we could just run maybe four more blocks and we'd be at the freeway overpass. Below it were the butt-ends of old roads closed off when the freeway had been built. You could hide there the rest of your life and no one would find you. But Angel made me turn right and go down a block to this rundown crack-in-the-wall called Stan's Jigger. I'd never been in there—I'd never made it a practice to go into bars—but the Angel was pushing too hard to argue.

Inside it was smelly and dark and not too happy. The Angel and I went down to the end of the bar and stood under a blood-red light while he searched his pockets for money.

Enough for one drink apiece, he said.

I don't want anything.

You can have soda or something.

The Angel ordered from the bartender, who was suspicious. This was a place for regulars and nobody else, and certainly nobody else like me or the Angel. The Angel knew that even stronger than I did but he just stood and pretended to sip his drink without looking at me. He was all pulled into himself and I was hovering around the edges. I knew he was still pretty panicked and trying to figure out what he could do next. As close as I was, if he had to get real far away, he was going to have a problem and so was I. He'd have to tow me along with him and that wasn't the most practical thing to do.

Maybe he was sorry now he'd let me take him home. But he'd been so weak then, and now with all the filtering and stuff I'd done for him, he couldn't just cut me off without a lot of pain.

I was trying to figure out what I could do for him now when the bartender came back and gave us a look that meant order or get out, and he'd have liked it better if we got out. So would everyone else there. The few other people standing at the bar weren't looking at us, but they knew right where we were, like a sore spot. It wasn't hard to figure out what they thought about us, either, maybe because of me or because of the Angel's beautiful face.

We got to leave, I said to the Angel but he had it in his head this was good camouflage. There wasn't enough money for two more drinks so he smiled at the bartender and slid his hand across the bar and put it on top of the bartender's. It was tricky doing it this way; bartenders and waitresses took more persuading because it wasn't normal for them just to give you something.

The bartender looked at the Angel with his eyes half closed. He seemed to be thinking it over. But the Angel had just blown a lot going through the fence instead of climbing over it and the fear was scuttling his concentration and I just knew that it wouldn't work. And maybe my knowing that didn't help, either.

The bartender's free hand dipped down below the bar and came up with a small club. "Faggot!" he roared and caught Angel just over the ear. Angel slammed into me and we both crashed to the floor. Plenty of emotional kinetic energy in here, I thought dimly as the guys standing at the bar fell on us, and then I didn't think anything more as I curled up into a ball under their fists and boots.

We were lucky they didn't much feel like killing anyone. Angel went out the door first and they tossed me out on top of him. As soon as I landed on him, I knew we were both in trouble; something was broken inside him. So much for keeping out of harm's way. I rolled off him and lay on the pavement, staring at the sky and trying to catch my breath. There was blood in my mouth and my nose, and my back was on fire.

Angel? I said, after a bit.

He didn't answer. I felt my mind get kind of all loose and runny, like my brains were leaking out my ears. I thought about the trade we'd taken the money from and how I'd been scared of him and his friends and how silly that had been. But then, I was too harmless to live.

The stars were raining silver fireworks down on me. It didn't help.

Angel? I said again.

I rolled over onto my side to reach for him, and there she was. The car was parked at the curb and she had Angel under the armpits, dragging him toward the open passenger door. I couldn't tell if he was conscious or not and that scared me. I sat up.

She paused, still holding the Angel. We looked into each other's eyes, and I started to understand.

"Help me get him into the car," she said at last. Her voice sounded hard and flat and unnatural. "Then you can get in, too. In the *back* seat."

I was in no shape to take her out. It couldn't have been better for her if she'd set it up herself. I got up, the pain flaring in me so bad that I almost fell down again, and took the Angel's ankles. His ankles were so delicate, almost like a woman's, like *hers*. I didn't really help much, except to guide his feet in as she sat him on the seat and strapped him in with the shoulder harness. I got in the back as she ran around to the other side of the car, her steps all real light and peppy, like she'd found a million dollars lying there on the sidewalk.

We were out on the freeway before the Angel stirred in the shoulder harness. His head lolled from side to side on the back of the seat. I reached up and touched his hair lightly, hoping she couldn't see me do it.

Where are you taking me, the Angel said.

"For a ride," said the woman. "For the moment."

Why does she talk out loud like that? I asked the Angel.

Because she knows it bothers me.

"You know I can focus my thoughts better if I say things out loud," she said. "I'm not like one of your little pushovers." She glanced at me in the rear view mirror. "Just *what* have you gotten yourself into since you left, darling? Is that a boy or a girl?"

I pretended I didn't care about what she said or that I was too harmless to live or any of that stuff, but the way she said it, she meant it to sting.

Friends can be either, Angel said. It doesn't matter which. Where are you taking us?

Now it was *us*. In spite of everything, I almost could have smiled.

"Us? You mean, you and me? Or are you really referring to your little pet back there?"

My friend and I are together. You and I are *not*.

The way the Angel said it made me think he meant more than not together; like he'd been with her once the way he was with me now. The Angel let me know I was right. Silver fireworks started flowing slowly off his head down the back of the seat and I knew there was something wrong about it. There was too much all at once.

"Why can't you talk out loud to me, darling?" the woman said with fakey-sounding petulance. "Just say a few words and make me happy. You have a lovely voice when you use it."

That was true, but the Angel never spoke out loud unless he couldn't get out of it, like when he'd ordered from the bartender. Which had probably helped the bartender decide about what he thought we were, but it was useless to think about that.

"All right," said Angel, and I knew the strain was awful for him. "I've said a few words. Are you happy?" He sagged in the shoulder harness.

"Ecstatic. But it won't make me let you go. I'll drop your pet at the nearest hospital and then we'll go home." She glanced at the Angel as she drove. "I've missed you so much. I can't *stand* it without you, without you making things happen. Doing your little miracles. You knew I'd get addicted to it, all the things you could do to people. And then you just took off, I didn't know what had happened to you. And it *hurt*." Her voice turned kind of pitiful, like a little kid's. "I was in real *pain*. You must have been, too. Weren't you? Well, *weren't you*?"

Yes, the Angel said. I was in pain, too.

I remembered him standing on my corner, where I'd hung out all that time by myself until he came. Standing there in pain. I didn't know why or from what then, I just took him home, and after a little while, the pain went away. When he decided we were together, I guess.

The silvery flow over the back of the car seat thickened. I cupped my hands under it and it was like my brain was lighting up with pictures. I saw the Angel before he was my Angel, in this really nice house, the woman's house, and how she'd take him places, restaurants or stores or parties, thinking at him real hard so that he was all filled up with her and had to do what she wanted him to. Steal sometimes; other times, weird stuff, making people do silly things like suddenly start singing or taking their clothes off. That was mostly at the parties, though she made a waiter she didn't like burn himself with a pot of coffee. She'd get men, too, through the Angel, and they'd think it was the greatest idea in the world to go to bed with her. Then she'd make the Angel show her the others, the ones that had been sent here the way he had for crimes nobody could have understood, like the waitress with no face. She'd look at them, sometimes try to do things to them to make them uncomfortable or unhappy. But mostly she'd just stare.

It wasn't like that in the very beginning, the Angel said weakly and I knew he was ashamed.

It's okay, I told him. People can be nice at first, I know that. Then they find out about you.

The woman laughed. "You two are *so* sweet and pathetic. Like a couple of little children. I guess that's what you were looking for, wasn't it, darling? Except children can be cruel, too, can't they? So you got this—*creature* for yourself." She looked at me in the rear view mirror again as she slowed down a little, and for a moment I was afraid she'd seen what I was doing with the silvery stuff that was still pouring out of the Angel. It was starting to slow now. There wasn't much time left. I wanted to scream, but the Angel was calming me for what was coming next. "What happened to you, anyway?"

Tell her, said the Angel. To stall for time, I knew, keep her occupied.

I was born funny, I said. I had both sexes.

"A hermaphrodite!" she exclaimed with real delight.

She loves freaks, the Angel said, but she didn't pay any attention.

There was an operation, but things went wrong. They kept trying to fix it as I got older but my body didn't have the right kind of chemistry or something. My parents were ashamed. I left after awhile.

"You poor thing," she said, not meaning anything like that. "You were *just* what darling, here, needed, weren't you? Just a little nothing, no demands, no desires. For anything." Her voice got all hard. "They could probably fix you up now, you know."

I don't want it. I left all that behind a long time ago, I don't need it.

"*Just* the sort of little pet that would be perfect for you," she said to the Angel. "Sorry I have to tear you away. But I can't get along without you now. Life is so boring. And empty. And—" She sounded puzzled. "And like there's nothing more to live for since you left me."

That's not me, said the Angel. That's you.

"No, it's a lot of you, and you know it. You know you're addictive to human beings, you knew that when you came here—when they *sent* you here. Hey, you, *pet*, do you know what his crime was, why they sent him to this little backwater penal colony of a planet?"

Yeah, I know, I said. I really didn't, but I wasn't going to tell her that.

"What do you think about *that*, little pet neuter?" she said gleefully, hitting the accelerator pedal and speeding up. "What do you think of the crime of refusing to mate?"

The Angel made a sort of an out-loud groan and lunged at the steering wheel. The car swerved wildly and I fell backwards, the silver stuff from the Angel going all over me. I tried to keep scooping it into my mouth the way I'd been doing, but it was flying all over the place now. I heard the crunch as the tires left the road and went onto the shoulder. Something struck the side of the car, probably the guard rail, and made it fishtail, throwing me down on the floor. Up front the woman was screaming and cursing and the Angel wasn't making a sound, but, in my head, I could hear him sort of keening. Whatever happened, this would be it. The Angel had told me all that time ago, after I'd taken him home, that they didn't last long after they got here, the exiles from his world and other worlds. Things tended to *happen* to them, even if they latched on to someone like me or the woman. They'd be in accidents or the people here would kill them. Like antibodies in a human body rejecting something or fighting a disease. At least I belonged here, but it looked like I was going to die in a car accident with the Angel and the woman both. I didn't care.

The car swerved back onto the highway for a few seconds and then pitched to the right again. Suddenly there was nothing under us and then we thumped down on something, not road but dirt or grass or something, bombing madly up and down. I pulled myself up on the back of the seat just in time to see the sign coming at us at an angle. The corner of it started to go through the windshield on the woman's side and then all I saw for a long time was the biggest display of silver fireworks ever.

It was hard to be gentle with him. Every move hurt but I didn't want to leave him sitting in the car next to her, even if she was dead. Being in the back seat had kept most of the glass from flying into me but I was still shaking some out of my hair and the impact hadn't done much for my back.

I laid the Angel out on the lumpy grass a little ways from the car and looked around. We were maybe a hundred yards from the highway, near a road that ran parallel to it. It was dark but I could still read the sign that had come through the windshield and split the woman's head in half. It said, *Construction Ahead, Reduce Speed.* Far off on the other road, I could see a flashing yellow light and at first I was afraid it was the police or something but it stayed where it was and I realized that must be the construction.

"Friend," whispered the Angel, startling me. He'd never spoken aloud to me, not directly.

Don't talk, I said, bending over him, trying to figure out some way I could touch him, just for comfort. There wasn't anything else I could do now.

"I have to," he said, still whispering. "It's almost all gone. Did you get it?"

Mostly, I said. Not all.

"I meant for you to have it."

I know.

"I don't know that it will really do you any good." His breath kind of bubbled in his throat. I could see something wet and shiny on his mouth but it wasn't silver fireworks. "But it's yours. You can do as you like with it. Live on it the way I did. Get what you need when you need it. But you can live as a human, too. Eat. Work. However, whatever."

I'm not human, I said. I'm not any more human than you, even if I do belong here.

"Yes, you are, little friend. I haven't made you any less human," he said, and coughed some. "I'm not sorry I wouldn't mate. I couldn't mate with my own. It was too . . . I don't know, too little of me, too much of them, something. I couldn't bond, it would have been nothing but emptiness. The Great Sin, to be unable to give, because the universe knows only less or more and I insisted that it would be good or bad. So they sent me here. But in the end, you know, they got their way, little friend." I felt his hand on me for a moment before it fell away. "I did it after all. Even if it wasn't with my own."

The bubbling in his throat stopped. I sat next to him for awhile in the dark. Finally I felt it, the Angel stuff. It was kind of fluttery-churny, like too much coffee on an empty stomach. I closed my eyes and lay down on the grass, shivering. Maybe some of it was shock but I don't think so. The silver fireworks started, in my head this time, and with them came a lot of pictures I couldn't understand. Stuff about the Angel and where he'd come from and the way they mated. It was a lot like how we'd been together, the Angel and me. They looked a lot like us but there were a lot of differences, too, things I couldn't make out. I couldn't make out how they'd sent him here, either—by *light*, in, like, little bundles or something. It didn't make any sense to me, but I guessed an Angel could be light. Silver fireworks.

I must have passed out, because when I opened my eyes, it felt like I'd been laying there a long time. It was still dark, though. I sat up and reached for the Angel, thinking I ought to hide his body.

He was gone. There was just a sort of wet sandy stuff where he'd been.

I looked at the car and her. All that was still there. Somebody was going to see it soon. I didn't want to be around for that.

Everything still hurt but I managed to get to the other road and start walking back toward the city. It was like I could *feel* it now, the way the Angel must have, as though it were vibrating like a drum or ringing like a bell with all kinds of stuff, people laughing and crying and loving and hating and being afraid and everything else that happens to people. The stuff that the Angel took in, energy, that I could take in now if I wanted.

And I knew that taking it in that way, it would be bigger than anything all those people had, bigger than anything I could have had if things hadn't gone wrong with me all those years ago.

I wasn't so sure I wanted it. Like the Angel, refusing to mate back where he'd come from. He wouldn't, there, and I couldn't, here. Except now I could do something else.

I wasn't so sure I wanted it. But I didn't think I'd be able to stop it, either, any more than I could stop my heart from beating. Maybe it wasn't really such a good thing or a right thing. But it was like the Angel said: the universe doesn't know good or bad, only less or more.

Yeah. I heard *that*.

I thought about the waitress with no face. I could find them all now, all the ones from the other places, other worlds that sent them away for some kind of alien crimes nobody would have understood. I could find them all. They threw away their outcasts, I'd tell them, but here, we *kept* ours. And here's how. Here's how you live in a universe that only knows less or more.

I kept walking toward the city.

Curse of the Angel's Wife
by
Bruce Boston

Bruce Boston has published poetry and short fiction in a wide variety of markets. He is a recipient of the Pushcart Prize for short fiction, has won the prestigious Rhysling Award for poetry, and has twice won the annual Asimov's Readers Award *poll for the year's best poem. His most recent book is a poetry collection,* Accursed Wives.

*   *   *

The milk silken embrace
of his six-foot wingspan
drapes her in a coverlet
of staid domestic desire.
The loose feathers she must
vacuum on a daily basis

drive her up the wall.
He is perfect to be sure.
Just like their marriage.
Just like their lives.
A spacious townhouse
in an affluent suburb

of the Celestial City.
Two and a half children.
Summer vacations in Jamaica.
Thanksgiving with her parents
in Denver or his in Rochester.
Christmas at God's doorstep

with the Hallelujah Chorus.
Only there are no Roman candles.
No dicey dives into the ink blue
waters of some icy Adriatic
while the stars shine on.
What should be the limitless

reaches of Heaven have become
for her a precise Purgatory.
And as she moves incessantly
from one color-coordinated room
to the next, upstairs and down,
she knows it will always be such.

Always she will welcome him home.
Always she will be a mother of two
pregnant with this barely half a child.
"Hallelujah!" they will shout and they
will sing until their lungs are bursting.
Loose feathers blowing everywhere.

Sleepers Awake
by
Jamil Nasir

New writer Jamil Nasir makes his home in Maryland, where he is a practicing attorney. His stories have appeared in Asimov's Science Fiction, Interzone, Aboriginal Science Fiction, *and all three volumes of Robert Silverberg and Karen Haber's* Universe *anthology series.*

Here's a chilling and yet oddly lyrical look at the end of everything—which may turn out to be not as bad as you feared it would be . . .

I

It all started with a flash.

It had been a mild October Sunday, yellow leaves fluttering down against a blue sky, the barking of a neighborhood dog and the tang of wood smoke coming faintly on the still air, warm enough to sit on your back deck all day. I had sat on mine till evening, reading, dozing, and watching the light turn long and yellow, then blue. Even when it got chilly and too dark to follow my spy book, where a beautiful girl in a parking garage was begging the hero to help her escape from terrorists, I didn't want to go in. I was leaning my chair against the cool brick of the house, listening to the trilling of crickets and an occasional car down on Thayer Avenue, when it came: a split-second of flashbulb blue piercing the neighborhood like an X-ray.

My chair thumped down on four legs. Another chair scraped back in the kitchen. Vicki slid the glass door open, a magazine in her hand. "What was that?"

We went and stood by the deck railing. The evening air was still and deep, two early stars shining through the branches of our backyard oak.

The screen door next door slammed and Mrs. Romer's old, hoarse voice said: "Going to rain, I imagine."

"There aren't any clouds," said Vicki.

"What?"

"There aren't any clouds. It wasn't lightning," Vicki yelled.

"Maybe an electric short in the circuit box down the street. Big one. Somebody ought to call the electric company," I told Vicki.

I got her to go in and call. I stood looking up into the darkness, crickets rippling the silence softly. Three houses down, Cindy Lipman stood in her back yard holding her baby, face a white blur looking up into the air.

"You can bet it's some kind of bad weather, anyhow," said Mrs. Romer sourly, and went back inside, screen door slamming behind her.

Looking up through the branches of the oak, I thought I heard, very faintly, the ringing of tiny bells blending with the crickets' song.

Vicki came back out. "The line's busy. Probably a lot of people—"

"Listen," I hissed.

"What?"

I strained my ears. The ringing seemed to have retreated back into my imagination.

But that night, on the edge of sleep, I thought I heard it again, sweet and distant, very faint.

"You hear that?" I whispered to Vicki.

"Mmm?"

"Bells."

Pause.

"Go to sleep."

II

Things were screwed up at work the next day. For one thing, the phones were broken. I had an important call to make to Syracuse, New York, but I kept getting whistling and crackling noises instead. The operator wouldn't answer. I finally told Rose to report it to the office manager, and spent the rest of the morning talking into my dictaphone. When I got back from lunch, Rose had the transcription on my chair. I put my feet on the desk with a contented sigh, uncapped a red pen, turned back the cover sheet, and read:

Sleepers Awake
Sleepers awake, the voice is calling,
On battlements the watchmen cry:
Wake, city of Jerusalem! . . .

The telephone rang. I groped for it.

"Bill Johnson, please," said a faraway, staticky voice.

"You have the wrong number."

"This isn't Johnson's Formal Wear in Des Moines, Iowa?"

I said no, hung up, and buzzed Rose, handed her the memo as the phone rang again.

"Bill Johnson, please," said a faraway, staticky voice.

I hung up. Rose was staring at the memo blankly. "That's funny. Something must be wrong with the word-processing system. I'll try to . . ."

The phone rang. I answered it, watching her out of the office suspiciously.

"Bill Johnson? Of Des Moines, Iowa?"

"No, Bob Wilson, of Washington, D.C., the same guy you've gotten the last half-dozen times."

"Sorry about that, Mr. Wilson. Tom Gibbs from New York City. I'm in Formal Wear. How are the phones down your way?"

"Screwed up."

"Same here. I've been trying to get through to Des Moines all morning. Seems like the trunk lines are out of whack. I can get Washington, Boston, Chicago, and L.A. okay, but the farm lands don't answer. Funny."

The phone rang once more that afternoon. I picked it up, expecting Tom Gibbs, but it wasn't Tom Gibbs; it was a wide, distant hum, a faint gabble of ten thousand crossed lines overlaid with the electronic buzz of some vast malfunction, like a telephone call from Entropy itself. I hung up with a shiver and a quick prayer that It didn't intend to come visit in person.

III

I was in a bad mood when I got home.

"Where's the newspaper?" I complained, after searching the living room for it. "You didn't throw it away again, did you?"

"It didn't come," Vicki called from upstairs. "I left you some green beans on the stove."

"Green beans?" I went and looked at them mournfully.

"I've got rehearsal, honey." She came downstairs, beautiful in a blue skirt and pink, floppy sweater, eyes vivid with makeup, gave me a barely touching kiss that wouldn't smear her lipstick. "And when I get back we have to go over to Mrs. Romer's. She swears she has ghosts. I promised we'd come and make sure there aren't any. I think she's gone crazy, poor old lady."

"Ghosts? Honey, I don't want to go over there tonight. I'm tired. You wouldn't believe—"

In the back yard, crickets trilled in subtly shifting patterns, the air still and just a little damp. Moonlight cast a dark deck shadow on the grass. I was leaning on the railing before going back inside to my spy book, when I heard the faint, sweet sound of bells.

I held my breath. The lights of Vicki's car had just disappeared down the hill. The sound seemed to be coming from around the side of the house.

I tiptoed down wooden steps and through crackling leaves, poked my head past the gutter downspout at the corner.

High in a young maple in Arland Johnston's side yard, unseasonable firefly lights floated.

I snuck forward, the soft earth of iris beds silencing my steps. For a second it crossed my mind that Arland had hung out Christmas lights: I thought I saw tiny haloed saints and angels with trumpets. Then they all winked out at once.

I stood looking up into the tree, lit pale by the moon. As I watched, a single leaf let go and fluttered down. Then I heard the bells again, faint and faraway.

The firefly lights were floating around a tree in old Mr. Jakeway's back yard, down at the bottom of the street.

I crept across silent asphalt that was moon-tinted the same deep, dusty blue as the sky, along the sidewalk in tree-shadows, pushed through a hole in Mr. Jakeway's hedge, getting scratched and poked. I picked my way through his quarter-acre back yard, trying to tell clumps of weeds from junk auto parts that could break your leg in the dark. Gnarled tree-branches hung almost to the ground.

A cobra blur coiled around my leg and yanked me into the air.

I tried to scream, but only a faint gurgling came out. I hung upside down, breath knocked out of me, spinning slowly, arms and free leg struggling wildly in the air.

The rope around my ankle jerked. There were grunts from above, and I started going up again, slowly. Hands took hold of me and pulled me onto a thick tree-branch four stories off the ground.

An old man squatted on the branch. For a second I thought he was Mr. Jakeway, but then I saw that he was even older, with a sour, wrinkled face, and no hair. He wore a long, dingy robe that the moon lit grey, with big buttons down the front. He peered at me through wire-rimmed spectacles. Around him crouched half a dozen kids in their early teens, watching me solemnly. Three of them held me onto the branch.

The old man croaked: "I am the Angel of Death."

I stared at him. Then I did something I would never have expected: I started to cry. I could see our house far below, yard awash in pale leaves, my old Datsun parked in front, a bag of newspapers on the walk waiting for the recycling truck. I had never seen the neighborhood from up here; already it looked faraway and out of reach, like a picture of someplace you used to live but will never see again.

"Please stop crying," said the old man irritably. "I'm not going to take you yet. At least, not if you promise to stop poking around where you have no business. We're having enough trouble right now without you."

I wiped my shirtsleeve across my nose hopefully.

"Do you promise to stop snooping? To leave those little lights alone? And not to tell anyone about us?"

I nodded eagerly. One of the teenage kids looped the end of the rope they had pulled off my ankle around my chest.

"See that you don't," the old man croaked as they lowered me rotating toward the earth. "If you do—"

When I reached the ground, I struggled out of the rope and ran blindly until I was inside my house, locked the door, drew all the curtains, and dialed 911.

It took them a long time to answer. After I had given my name and address, I said: "There's a weirdo in a tree at the end of my block who claims he's the Angel of Death. He's got some kids with him. They've got a rope snare rigged up that almost broke my back. This guy is dangerous, officer—if you could see his face—"

"Angel of Death—up in a tree—rope snare—" the heavy voice on the other end repeated slowly; obviously he was writing it down. "And what address would this be at, Mr. Wilson?"

"It's the first house on your right as you turn onto Thayer Place. I don't know the exact address. You're sending somebody right over?"

"It'll probably be half an hour, Mr. Wilson, before we can get to it. We've—"

"Half an *hour?* Officer, there's a dangerous maniac—"

"If you'll let me finish, Mr. Wilson, we've got thirty other emergency calls, and we just don't have the cars to cover them. I suggest you stay inside and keep your doors locked until we can get out there, but I wouldn't panic. The other wild calls we've had tonight have turned out to be hoaxes."

"This isn't a hoax!"

"I didn't say it was, sir. But look, we've got a report of a giant lizard prowling around Sligo Creek—ate somebody's dog, says here. We've got a report of a *mushroom cloud* over on Colesville Road. We've got ghosts all over town. We figure it's one of these kids' Dungeons and Dragons clubs or some people very confused about when Halloween is, so I wouldn't get too concerned. Just stay inside until the officer gets there."

As soon as I put down the phone, a scream sounded faintly from next door.

I spent a minute that felt like an hour chewing the end off my thumb. I figured the Angel of Death guy and his kids were murdering Mrs. Romer. I wondered what I should do about that.

Another scream.

I banged out along leaf-deep sidewalks. All of Mrs. Romer's windows were lit and her front door was ajar. Mrs. Romer herself was standing in the middle of her small, well-furnished living room, wrinkled hands on her hips, looking around with solemn belligerence.

"He's back," she announced in her hoarse voice as I stopped in the doorway. "Him and his alcoholic mother and his sponging sister."

"Who?" I yelled, trying to keep my teeth from chattering.

"Terrell."

"I—I thought he was dead."

"It was such a relief to me. I learned to love him afterward; he left me this house and a lot of money. God bless him. But he's back. Him and his alcoholic, sponging family."

"Mrs. Romer, I've got a terrible emergency—"

"You look in the basement," she told me. "I'll go upstairs. If we can't find them, we'll have to look in the attic."

And she started up the stairs, yelling quaveringly: "Terrell! Terrell! You come out right now!"

It took me awhile to get her calmed down. She wouldn't let me leave until I had crawled around in her attic, poking a flashlight into dusty, cobwebbed corners. Maybe I didn't hurry as much as I could have; with the Angel of Death guy prowling the neighborhood, Mrs. Romer's attic felt comfortably remote and full of dark hiding places. Thankfully, I didn't find her dead in-laws crouching in any of them. When I peeked out her front door twenty minutes later, I was relieved to see the red and blue lights of a police car rotating silently at the end of the street.

I walked down to where a policeman and old Mr. Jakeway stood by a purring squad car, the mist of their breath rising into blue depths where the moon shone mistily. Another policeman was crashing around in the brush behind Mr. Jakeway's house, shining a flashlight up into the trees.

"Hey there, Bobby," said Mr. Jakeway. "Officer here tells me you saw some kids up in my trees."

"An old man and some kids. But that was an hour ago."

"Well, they're gone now," said the policeman.

"Officer, I know it sounds strange, but they were there. They pulled me—"

"You're not the only report we have on them," said the policeman, looking at a clipboard with his flashlight. "At least the old man. We got a call over on Pershing Drive, an old man fitting that description trampling through people's flower beds. Went off in a big foreign car, says here."

"You think they're foreigners? Terrorists?" asked Mr. Jakeway, thrusting his old, grizzled head forward.

"I don't know what they are. We've gotten a lot of strange calls tonight, is all I know."

"Psychological warfare, maybe," said Mr. Jakeway, nodding and looking into our eyes one at a time. "Could be. You never know what they're inventing in those laboratories. Some kind of gas, maybe, makes you see people up in trees when there aren't any."

The other policeman crashed out of the bushes, looking scratched and out of breath.

"You ought to cut down some of those weeds back there," he told Mr. Jakeway.

IV

I had left the house door open; it spilled a rectangle of light onto the front walk in the still, cricket-trilled air, and I could hear the phone ringing half a block away as I walked back up from Mr. Jakeway's.

I rushed in and answered it.

It was Vicki. "Bob? Hi."

She never calls me "Bob" unless somebody is listening. In the background I could hear music and voices.

"I'm going to be a little late tonight. Something wonderful has happened."

"Where are you? Are you all right?"

"Of course I'm all right. I'm at rehearsal. Honey, you'll never guess what happened."

"Are you coming home? There's some weird things—"

"I'm going to be a little late. Honey, there was a producer at rehearsal tonight. None of us knew it. Stuart introduced us afterward. His name is Ken, and he's doing a show at the Kennedy Center in March. And he *signed me up for a part*. With *Tim Curry*."

"That's great, honey, great! But I wish you'd come home, because—"

"Honey? The line's getting staticky. We're going out to celebrate and sign the contract. Can you hear me?"

"I can hear you fine—"

"Hello? Bob? Oh, he's gone," she said disappointedly to someone at her end, and hung up.

Aside from a few distant crackles, the phone was dead.

I got my keys, locked the front door behind me. The gas station at Dale and Piney Branch glared with white neon, self-serve customers dawdling over their hoses. Overfed diners tottered out the door of the Chesapeake Crab House. I pointed the Datsun toward town. Half an hour later I was banging on the locked door of the Souris Studio storefront on 14th Street, cupping my hands on the glass to peer into a dim entrance area with a coatrack, a few shabby chairs, and a display stand for theater programs, but no people. I stood in the smoky, run-down darkness trying to imagine where one would go to celebrate a contract. Then I walked back to the parking garage.

My car was on the third sublevel. I went down urine-smelling concrete steps, crossed the oil-stained, neon-lit ramp. I had the door unlocked when a voice behind me said: "Can you give me a ride?"

The ramp had been deserted a second before. "No," I said, and yanked the door open.

"Please. Someone is following me. Please."

That made me turn and look.

She was small, slim, with fashionably tousled blonde hair, breathtaking dark eyes. She wore black tights, a black leather jacket, little pink ballerina shoes. Her face was wild, lips trembling. She came closer between the cars.

"Please," she said.

The heavy throb of an engine echoed down the ramp, and her pupils dilated crazily. Her breath came in tearing gasps.

Déjà vu. I moved away from the car door with a quick gesture. She scrambled to the floor of the passenger seat and crouched there, head down.

I got in, backed out of my space, and headed up the ramp. At the first turn I had to edge past a black Mercedes limo coming down. I edged close enough to see through the tinted glass of the back seat.

An old man with a bald, wrinkled face sat there. He wore a grey robe with big buttons, wire-rimmed spectacles. He didn't see me; his eyes were straining through the windshield as if looking for something.

My heart pounded. I paid the garage attendant in his cubicle of light with a shaking hand.

We were rattling over potholes on 14th Street before the woman said: "You know him." She was staring up at me.

"I'm going to call the police."

She laughed shortly. "The police," she sneered. She threw herself into the passenger seat. "Take a right here. You can use my phone."

As we drove it began to rain. A few minutes later, turning down 22nd Street, I suddenly had the feeling that I was leaving behind everything familiar to me, my whole life.

A few blocks down 22nd, I pulled over by a brick building with wide front steps between worn stone lions, brass-and-glass entrance doors glittering with chandelier light. The building elevator was elderly but highly polished. The third floor hall was silent, lit discreetly by brass leaves with bulbs behind them, carpeted in a red floral pattern. The woman unlocked a door near the end, locked and bolted it behind us.

"Phone's over there," she said, her hand a pale blur in the dark. She hurried into another room.

Rain pattered on the sills of open windows, and the glare of streetlight showed black and white outlines of magazines, clothes, and dishes scattered over deep chairs and a sofa, low glass-and-metal tables. Shelves held powerful stereo components, books, and vases. Shadowy art prints hung on the walls.

The woman was opening and closing drawers in the other room. She hadn't turned on any lights. I dialed 911 on a telephone shaped like a banana. It was busy.

"You have a phone book?" I called.

"Somewhere." She sounded preoccupied.

A phone book-sized binder lay on a table at the end of the sofa; but when I opened it, I found myself looking at an eight-by-ten glossy photograph of her wearing only a gold necklace, her delicate, muscular body stretched out on a bed. I closed the book with a snap. From where I stood I could see out the window.

The woman's voice said behind me: "Look, I need a ride somewhere. It's a matter of life and death. Can you help me?"

"No," I said. "Not yet."

She came around the sofa. She was wearing a white plastic raincoat over a white dress and white stockings, carrying an overnight bag. I held her so she wouldn't get too near the window. Streetlight glow lit her face silver-grey.

A black Mercedes limousine was parked across the street.

"Oh my God," she whispered. She started to shake.

I got her by both wrists, whispering: "Shh." I was imagining the Angel of Death and his chauffeur listening in the hall outside.

"No!" she screamed in a sudden frenzy. "No!" She tried to wrench her wrists away from me.

I wrapped my left hand around her face, pinioned her arms with my right, and dragged her struggling into the next room. One of her blue rubber boots kicked off and hit the wall. I crushed her down on a big, unmade bed, held a pillow over her head to muffle her screams. After awhile, lack of air made her quiet.

I took the pillow away enough to say in her ear: "Maybe they don't know we're here."

She lay still.

I helped her sit up. Her face was red, swollen, wet, her breath gasping with sobs. I put my finger to my lips and crept back into the living room, listened at the front door. The elevator opened once, but voices and footsteps went away in another direction.

There was no other sound. I tried the telephone. There were only buzzing and crackling noises on it now. I sat down against the wall behind the front door, my ears straining against the patter of rain and the sound of traffic.

After a long time I peered out the window again. Streetlight glittered on wet pavement. The black limo was gone.

The woman was asleep in her coat, one boot on, her face calm and intent like a child's. She woke with a start when I touched her.

"They're gone," I told her. My voice seemed to come from far off somewhere. I had started to shake.

She looked up into my face for a minute. Then she began fumbling with the buttons on her dress, breath quickening.

V

I woke up next to her after midnight, exhausted. Her skin seemed to glow faintly in the dark, as if there was a light inside her.

I lay and watched her. Gradually she woke up too.

When she was awake, I said: "I don't understand what's happening."

She propped herself up, sitting against the head of the bed, got a cigarette from the night table. Tendrils of smoke curled around her pale hair, pale shoulders.

"You're dead," she said.

I didn't say anything to that.

"Everybody's dead. Everybody at once," she went on. "All together. Whoosh. A wholesale global disaster, Sunday evening about five-thirty. You might have seen a flash or felt a sharp pain. I won't tell you what it was, since it's no longer your business, but almost a billion people died in the first half-hour, and more are coming in all the time.

"Almost nobody noticed. But now you're starting to notice. Now your comfortable consensual reality is starting to break down, to be rebuilt by more powerful forces: desires, obsessions, fears."

I got out of bed. I felt dizzy.

"I have to go," I said. "Home."

"You don't have a home anymore. Just a blackened spot on a

tiny piece of dust buzzing around a spark of light in a far corner of the universe. And a dream image that could vanish any second. You might as well stay here." She smiled, letting a wisp of smoke curl out through her lips.

"I can't," I said thickly, hunting for my underwear in the pile of clothes by the bed. "My wife—"

VI

By the time I turned the Datsun onto Thayer Place, it had stopped raining. Untidy maple branches looming over the front walk in the dark dripped on the limp, waterlogged bag of newspapers. I was heading shakily for the front door when there were steps behind me on the sidewalk.

A bent figure was jogging painfully up the hill. I stumbled backward, the adrenaline of fear flashing through me, but it was only Mr. Jakeway, unshaven jowls wagging, sunken eye-sockets filled with shadow.

"Bobby," he rasped. His thin, trembling hands took hold of my shoulders and he leaned on me, breathing hard. "Have they got you too? Or are you awake?" His breath smelled faintly alcoholic.

Before I could answer he went on: "They're lying, Bobby. Nothing's happened. Nobody's *dead*. Don't believe 'em, boy." He leaned on me harder, put his arm around my shoulder. "They want us to move aside. Just move aside and give up. They're using some kind of gas. Black gas. Thank goodness I found you, Bobby," he said hoarsely. "Everybody else is walking around in a dream."

I stared at the glitter of his eyes in the dark. I felt strange.

"Who?" I finally blurted out. "Who?"

"I don't know *who*," he whispered hoarsely. "But they're not from here. Aliens, maybe. I seen them walking through the streets, spraying black gas. We've got to do something, Bobby, before they—"

"Somebody told me it was a worldwide disaster—" I stammered miserably.

"That's what *they* say! That's *their* story! But it's a *lie*, Bobby. They want us to—"

"So what do we—what do we *do*?"

The question seemed to agitate him. "We have to wake up the others! We have to wake everybody up! Quick! Where's your wife? I'll go after Arland. Come on!"

His panic infected me. I ran up the walk to our front door.

The living room—tidy and familiar, yellowish light from the floor lamp by the couch throwing familiar shadows—turned my panic into cold, jittery sweat.

"Vicki?" I called.

No answer.

Out the window, Mrs. Romer's brightly lit kitchen caught my eye. Something was going on in there.

A man and a woman sat at a table by the kitchen window, talking tensely. I couldn't hear what they were saying. The woman looked vaguely like Mrs. Romer, but young, with an obsolete hairdo. The man was unshaven, jowly, tired-looking.

There was a muffled scream, and the woman dived across the table and buried a paring knife in the tired-looking man's forehead. They tumbled down out of sight, the woman screaming wildly.

My heart pounded. A darkness came over my eyes. I sat down heavily on the couch.

When I started to think again, I was exhausted, drained, too tired even to see clearly: the wall, floor lamp, and coffee table next to me looked fuzzy, translucent, unreal.

Voices, laughter, and footsteps were approaching along the front walk. The front door flew open and a dozen people came in. As they did, the living-room changed. The walls turned from blue to peach and fled outward in a long, curving line; the hardwood floor became plush blond carpet and sagged to shape a huge sunken living-room with grand piano, Chinese screens, round, furry chairs and sofas, dark lacquered cabinets, soft lighting, tropical plants. My body felt peculiarly stiff. I looked down with difficulty. All I could see of myself was a large Chinese vase displayed on a carved stand.

The people who piled through the arched, oak front door looked too grown-up to be carrying on the way they were. The men wore tuxedos with flowers in the lapels, the women glittery outfits that seemed to be half evening gown, half bikini. They were all young and beautiful. They crowded, laughing, chattering, and squealing, up a wide, curved staircase.

I was still too tired to move, so I sat numbly for another few minutes, until two people came back down the stairs. Music and merrymaking sounds came faintly from above.

The two people, a man and a woman, leaned on the grand piano not more than a stone's throw from me. The man was broad-shouldered and tall, with the kind of face Michelangelo used to carve out of marble, hair curling carelessly over his collar. He gazed at the woman as if there was nothing else to see in the world.

She was my wife. A little bigger in some places, a little smaller in others than I remembered her, dark ringlets thicker, the West Virginia jawline trimmed down some, but unmistakably Victoria Wilson. She was wearing a tight, slithery dress of gold sequins that showed off most of one leg and that I had to admit looked great, even though it was embarrassing the hell out of me.

I tried to stand up and make a fuss. I couldn't move or talk.

"You haven't given me your answer, darling," murmured the man, gazing down at her. She was gazing at him too, in a way I didn't like. "You can't leave me hanging like this. Please . . ."

"How *can* I answer? How can I even *think* right now, Billy? Everything is so wonderful! I feel as if I'm in heaven!" She put her drink on the piano and kicked off her high heels. "Do you think it's a dream? An Oscar nomination, a box-office smash—"

"And all because of you," he said. "You made that film what it is. Without you it would have been nothing."

"Oh, Billy—"

He drew her close in his strong arms, crushing her to him with barely controlled passion, and as their lips touched a shudder went through him.

"Hey!" I managed to yell in outrage.

I thought Vicki glanced at me, but the man didn't seem to hear.

"It's funny," he said when they were done slobbering on each other. He seemed ready to cry. "Here I am, the most powerful man in Hollywood—I really thought I had it made. Any woman in the world would do anything to get in my next picture. But the one I really want—the one I *must* have—won't have me."

He knelt down in front of her, looking up with imploring eyes.

"Please," he whispered. "Please . . ."

"Oh, brother!" I groaned.

"Will you shut *up?*" Vicki screamed at me, stamping her foot. "What are you doing here? I didn't come snooping around your stupid, corny private eye scene with that slut, did I? Get out of here! Leave me alone!"

Her rage hit me like a wave. Everything turned fuzzy and translucent again, Vicki and the Hollywood producer like ghosts with lights glowing inside them. The producer didn't seem to have noticed Vicki yelling—he stood up and took her in his arms again. And as they kissed, something funny happened: the light inside Vicki seemed to flicker and go dim, while the light inside the producer got stronger, as if he had drawn some of her light into himself.

And there was something else—someone I hadn't noticed before, sitting on a distant love seat, half hidden by a dwarf palm, hands clasped patiently over his long grey robe, wire-rimmed glasses patiently watching the oblivious lovers.

I struggled, trying to shout a warning, but I couldn't move or make a sound.

Ghostly music played. Vicki and the producer started to dance, close and slow, gradually swaying over near where I sat stiff and dumb. Soon the producer's tuxedoed bottom swayed languidly in front of my face. I lunged forward with all my strength, and bit it desperately hard. He screamed and jumped out of her arms, whirling in astonishment and rubbing himself.

Vicki's face was ugly with rage as she kicked me off my stand to shatter against the wall.

VII

I stood in the trough of a mountain in heavy night rain, showing my thumb to Interstate traffic that made a pale ribbon through murky darkness up the mountain's shoulder. Every few minutes lightning struck the summit, lighting wooded hills and sending out a crackling boom. I wore an old army surplus poncho, I was seventeen, the rain was warm, and the crowded, lonely highway made me feel somehow alive, vital, like a sailor on an uncharted ocean. When a little white car pulled out of traffic up the shoulder, I ran, lugging my knapsack, and climbed into the front seat next to a girl.

She was slender and young, wearing jeans and a floppy sweater, tousled blonde hair falling to her shoulders, dark eyes that flashed at me, then watched the mirror for an opening in traffic. Her pale hair and skin seemed to glow in the dark.

"Where are you going?" she asked.

It seemed strange that I couldn't remember. To hide my confusion, I pulled the poncho off over my head, getting water on the front seat. I felt the car accelerate.

"Okay," she said softly. "Come and say goodbye."

We climbed the mountain toward the storm, which now sent out a flash and a boom.

High up, the highway was bordered by jutting boulders and pines, the mountaintop bulking black in the gloom. At a sign that said "Authorized Vehicles Only," the girl jerked the steering wheel to the right and we were climbing a rutted track among the boulders, the lights of the highway abruptly left behind. Pine trees swayed and moaned in the rain and wind, dead leaves whirled and scattered before our lights. There was a blinding flash that seemed to obliterate everything, and a splitting bang that shook the mountain.

The track turned steeply up, and the little car's engine strained, its wheels spinning. At last we came to a slope it wouldn't climb. The girl killed the engine and lights and we got out into wet, rushing air that smelled of ozone and scorched rock. My skin prickled with electricity. Not far above, black clouds roiled, muttering heavily.

She was a pale blur scrambling through high grass that bent hissing in the wind. I scrambled up the slope after her.

Something loomed above me: a huge rock cropping out of the very top of the mountain. She was climbing it.

"Hey!" I yelled, laughing. "This is crazy! We've got to get out of here!" The storm scattered my words. I started after her, fingers straining on narrow holds, tennis-shoes slipping on wet rock, wind and rain tearing at me blindingly. When I reached the top, I was gasping.

The girl was naked, standing on the topmost pinnacle of rock, arching her body upward, straining her hands toward the clouds and moaning. The rock steamed, and the smell of burning and electricity was strong.

The glow of her skin reminded me of something. I stood at the edge of the rock, suddenly trembling, dizzy chasms of wind rushing below me.

"Don't be afraid," said the girl. "We're here to help you. To smooth your way from this world to the next."

"No," I whimpered.

But somehow I knew it was what I had always wanted.

I pulled off my clothes, throwing them out into the blackness. The rock was hot and charred under my feet.

I reached for the girl's upstraining body.

A livid blue spark jumped between us, lighting for a second her white skin, her crazy eyes, the hair standing out from her head like a silver mane. Then she was clawing at me, pulling me desperately to her, and we wrestled, standing, kneeling, and lying, until the mountain seemed to rock thundering on the roots of the world.

There was an enormous flash that cut the flesh from us in an instant, and I was illuminated from within: I saw our bodies flaming in the rushing air, and all the cracks and straining strength of rock under us, pushed up to the air from the liquid searing center of the earth, saw the live green things that crept and grew over the mountain toward the light, pushing upward by millimeters even in that second, saw birds huddled in their nests in swaying branches, saw animals crouching in their holes, a little river frothing at the foot of the mountain, and all rivers running to the oceans, the whales gliding silent and deep through the cold blue oceans, birds singing over the nests of their young in the evening, saw a young man leaning on a bridge in the evening, staring down into quiet water.

And as the vision faded and I plunged through darkness like a dying spark from a Fourth of July rocket, I saw, seated in the midst of everything, an old, old man in a grey robe, hands folded patiently on his stomach.

VIII

. . . a fresh October day with pale blue sky, yellow leaves fluttering down. I was sitting on my back deck, so tired that it was an effort to breathe, to hold my head up, so tired that the long yellow sunlight seemed aged and brittle, the breeze cold. Vicki sat in the chair next to mine, head bowed, hands lying useless in her lap like an old woman's.

Slow footsteps came along the flagstones at the side of the house, with a heavy *clunk*, as if whoever walked there leaned on a staff. The footsteps climbed the wooden steps, and an old man came into view. He was tall and stooped in his grey robe, bald, wrinkled face grave and thoughtful.

He stood looking down at us for a few minutes. Then he intoned in a strong, old voice: "The first seed of Life is desire. Life is the unwinding of desire, like the unwinding of a spring. When desire is burned away, the next world comes.

"I sent you images, reflections of your own desires, to help you to the next world."

Then a profound blue light shone from him, dimming the sun, and it was as if his body had turned inside out, had become hollow—had become an opening or doorway in the air of our back yard through which blue light shone from some other place, where I thought I could see stars. Flanking the door were two tall, shining figures in chain mail, leaning on heavy spears.

Then they and the door and the old man were gone.

A haze had come over the afternoon sun, making the sky pale. Mist was creeping through the bushes at the bottom of the garden. Birds sang and fluttered on the old grape arbor in Mrs. Romer's back yard. I was too tired to move, or even think, almost too tired to watch the mist roll in silently, softening the outlines of trees down on Thayer Avenue. After awhile the yellow leaves of our oak dripped with it, and the sky had turned twilight grey. The few sleepy songs of birds were muffled in the still air.

Fog thickened, so now I could only see halfway down the hill. Mrs. Romer's grape arbor began to slip out of sight. My hand had somehow gotten locked with Vicki's, but I couldn't turn to look at her. A surf, invisible in the fog, seemed to roll under us now, as if the ocean washed around the foundations of the house. Soon I could only see the horizontal bar of the deck railing in the mist, and the oak tree's shadow leaning over us as soft grey silence closed around.

My eyes were heavy and my chin drooped to my chest, but somewhere, maybe deep inside, someone seemed to be shaking me gently and saying "wake up, wake up."

Then I fell asleep.

And the Angels Sing
by
Kate Wilhelm

*Kate Wilhelm began publishing in 1956, and by now is widely
regarded as one of the best of today's writers—outside the genre
as well as in it. Her work has never been limited to the strict
boundaries of the field, and she has published mysteries, main-
stream thrillers, and comic novels as well as science fiction.
Wilhelm won a Nebula Award in 1968 for her short story "The
Planners," took a Hugo in 1976 for her well-known novel* Where
Late the Sweet Birds Sang, *added another Nebula to her collec-
tion in 1987 for her story "The Girl Who Fell into the Sky," and
won yet another Nebula the following year for her story "Forever
Yours, Anna." Her many books include the novels* Margaret and I;
Fault Lines; The Clewiston Test; Juniper Time; Welcome, Chaos;
Oh, Susannah!; Huysman's Pets; *and* Cambio Bay; *the mystery
novels* Smart House; Sweet, Sweet Poison; Seven Kinds of Death;
The Hamlet Trap; *and* Death Qualified; *and the collections* The
Downstairs Room, Somerset Dreams; The Infinity Box; Listen,
Listen; *and* Children of the Wind. *Her most recent books are a
collection,* And the Angels Sing, *and a mystery novel,* Justice for
Some. *Wilhelm and her husband, writer Damon Knight, ran the
Milford Writer's Conference for many years, and both are still
deeply involved in the operation of the* Clarion *workshop for new
young writers. She lives with her family in Eugene, Oregon.*

*Here she gives us a bittersweet story concerned, like much of
her best work, with the making of some very hard choices . . .*

* * *

Eddie never left the office until one or even two in the morning on
Sundays, Tuesdays, and Thursdays. The *North Coast News* came
out three times a week, and it seemed to him that no one could
publish a paper unless someone in charge was on hand until the
press run. He knew that the publisher, Stuart Winkle, didn't
particularly care, as long as the advertising was in place, but it

wasn't right. Eddie thought. What if something came up, something went wrong? Even out here at the end of the world there
could be a late-breaking story that required someone to write it, to
see that it got placed. Actually, Eddie's hopes for that event, high
six years ago, had diminished to the point of needing conscious
effort to recall. In fact, he liked to see his editorials before he
packed it in.

This night, Thursday, he read his own words and then bellowed,
"Where is she?" She was Ruthie Jenson, and *she* had spelled
frequency with one *e* and an *a*. Eddie stormed through the deserted
outer office, looking for her, and caught her at the door just as she
was wrapping her vampire cloak about her thin shoulders. She was
thin, her hair was cut too short, too close to her head, and she
was too frightened of him. And, he thought with bitterness, she
was crazy, or she would not wait around three nights a week for
him to catch her at the door and give her hell.

"Why don't you use the goddamn dictionary? Why do you
correct my copy? I told you I'd wing your neck if you touched my
copy again!"

She made a whimpering noise and looked past him in terror,
down the hallway, into the office.

"I . . . I'm sorry. I didn't mean . . ." Fast as quicksilver then,
she fled out into the storm that was still howling. He hoped the
goddamn wind would carry her to Australia or beyond.

The wind screamed as it poured through the outer office,
scattering a few papers, setting a light adance on a chain. Eddie
slammed the door against it and surveyed the space around him,
detesting every inch of it at the moment. Three desks, the
fluttering papers that Mrs. Rondale would heave out because
anything on the floor got heaved out. Except dirt; she seemed
never to see quite all of it. Next door the presses were running;
people were doing things, but the staff that put the paper together
had left now. Ruthie was always next to last to go, and then Eddie.
He kicked a chair on his way back to his own cubicle, clutching
the ink-wet paper in his hand, well aware that the ink was
smearing onto skin.

He knew that the door to the pressroom had opened and softly closed again. In there they would be saying Fat Eddie was in a rage. He knew they called him Fat Eddie, or even worse, behind his back, and he knew that no one on Earth cared if the *North Coast News* was a mess except him. He sat at his desk, scowling at the editorial—one of his better ones, he thought—and the word *frequency* leaped off the page at him; nothing else registered. What he had written was "At this time of year the storms bear down onshore with such regularity, such frequency, that it's as if the sea and air are engaged in the final battle." It got better, but he put it aside and listened to the wind. All evening he had listened to reports from up and down the coast, expecting storm damage, light outages, wrecks, something. At midnight he had decided it was just another Pacific storm and had wrapped up the paper. Just the usual: Highway 101 under water here and there, a tree down here and there, a head-on, no deaths. . . .

The wind screamed and let up, caught its breath and screamed again. Like a kid having a tantrum. And up and down the coast the people were like parents who had seen too many kids having too many tantrums. Ignore it until it goes away and then get on about your business, that was their attitude. Eddie was from Indianapolis, where a storm with eighty-mile-per-hour winds made news. Six years on the coast had not changed that. A storm like this, by God, should make news!

Still scowling, he pulled on his own raincoat, a great black waterproof garment that covered him to the floor. He added his black, wide-brimmed hat and was ready for the weather. He knew that behind his back they called him Mountain Man, when they weren't calling him Fat Eddie. He secretly thought that he looked more like The Shadow than not.

He drove to Connally's Tavern and had a couple of drinks, sitting alone in glum silence, and then offered to drive Truman Cox home when the bar closed at two.

The town of Lewisburg was south of Astoria, north of Cannon Beach, population nine hundred eighty-four. And at two in the morning they were all sleeping, the town blacked out by rain. There were the flickering night-lights at the drugstore, and the lights from the newspaper building, and two traffic lights, al-

though no other traffic moved. Rain pelted the windshield and
made a river through Main Street, cascaded down the side streets
on the left, came pouring off the mountain on the right. Eddie
made the turn onto Third and hit the brakes hard when a figure
darted across the street.

"Jesus!" he grunted as the car skidded, then caught and righted
itself. "Who was that?"

Truman was peering out into the darkness, nodding. The figure
had vanished down the alley behind Sal's Restaurant. "Bet it was
the Boland girl, the younger one. Not Norma. Following her
sister's footsteps."

His tone was not condemnatory, even though everyone knew
exactly where those footsteps would lead the kid.

"She sure earned whatever she got tonight," Eddie said with a
grunt and pulled up into the driveway of Truman's house. "See
you around."

"Yep. Probably will. Thanks for the lift." He gathered himself
together and made a dash for his porch.

But he would be soaked anyway, Eddie knew. All it took was a
second out in this driving rain. That poor, stupid kid, he thought
again as he backed out of the drive, retraced his trail for a block
or two, and headed toward his own little house. On impulse he
turned back and went down Second Street to see if the kid was still
scurrying around; at least he could offer her a lift home. He knew
where the Bolands lived, the two sisters, their mother, all in the
trade now, apparently. But God, he thought, the little one couldn't
be more than twelve.

The numbered streets were parallel to the coastline; the cross
streets had become wind tunnels that rocked his car every time he
came to one. Second Street was empty, black. He breathed a sigh
of relief. He hadn't wanted to get involved anyway, in any manner,
and now he could go on home, listen to music for an hour or two,
have a drink or two, a sandwich, and get some sleep. If the wind
ever let up. He slept very poorly when the wind blew this hard.
What he most likely would do was finish the book he was reading,
possibly start another one. The wind was good for another four or
five hours. Thinking this way, he made another turn or two and

then saw the kid again, this time sprawled on the side of the road.

If he had not already seen her once, if he had not been thinking about her, about her sister and mother, if he had been driving faster than five miles an hour, probably he would have missed her. She lay just off the road, facedown. As soon as he stopped and got out of the car, the rain hit his face, streamed from his glasses, blinding him almost. He got his hands on the child and hauled her to the car, yanked open the back door and deposited her inside. Only then he got a glimpse of her face. Not the Boland girl. No one he had ever seen before. And as light as a shadow. He hurried around to the driver's side and got in, but he could no longer see her now from the front seat. Just the lumpish black raincoat that gleamed with water and covered her entirely. He wiped his face, cleaned his glasses, and twisted in the seat; he couldn't reach her, and she did not respond to his voice.

He cursed bitterly and considered his next move. She could be dead, or dying. Through the rain-streaked windshield the town appeared uninhabited. It didn't even have a police station, a clinic, or a hospital. The nearest doctor was ten or twelve miles away, and in this weather. . . . Finally he started the engine and headed for home. He would call the state police from there, he decided. Let them come and collect her. He drove up Hammer Hill to his house and parked in the driveway at the walk that led to the front door. He would open the door first, he had decided, then come back and get the kid; either way he would get soaked, but there was little he could do about that. He moved fairly fast for a large man, but his fastest was not good enough to keep the rain off his face again. If it would come straight down, the way God meant rain to fall, he thought, fumbling with the key in the lock, he would be able to see something. He got the door open, flicked on the light switch, and went back to the car to collect the girl. She was as limp as before and seemed to weigh nothing at all. The slicker she wore was hard to grasp, and he did not want her head to loll about for her to brain herself on the porch rail or the door frame, but she was not easy to carry, and he grunted although her weight was insignificant. Finally he got her inside, and kicked the door shut, and made his way to the bedroom, where he dumped her on the bed.

Then he took off his hat that had been useless, and his glasses that had blinded him with running water, and the raincoat that was leaving a trail of water with every step. He backed off the Navaho rug and out to the kitchen to put the wet coat on a chair, let it drip on the linoleum. He grabbed a handful of paper toweling and wiped his glasses, then returned to the bedroom.

He reached down to remove the kid's raincoat and jerked his hand away again. "Jesus Christ!" he whispered and backed away from her. He heard himself saying it again, and then again, and stopped. He had backed up to the wall, was pressed hard against it. Even from there he could see her clearly. Her face was smooth, without eyebrows, without eyelashes, her nose too small, her lips too narrow, hardly lips at all. What he had thought was a coat was part of her. It started on her head, where hair should have been, went down the sides of her head where ears should have been, down her narrow shoulders, the backs of her arms that seemed too long and thin, almost boneless.

She was on her side, one long leg stretched out, the other doubled up under her. Where there should have been genitalia, there was too much skin, folds of skin.

Eddie felt his stomach spasm; a shudder passed over him. Before, he had wanted to shake her, wake her up, ask questions; now he thought that if she opened her eyes, he might pass out. And he was shivering with cold. Moving very cautiously, making no noise, he edged his way around the room to the door, then out, back to the kitchen where he pulled a bottle of bourbon from a cabinet and poured half a glass that he drank as fast as he could. He stared at his hand. It was shaking.

Very quietly he took off his sodden shoes and placed them at the back door, next to his waterproof boots that he invariably forgot to wear. As soundlessly as possible he crept to the bedroom door and looked at her again. She had moved, was now drawn up in a huddle as if she was as cold as he was. He took a deep breath and began to inch around the wall of the room toward the closet, where he pulled out his slippers with one foot and eased them on, and then tugged on a blanket on a shelf. He had to let his breath out; it sounded explosive to his ears. The girl shuddered and made herself into a tighter ball. He moved toward her slowly, ready to turn and run, and finally was close enough to lay the blanket over her. She was shivering hard. He backed away from her again and this time went to the living room, leaving the door open so that he could see her, just in case. He turned up the thermostat, retrieved his glass from the kitchen, and went to the door again and again to peer inside. He should call the state police, he knew, and made no motion toward the phone. A doctor? He nearly laughed. He wished he had a camera. If they took her away, and they would, there would be nothing to show, nothing to prove she had existed. He thought of her picture on the front page of the *North Coast News* and snorted. *The National Enquirer*? This time he muttered a curse. But she was news. She certainly was news.

Mary Beth, he decided. He had to call someone with a camera, someone who could write a decent story. He dialed Mary Beth, got her answering machine, and hung up, dialed it again. At the fifth call her voice came on. "Who the hell is this, and do you know that it's three in the fucking morning?"

"Eddie Delacort. Mary Beth, get up, get over here, my place, and bring your camera."

"Fat Eddie? What the hell—"

"Right now, and bring plenty of film." He hung up.

A few seconds later his phone rang; he took it off the hook and laid it down on the table. While he waited for Mary Beth, he surveyed the room. The house was small, with two bedrooms, one that he used for an office, on the far side of the living room. In the living room there were two easy chairs covered with fine, dark green leather, no couch, a couple of tables, and many bookshelves, all filled. A long cabinet held his sound equipment, a stereo, hundreds of albums. Everything was neat, arranged for a large man to move about easily, nothing extraneous anywhere. Underfoot was another Navaho rug. He knew the back door was securely locked; the bedroom windows were closed, screens in place. Through the living room was the only way the kid on his bed could get out, and he knew she would not get past him if she woke up and tried to make a run. He nodded, then moved his two easy chairs so that they faced the bedroom; he pulled an end table between them, got another glass, and brought the bottle of bourbon. He sat down to wait for Mary Beth, brooding over the girl in his bed. From time to time the blanket shook hard; a slight movement that was nearly constant suggested that she had not yet warmed up. His other blanket was under her, and he had no intention of touching her again in order to get to it.

Mary Beth arrived as furious as he had expected. She was his age, about forty, graying, with suspicious blue eyes and no makeup. He had never seen her with lipstick on, or jewelry of any kind except for a watch, or in a skirt or dress. That night she was in jeans and a sweatshirt and a bright red hooded raincoat that brought the rainstorm inside as she entered, cursing him. He noted with satisfaction that she had her camera gear. She cursed him expertly as she yanked off her raincoat and was still calling him names when he finally put his hand over her mouth and took her by the shoulder, propelled her toward the bedroom door.

"Shut up and look," he muttered. She was stronger than he had realized and now twisted out of his grasp and swung a fist at him. Then she faced the bedroom. She looked, then turned back to him red-faced and sputtering. "You . . . you got me out . . . a floozy in your bed. . . . So you really do know what that thing you've got is used for! And you want pictures! Jesus God!"

"Shut up!"

This time she did. She peered at his face for a second, turned and looked again, took a step forward, then another. He knew her reaction was to his expression, not the lump on the bed. Nothing of that girl was visible, just the unquiet blanket and a bit of darkness that was not hair but should have been. He stayed at Mary Beth's side, and his caution was communicated to her; she was as quiet now as he was.

At the bed he reached out and gently pulled back the blanket. One of her hands clutched it spasmodically. The hand had four apparently boneless fingers, long and tapered, very pale. Mary Beth exhaled too long, and neither of them moved for what seemed minutes. Finally she reached out and touched the darkness at the girl's shoulder, touched her arm, then her face. Abruptly she pulled back her hand. The girl on the bed was shivering harder than ever, in a tighter ball that hid the many folds of skin at her groin.

"It's cold," Mary Beth whispered.

"Yeah." He put the blanket back over the girl.

Mary Beth went to the other side of the bed, squeezed between it and the wall and carefully pulled the bedspread and blanket free, and put them over the girl also. Eddie took Mary Beth's arm, and they backed out of the bedroom. She sank into one of the chairs he had arranged and automatically held out her hand for the drink he was pouring.

"My God," Mary Beth said softly after taking a large swallow, "what is it? Where did it come from?"

He told her as much as he knew, and they regarded the sleeping figure. He thought the shivering had subsided, but maybe she was just too weak to move so many covers.

"You keep saying it's a she." Mary Beth said. "You know that thing isn't human, don't you?"

Reluctantly he described the rest of the girl, and this time Mary Beth finished her drink. She glanced at her camera bag but made no motion toward it yet. "It's our story," she said. "We can't let them have it until we're ready. Okay?"

"Yeah. There's a lot to consider before we do anything."

Silently they considered. He refilled their glasses, and they sat watching the sleeping creature on his bed. When the lump flattened out a bit, Mary Beth went in and lifted the covers and examined her, but she did not touch her again. She returned to her chair very pale and sipped bourbon. Outside the wind moaned, but the howling had subsided, and the rain was no longer a driving presence against the front of the house, the side that faced the sea.

From time to time one or the other made a brief suggestion.

"Not radio," Eddie said.

"Right," Mary Beth said. She was a stringer for NPR.

"Not newsprint," she said later.

Eddie was a stringer for AP. He nodded.

"It could be dangerous when it wakes up," she said.

"I know. Six rows of alligator teeth, or poison fangs, or mind rays."

She giggled. "Maybe right now there's a hidden camera taking in all this. Remember that old TV show?"

"Maybe they sent her to test us, our reaction to *them*."

Mary Beth sat up straight. "My God, more of them?"

"No species can have only one member," he said very seriously. "A counterproductive trait." He realized that he was quite drunk. "Coffee," he said and pulled himself out of the chair, made his way unsteadily to the kitchen.

When he had the coffee ready, and tuna sandwiches, and sliced onions and tomatoes, he found Mary Beth leaning against the bedroom door, contemplating the girl.

"Maybe it's dying," she said in a low voice. "We can't just let it die, Eddie."

"We won't," he said. "Let's eat something. It's almost daylight."

She followed him to the kitchen and looked around it. "I've never been in your house before. You realize that? All the years I've known you, I've never been invited here before."

"Five years," he said.

"That's what I mean. All those years. It's a nice house. It looks like your house should look, you know?"

He glanced around the kitchen. Just a kitchen—stove, refrigerator, table, counters. There were books on the counter and piled on the table. He pushed the pile to one side and put down plates. Mary Beth lifted one and turned it over. Russet-colored, gracefully shaped pottery from North Carolina, signed by Sara. She nodded, as if in confirmation. "You picked out every single item individually, didn't you?"

"Sure. I have to live with the stuff."

"What are you doing here, Eddie? Why here?"

"The end of the world, you mean? I like it."

"Well, I want the hell out. You've been out and chose to be here. I choose to be out. That thing on your bed will get me out."

From the University of Indiana to a small paper in Evanston, on to Philadelphia, New York. He felt he had been out plenty, and now he simply wanted a place where people lived in individual houses and chose the pottery they drank their coffee from. Six years ago he had left New York, on vacation, he had said, and he had come to the end of the world and stayed.

"Why haven't you gone already?" he asked Mary Beth.

She smiled her crooked smile. "I was married, you know that? To a fisherman. That's what girls on the coast do, marry fishermen or lumbermen or policemen. Me, Miss Original No-Talent herself. Married, playing house forever. He's out there somewhere. Went out one day and never came home again. So I got a job with the paper, this and that. Only one thing could be worse than staying here at the end of the world, and that's being in the world broke. Not my style."

She finished her sandwich and coffee and now seemed too restless to sit still. She went to the window over the sink and gazed out. The light was gray. "You don't belong here any more than I do. What happened? Some woman tell you to get lost? Couldn't get the job you wanted? Some young slim punk worm in front of you? You're dodging just like me."

All the above, he thought silently, and said, "Look, I've been thinking. I can't go to the office without raising suspicion, in case anyone's looking for her, I mean. I haven't been in the office before one or two in the afternoon for more than five years. But you can. See if anything's come over the wires, if there's a search on, if there was a wreck of any sort. You know. If the FBI's nosing around, or the military. Anything at all." Mary Beth rejoined him at the table and poured more coffee, her restlessness gone, an intent look on her face. Her business face, he thought.

"Okay. First some pictures, though. And we'll have to have a story about my car. It's been out front all night," she added crisply. "So, if anyone brings it up, I'll have to say I keep you company now and then. Okay?"

He nodded and thought without bitterness that that would give them a laugh at Connally's Tavern. That reminded him of Truman Cox. "They'll get around to him eventually, and he might remember seeing her. Of course, he assumed it was the Boland girl. But they'll know we saw someone."

Mary Beth shrugged. "So you saw the Boland girl and got to thinking about her and her trade and gave me a call. No problem."

He looked at her curiously. "You really don't care if they start that scuttlebutt around town about you and me?"

"Eddie," she said almost too sweetly, "I'd admit to fucking a pig if it would get me the hell out of here. I'll go on home for a shower, and by then maybe it'll be time to get on my horse and go to the office. But first some pictures."

At the bedroom door he asked in a hushed voice, "Can you get them without using the flash? That might send her into shock or something."

She gave him a dark look. "Will you for Christ's sake stop calling it a her!" She scowled at the figure on the bed. "Let's bring in a lamp, at least. You know I have to uncover it."

He knew. He brought in a floor lamp, turned on the bedside light, and watched Mary Beth go to work. She was a good photographer, and in this instance she had an immobile subject; she could use time exposures. She took a roll of film and started a second one, then drew back. The girl on the bed was shivering hard again, drawing up her legs, curling into a tight ball.

"Okay. I'll finish in daylight, maybe when she's awake."

Mary Beth was right, Eddie had to admit; the creature was not a girl, not even a female probably. She was elongated, without any angles anywhere, no elbows or sharp knees or jutting hipbones. Just a smooth long body without breasts, without a navel, without genitalia. And with that dark growth that started high on her head and went down the backs of her arms, covered her back entirely. Like a mantle, he thought, and was repelled by the idea. Her skin was not human, either. It was pale with yellow rather than pink undertones. She obviously was very cold; the yellow was fading to a grayish hue. Tentatively he touched her arm. It felt wrong, not yielding the way human flesh covered with skin should yield. It felt like cool silk over something firmer than human flesh.

Mary Beth replaced the covers, and they backed from the room as the creature shivered. "Jesus," Mary Beth whispered. "You'd think it would have warmed up by now. This place is like an oven, and all those covers." A shudder passed through her.

In the living room again, Mary Beth began to fiddle with her camera. She took out the second roll of film and held both rolls in indecision. "If anyone's nosing around, and if they learn that you might have seen it, and that we've been together, they might snitch my film. Where's a good place to stash it?"

He took the film rolls and she shook her head. "Don't tell me. Just keep it safe." She looked at her watch. "I won't be back until ten or later. I'll find out what I can, make a couple of calls. Keep an eye on it. See you later."

He watched her pull on her red raincoat and went to the porch with her, where he stood until she was in her car and out of sight. Daylight had come; the rain had ended, although the sky was still overcast and low. The fir trees in his front yard glistened and shook off water with the slightest breeze. The wind had turned into no more than that, a slight breeze. The air was not very cold, and it felt good after the heat inside. It smelled good, of leaf mold and sea and earth and fish and fir trees. . . . He took several deep breaths and then went back in. The house really was like an oven, he thought, momentarily refreshed by the cool morning and now once again feeling logy. Why didn't she warm up? He stood in the doorway to the bedroom and looked at the huddled figure. Why didn't she warm up?

He thought of victims of hypothermia; the first step, he had read, was to get their temperature back up to normal, any way possible. Hot water bottle? He didn't own one. Hot bath? He stood over the girl and shook his head slightly. Water might be toxic to her. And that was the problem; she was an alien with unknown needs, unknown dangers. And she was freezing.

With reluctance he touched her arm, still cool in spite of all the covering over her. Like a hothouse plant, he thought then, brought into a frigid climate, destined to die of cold. Moving slowly, with even greater reluctance than before, he began to pull off his trousers, his shirt, and when he was down to undershirt and shorts, he gently shifted the sleeping girl and lay down beside her, drew her to the warmth of his body.

The house temperature by then was close to eighty-five, much too warm for a man with all the fat that Eddie had on his body; she felt good next to him, cooling, even soothing. For a time she made no response to his presence, but gradually her shivering lessened, and she seemed to change subtly, lose her rigidity; her legs curved to make contact with his legs; her torso shifted, relaxed, flowed into the shape of his body; one of her arms moved over his chest, her hand at his shoulder, her other arm bent and fitted itself against him. Her cool cheek pressed against the pillows of flesh over his ribs. Carefully he wrapped his arms about her and drew her closer. He dozed, came awake with a start, dozed again. At nine he woke up completely and began to disengage himself. She made a soft sound, like a child in protest, and he stroked her arm and whispered nonsense. At last he was untangled from her arms and legs and stood up and pulled on his clothes again. The next time he looked at the girl, her eyes were open, and he felt entranced momentarily. Large, round, golden eyes, like pools of molten gold, unblinking, inhuman. He took a step away from her.

"Can you talk?"

There was no response. Her eyes closed again and she drew the covers high up onto her face, buried her head in them.

Wearily Eddie went to the kitchen and poured coffee. It was hot and tasted like tar. He emptied the coffee maker and started a fresh brew. Soon Mary Beth would return and they would make the plans that had gone nowhere during the night. He felt more tired than he could remember and thought ruefully of what it was really like to be forty-two and a hundred pounds overweight and miss a night's sleep.

"You look like hell," Mary Beth said in greeting at ten. She looked fine, excited, a flush on her cheeks, her eyes sparkling. "Is it okay? Has it moved? Come awake yet?" She charged past him and stood in the doorway to the bedroom. "Good. I got hold of Homer Carpenter, over in Portland. He's coming over with a video camera around two or three. I didn't tell him what we have, but I had to tell him something to get him over. I said we have a coelacanth."

Eddie stared at her. "He's coming over for that? I don't believe it."

She left the doorway and swept past him on her way to the kitchen. "Okay, he doesn't believe me, but he knows it's something big, something hot, or I wouldn't have called him. He knows me that well, anyway."

Eddie thought about it for a second or two, then shrugged. "What else did you find out?"

Mary Beth got coffee and held the cup in both hands, surveying him over the top of it. "Boy oh boy, Eddie! I don't know who knows what, or what it is they know, but there's a hunt on. They're saying some guys escaped from the pen over at Salem, but that's bull. Roadblocks and everything. I don't think they're telling anyone anything yet. The poor cops out there don't know what the hell they're supposed to be looking for, just anything suspicious, until the proper authorities get here."

"Here? They know she's here?"

"Not here here. But somewhere on the coast. They're closing in from north and south. And that's why Homer decided to get his ass over here, too."

Eddie remembered the stories that had appeared on the wire services over the past few weeks about an erratic comet that was being tracked. Stuart Winkle, the publisher and editor in chief, had not chosen to print them, but Eddie had seen them. And more recently the story about a possible burnout in space of a Soviet capsule. Nothing to worry about, no radiation, but there might be bright lights in the skies, the stories had said. Right, he thought.

Mary Beth was at the bedroom door again, sipping her coffee. "I'll owe you for this, Eddie. No way can I pay for what you're giving me." He made a growly noise, and she turned to regard him, suddenly very serious.

"Maybe there is something," she said softly. "A little piece of the truth. You know you're not the most popular man in town, Eddie. You're always doing little things for people, and yet, do they like you for it, Eddie? Do they?"

"Let's not do any psychoanalysis right now," he said coldly. "Later."

She shook her head. "Later I won't be around. Remember?" Her voice took on a mocking tone. "Why do you suppose you don't get treated better? Why no one comes to visit? Or invites you to the clambakes, except for office parties, anyway? It's all those little things you keep doing, Eddie. Overdoing maybe. And you won't let anyone pay you back for anything. You turn everyone into a poor relation, Eddie, and they begin to resent it."

Abruptly he laughed. For a minute he had been afraid of her, what she might reveal about him. "Right," he said. "Tell that to Ruthie Jenson."

Mary Beth shrugged. "You give poor little Ruthie exactly what she craves—mistreatment. She takes it home and nurtures it. And then she feels guilty. The Boland kid you intended to rescue. You would have had her, her sister, and their mother all feeling guilty. Truman Cox. How many free drinks you let him give you, Eddie? Not even one, I bet. Stuart Winkle? You run his paper for him. You ever use that key to his cabin? He really wants you to use it, Eddie. A token repayment. George Allmann. Harriet Davies . . . it's a long list, Eddie, the people you've done little things for. The people who go through life owing you, feeling guilty about not liking you, not sure why they don't. I was on that list, too, Eddie, but not now. I just paid you in full."

"Okay," he said heavily. "Now that we've cleared up the mystery about me, what about her?" He pointed past Mary Beth at the girl on his bed.

"It, Eddie. It. First the video, and make some copies, get them into a safe place, and then announce. How does that sound?"

He shrugged. "Whatever you want."

She grinned her crooked smile and shook her head at him. "Forget it, Eddie. I'm paid up for years to come. Look, I've got to get back to the office. I'll keep my eyes on the wires, anything coming in, and as soon as Homer shows, we'll be back. Are you okay? Can you hold out for the next few hours?"

"Yeah, I'm okay." He watched her pull on her coat and walked to the porch with her. Before she left, he said, "One thing, Mary Beth. Did it even occur to you that some people like to help out? No ulterior motive or anything, but a little human regard for others?"

She laughed. "I'll give it some thought, Eddie. And you give some thought to having perfected a method to make sure people leave you alone, keep their distance. Okay? See you later." He stood on the porch, taking deep breaths. The air was mild; maybe the sun would come out later on. Right now the world smelled good, scoured clean, fresh. No other house was visible. He had let the trees and shrubbery grow wild, screening everything from view. It was like being the last man on Earth, he thought suddenly. The heavy growth even screened out the noise from the little town. If he listened intently, he could make out engine sounds, but no voices, no one else's music that he usually detested, no one else's cries or laughter.

Mary Beth never had been ugly, he thought then. She was good-looking in her own way even now, going on middle age. She must have been a real looker as a younger woman. Besides, he thought, if anyone ever mocked her, called her names, she would slug the guy. That would be her way. And he had found his way, he added, then turned brusquely and went inside and locked the door after him.

He took a kitchen chair to the bedroom and sat down by her. She was shivering again. He reached over to pull the covers more tightly about her, then stopped his motion and stared. The black mantle thing did not cover her head as completely as it had before. He was sure it now started farther back. And more of her cheeks was exposed. Slowly he drew away the cover and then turned her over. The mantle was looser, with folds where it had been taut before. She reacted violently to being uncovered, shuddering long spasmlike movements.

He replaced the cover.

"What the hell are you?" he whispered. "What's happening to you?"

He rubbed his eyes hard and sat down, regarding her with a frown. "You know what's going to happen, don't you? They'll take you somewhere and study you, try to make you talk, if you can, find out where you're from, what you want, where there are others. . . . They might hurt you. Even kill you."

He thought again of the great golden pools that were her eyes, of how her skin felt like silk over a firm substance, of the insubstantiality of her body, the lightness when he carried her.

"What do you want here?" he whispered. "Why did you come?"

After a few minutes of silent watching, he got up and found his dry shoes in the closet and pulled them on. He put on a plaid shirt that was very warm, and then he wrapped the sleeping girl in the blanket and carried her to his car and placed her on the backseat. He went back inside for another blanket and put that over her, too.

He drove up his street, avoiding the town, using a back road that wound higher and higher up the mountain. Stuart Winkle's cabin, he thought. An open invitation to use it any time he wanted. He drove carefully, taking the curves slowly, not wanting to jar her, to roll her off the backseat. The woods pressed in closer when he left the road for a log road. From time to time he could see the ocean, then he turned and lost it again. The road clung to the steep mountainside, climbing, always climbing; there was no other traffic on it. The loggers had finished with this area; this was state land, untouchable, for now anyway. He stopped at one of the places where the ocean spread out below him and watched the waves rolling in forever and ever, unchanging, unknowable. Then he drove on. The cabin was high on the mountain. Up here the trees were mature growth, mammoth and silent, with deep shadows beneath them, little understory growth in the dense shade. The cabin was redwood, rough, heated with a wood stove, no running water, no electricity. There was oil for a lamp, and plenty of dry wood stacked under a shed, and a store of food that Stuart had said he should consider his own. There were twin beds in the single bedroom and a couch that opened to a double bed in the living room. Those two rooms and the kitchen made up the cabin.

He carried the girl inside and put her on one of the beds; she was entirely enclosed in blankets like a cocoon. Hurriedly he made a fire in the stove and brought in a good supply of logs. Like a hothouse orchid, he thought; she needed plenty of heat. After the cabin started to heat up, he took off his outer clothing and lay down beside her, the way he had done before, and as before, she conformed to his body, melted into him, absorbed his warmth. Sometimes he dozed, then he lay quietly thinking of his childhood, of the heat that descended on Indiana like a physical substance, of the tornadoes that sometimes came, murderous funnels that sucked life away, shredded everything. He dozed and dreamed and awakened and dreamed in that state also.

He got up to feed the fire and tossed in the film Mary Beth had given him to guard. He got a drink of water at the pump in the kitchen and lay down by her again. His fatigue increased, but pleasurably. His weariness was without pain, a floating sensation that was between sleep and wakefulness. Sometimes he talked quietly to her, but not much, and what he said he forgot as soon as the words formed. It was better to lie without sound, without motion. Now and then she shook convulsively and then subsided again. Twilight came, darkness, then twilight again. Several times he aroused enough to build up the fire.

When it was daylight once more, he got up, reeling as if drunken; he pulled on his clothes and went to the kitchen to make instant coffee. He sensed her presence behind him. She was standing up, nearly as tall as he was, but incredibly insubstantial, not thin, but as slender as a straw. Her golden eyes were wide open. He could not read the expression on her face.

"Can you eat anything?" he asked. "Drink water?"

She looked at him. The black mantle was gone from her head; he could not see it anywhere on her as she faced him. The strange folds of skin at her groin, the boneless appearance of her body, the lack of hair, breasts, the very color of her skin looked right now, not alien, not repellent. The skin was like cool silk, he knew. He also knew this was not a woman, not a she, but something that should not be here, a creature, an it.

"Can you speak? Can you understand me at all?"

Her expression was as unreadable as that of a wild creature, a forest animal, aware, intelligent, unknowable.

Helplessly he said, "Please, if you can understand me, nod. Like this." He showed her, and in a moment she nodded. "And like this for no," he said. She mimicked him again.

"Do you understand that people are looking for you?"

She nodded slowly. Then very deliberately she turned around, and instead of the black mantle that had grown on her head, down her back, there was an iridescence, a rainbow of pastel colors that shimmered and gleamed. Eddie sucked in his breath as the new growth moved, opened slightly more.

There wasn't enough room in the cabin for her to open the wings all the way. She stretched them from wall to wall. They looked like gauze, filmy, filled with light that was alive. Not realizing he was moving, Eddie was drawn to one of the wings, reached out to touch it. It was as hard as steel and cool. She turned her golden liquid eyes to him and drew her wings in again.

"We'll go someplace where it's warm," Eddie said hoarsely. "I'll hide you. I'll smuggle you somehow. They can't have you!" She walked through the living room to the door and studied the handle for a moment. As she reached for it, he lumbered after her, lunged toward her, but already she was opening the door, slipping out.

"Stop! You'll freeze. You'll die!"

In the clearing of the forest, with sunlight slanting through the giant trees, she spun around, lifted her face upward, and then opened her wings all the way. As effortlessly as a butterfly, or a bird, she drew herself up into the air, her wings flashing light, now gleaming, now appearing to vanish as the light reflected one way and another.

"Stop!" Eddie cried again. "Please! Oh, God, stop! Come back!"

She rose higher and looked down at him with her golden eyes. Suddenly the air seemed to tremble with sound, trills and arpeggios and flutings. Her mouth did not open as the sounds increased until Eddie fell to his knees and clapped his hands over his ears, moaning. When he looked again, she was still rising, shining, invisible, shining again. Then she was gone. Eddie pitched forward into the thick layer of fir needles and forest humus and lay still. He felt a tugging on his arm and heard Mary Beth's furious curses but as if from a great distance. He moaned and tried to go to sleep again. She would not let him.

"You goddamn bastard! You filthy son of a bitch! You let it go! Didn't you? You turned it loose!"

He tried to push her hands away.

"You scum! Get up! You hear me? Don't think for a minute,

Buster, that I'll let you die out here! That's too good for you, you lousy tub of lard. Get up!"

Against his will he was crawling, then stumbling, leaning on her, being steadied by her. She kept cursing all the way back inside the cabin, until he was on the couch, and she stood over him, arms akimbo, glaring at him.

"Why? Just tell me why. For God's sake, tell me Eddie, why?" Then she screamed at him, "Don't you dare pass out on me again. Open those damn eyes and keep them open!"

She savaged him and nagged him, made him drink whiskey that she had brought along, then made him drink coffee. She got him to his feet and made him walk around the cabin a little, let him sit down again, drink again. She did not let him go to sleep, or even lie down, and the night passed.

A fine rain had started to fall by dawn. Eddie felt as if he had been away a long time, to a very distant place that had left few memories. He listened to the soft rain and at first thought he was in his own small house, but then he realized he was in a strange cabin and that Mary Beth was there, asleep in a chair. He regarded her curiously and shook his head, trying to clear it. His movement brought her sharply awake.

"Eddie, are you awake?"

"I think so. Where is this place?"

"Don't you remember?"

He started to say no, checked himself, and suddenly he was remembering. He stood up and looked about almost wildly.

"It's gone, Eddie. It went away and left you to die. You would have died out there if I hadn't come, Eddie. Do you understand what I'm saying?"

He sat down again and lowered his head into his hands. He knew she was telling the truth.

"It's going to be light soon," she said. "I'll make us something to eat, and then we'll go back to town. I'll drive you. We'll come back in a day or so to pick up your car." She stood up and groaned. "My God, I feel like I've been wrestling bears all night. I hurt all over."

She passed close enough to put her hand on his shoulder briefly. "What the hell, Eddie. Just what the hell."

In a minute he got up also and went to the bedroom, looked at the bed where he had lain with her all through the night. He approached it slowly and saw the remains of the mantle. When he tried to pick it up, it crumbled to dust in his hand.

Grave Angels
by
Richard Kearns

A former editor of the SFWA Bulletin, *Richard Kearns has published stories in* Orbit 21, Dragons of Light, The Magazine of Fantasy and Science Fiction, *and* Isaac Asimov's Science Fiction Magazine. *He lives in Beverly Hills, California.*

Here he offers us a poignant and eloquent exploration of the ambiguous borderland between life and death . . .

*   *   *

I first met Mr. Beauchamps when he dug Aunt Fannie's grave, the day before she died. I can remember it very clearly.

School was over, the heat of summer had finally settled in, withering the last of spring's magnolia blossoms, and I had just turned ten. Bobby, my older brother, and his friends had gone to the swimming hole down by the Dalton place, but I hadn't gone with them—not because I didn't want to. The last time I'd gone, they'd stolen my clothes. I figured it'd be at least another week before it'd be safe to go with them.

So I'd gone to the Evans Cemetery instead.

There were two cemeteries inside the Evans city limits—one for whites and one for blacks. It's still that way, as a matter of fact. But the white cemetery—the Evans Cemetery proper—had sixteen of the biggest oak trees in all of Long County, growing close enough together so you could move from one tree to the next without having to get down again. I liked to go there, especially on hot days, and climb the trees, read, watch the motorcars hurry in and out of Evans like big black bugs. There was always a breeze in the oaks, and I was sure it never touched the earth.

I used to sit in those branches for hours at a time, like a meadowlark or a squirrel, listening to that breeze. Underneath me, I could feel the trees bend and sway, creaking and rattling and bumping into one another, as if they were all alive and talking among themselves, elbowing each other and laughing sometimes.

I remember it was a Saturday, and I remember I'd brought *Robinson Crusoe* with me to read. I'd read it before, but it was a story I enjoyed—I liked pretending that I was entirely alone, free to do whatever I wanted.

I had just gotten comfortable on my branch when I heard someone humming down underneath me, and the sound of wood being tossed into a pile on the ground. Quietly, I closed my book and turned around to spy.

There was an old black man standing with his back to me, maybe thirty feet away from the tree I was in. He was dressed in blue and white striped overalls and a white long-sleeved shirt. On his head was an engineer's cap like the men wore down in the railway yard—it had blue and white stripes in it too. Next to him was a wheelbarrow—old, rust- and dirt-encrusted, its contents spilled on the ground: several two-by-fours of different lengths, painted white; a big tan canvas, all folded up; and digging tools.

He took his cap off, mopped his head with a big red bandanna handkerchief—he was partly bald—put the hat back on, stuffed the handkerchief in his pocket, and studied the graves for a moment, fists on his hips.

Then he sighed, shook his head, and, mumbling and grunting, squatted and scooped up the pieces of lumber in his arms. Their ends flailed the air every which way as he stood again.

He made his way over by Great-Great-Grandpa Evans's grave—the one with the angel sculpted in red granite—where, after deciding on a spot, he spent a couple of minutes meticulously arranging the two-by-fours so they formed a perfect white rectangle against the green grass. He then retrieved the canvas, spread it next to the area he'd staked out, rolled up his sleeves, took out a shovel, and started digging up the sod.

I was fascinated. He worked all morning without a stop, carefully placing shovelfuls of the caramel brown earth on top of the canvas, making sure that as he dug, the sides of the hole were straight, swinging the pickax in big arcs over his head, or chiseling at the sides with it in tiny hammerlike strokes, slow and steady. He hummed to himself, sang songs I'd never heard before, grunted a lot, talked to himself whenever he thought there was a problem keeping the sides straight up and down, chuckling more and more as he got deeper.

He stopped when the sun was overhead and he had dug up to his thighs. I could tell he was hot.

He crawled out, put the pickax and shovel in the wheelbarrow, and then spent a couple of minutes inspecting his work. After that, he walked straight toward the oaks, pulling the wheelbarrow behind him.

I had been pleased with my spying. I had hardly moved all morning, even when I got bored watching him, and watched the cars on Route 85 instead, or the lazy crows circle overhead. I hadn't made a sound.

But he walked right to the tree I was hiding in, parked the wheelbarrow, looked up through the leaves like he knew I was there the whole time, cupped his hands over his mouth, and called out: "Timothy Evans, you come down from there right now!"

I was so scared I dropped *Robinson Crusoe*. I watched it fall, sickeningly, right into his wheelbarrow. It took a long time to get there.

I didn't move, hoping he'd go away. He didn't.

"Timothy!"

"What makes you think Timothy Evans is up here?" I yelled back, trying to disguise my voice.

"Well, now, I know who's up there and who ain't, so you get your rear down here, Timothy Evans. No games!"

I slithered down a couple of levels, where we could see each other better, and changed tactics. "Why?"

"It's lunchtime."

"I have mine," I countered, showing him my brown bag.

"Mine's better," he said, pulling a tan wicker basket out from under his wheelbarrow. "Besides, I do believe I'll go home with your book if you don't come and get it."

"How'd you do that?"

"Do what?"

"Where'd the basket come from?"

He smiled. It was a pleasant smile, and I felt I liked him right away. He set the basket on the grass, took his hat off, and mopped his forehead with his sleeve. "If you don't come down, you'll never find out—will you?" With that, he bent over, produced a big red and white checkered tablecloth from the basket, spread it out in the shade under the next tree, sat down, and began to unpack the food.

I could smell the chicken from where I sat. He had potato salad, iced lemonade, and baking powder biscuits with butter and honey. "Promise you won't hurt me if I come down?"

"I ain't promising anything," he said, eating a drumstick, "'cept I'm going to eat all of this if you don't come down here and help me with it."

My stomach growled. Mama had made a peanut butter sandwich for me, with a couple of oranges for snacks. Fried chicken was a lot better. He looked old; I figured I could outrun him if I had to.

I came down in as expert and dignified a manner as possible, not slipping even once. From the bottom branch I dropped my lunch off to the side, swung by my hands briefly, and made a perfect landing by the wheelbarrow. Squatting next to it, I examined its underside, hoping to find the hook or shelf where the picnic basket had been hidden. There was nothing but pieces of rust caught in old cobwebs.

"Lunch is over here, boy," he yelled at me. I peered back at him over the top of the wheelbarrow. "You're not going to find anything to eat by looking over there." He laughed and went back to work on his drumstick.

I wiped my hands on my jeans, picked up my sack lunch, and retrieved *Robinson Crusoe* before I walked over to the tablecloth. I stood, book tucked under my arm, and watched him eat for a couple of seconds. "What's your name?" I asked.

He pulled a white paper napkin out of the basket, wiped his lips, chin, and fingers with it, and then looked up at me. "I am Mr. Beauchamps," he said, pronouncing it *bow-shomps*, like a foreigner, "and I am very pleased to meet you, Timothy." He took my hand, shook it, as if he were one of Papa's business partners. His hand was huge around mine, and felt warm and dry and crusty with calluses.

"Have a seat," he told me, nodding, while he lifted the hinged basket lid and fished around briefly. "You can't eat standing up." He produced a second blue and white china plate, dumped a second drumstick and three biscuits on it, and slid it over to me.

The chicken was good. So was the lemonade. I broke open one of the biscuits, which was hot, smeared butter all over it with a plastic knife, and dribbled honey on top of that. "How come you call yourself mister?" I asked. "None of the colored men I know call themselves mister. Only whites."

He leaned toward me on one elbow and plopped a pile of potato salad on my plate. "Three reasons," he said, sticking a plastic spoon in the mound and then sitting up. "First, 'cause I am eighty-three years old, and there are only two people in the whole city of Evans that are older than I am. Second, 'cause no one knows my first name, and I'm not telling what it is, so there's nothing I can be called *but* Mr. Beauchamps. Third," he said, leaning forward again, "'cause I am the gravedigger here. I buried 657 people in my time—white and colored, rich and poor, all of them the same. Ain't no boy does anybody's gravedigging."

"Oh."

He smiled and took a final bite out of his drumstick. "You weren't expected to know that, of course."

"Mr. Beauchamps." I smiled back at him. He was as remarkable up close as he was from a distance. His skin was the blackest I'd ever seen, like baker's chocolate or chicory coffee. His face was leathery and full of wrinkles, and his hands looked like they might have been tree roots. He had white hair, white eyebrows, even one or two white whiskers that curled out on his face from where he missed them shaving, I guess. They were easy to see because his skin was so dark.

I think the thing I remember most about him was his smile. His teeth weren't yellow, like most black folk I knew. They were bright white, and when he smiled, his whole face lit up, and all his wrinkles would mesh together and smile too.

"Isn't it kind of scary being a gravedigger?"

"Nope." He looked all around him. "Don't know what could make a day like today scary. The sun's out, shining bright; the grass is green, just like always; and if you're quiet enough, you can hear the birds singing away, two counties over. No boss to stand around and give me a hard time, lots of long lunches—if you take my meaning—my own shovel and pick and wheelbarrow, and new kinds of flowers blooming practically every time I come out here. Can't think of any place I'd rather work."

"But all those dead people—"

"Nonsense, Timothy. We're all going to be dead one day. I'm going to die, you're going to die, your mama and papa are going to die. It's part of life, part of living. The Lord says we can't enter the Kingdom of Heaven 'less we're born again. That's what dying is—being born again in God's Kingdom. We just can't see it so clear from this side."

I looked past him, back to where he'd been working. The old stone angel was standing guard over the spot. "Whose grave you digging now?"

"I ain't saying."

"How come?"

"I just ain't. 'Sides," he said, leaning back and stretching out on the grass, "it's your turn to do the talking now."

"My turn?"

"Sure. Read to me from your book."

So I read to him. I read the part where Robinson Crusoe found Friday—first in a dream, and then when he saved him from being eaten by other cannibals. Friday was the first human companion Robinson Crusoe had after living on the island by himself for years.

. . . never was a more faithful, loving, sincere servant than Friday was to me; without passions, sullenness, or designs; his very affections were tied to me, like those of a child to its father, and, I dare say, he would have sacrificed his life for my own, upon any occasion whatever.

I was greatly delighted with him, and made it my business to teach him everything that was proper and useful, and especially to make him speak, and understand me when I spoke. And he was a very apt scholar, and he was so merry, so diligent, and so pleased when he could understand me, or make me understand him, that it was very pleasant for me to talk to him. And now my life began to be very easy and happy.

Mr. Beauchamps chuckled when I finished reading, scratched his cheek, and said, "Now ain't that something."

"I like it. It's a good book."

"You would think Mr. Crusoe wanted a friend, after being lonely all the time."

"I think it would be fun to be alone like that."

"I see." He sat up and pawed through the picnic basket once again, but couldn't find anything for dessert, so each of us had an orange from my lunch. They were extra juicy, and we had a contest to see which one of us could spit the pits farther. Mr. Beauchamps won.

"Well," he said, sitting up and patting his stomach, "time for me to get back to work. Seeing as I found you, though, you're going to have to work with me, just like I was Mr. Crusoe."

"You found me!"

"'Course I did. Spying on me from the trees, just like some kind of savage. I could call you Saturday."

"I'm not a savage! My name is Timothy—"

"*All* children are savages! You take my word for it. That's what growing up consists of—civilizing you. You can be Saturday Evans."

"No!"

He chuckled again. "Very well," he said, hooking his thumbs in his suspenders, "I'll be more civilized than Mr. Crusoe was and let you keep your own name. Just so long as you keep me company, if you catch my drift."

"I don't mind that," I said, getting to my feet. "Do I get to watch you dig up close?"

"Of course you do. But we have to clean up here first."

Everything got packed, including my peanut butter sandwich. Then Mr. Beauchamps made the basket disappear by hiding it behind his back. He laughed when I asked him where it went, and told me he didn't know himself, but it hardly mattered until he was hungry again.

I watched him dig the rest of the grave that afternoon. I sat with my feet dangling in it sometimes, or lay on my stomach near the edge of it. The earth smelled rich and damp and somehow clean.

He talked about gravedigging, how it was a craft, how you had to know the earth, whether it was going to be wet enough to stay packed, or if it was going to be mud four feet down, or sand, or tree roots. He said early summer was the best time to dig, and told me how hard it was to dig graves in winter, or in the middle of a storm. But he said he couldn't stop digging graves just on account of the weather.

We sang together, sometimes songs I knew, sometimes songs he taught me. The breeze would brush by us every once in a while, and when we weren't talking or singing, I would just listen to the quiet, or to the sound of Mr. Beauchamps's shovel slicing through the earth.

It was late in the afternoon. Just as Great-Great-Grandpa Evans's angel started to touch the feet of the oaks with her shadow, we finished. The grave was deep—deeper than Mr. Beauchamps was tall.

He handed me the shovel, leaned the pickax in one corner of the grave, and climbed up on it like a stepladder. He hauled himself out from there. Then he took the shovel back, neatly hooked the head of the pickax with the back of the shovel's metal blade, and pulled it up.

"I have to go home now, sir."

He tipped his hat and bowed slightly. "Have a good evening then, Saturday."

"That's Timothy."

"Timothy."

"You have a good evening too, Mr. Beauchamps."

When I got home, I found my empty lunch bag folded up and stuck between the pages of *Robinson Crusoe*. I was sure I had put it in the picnic basket when we were cleaning up.

•   •   •

Aunt Fannie died Sunday afternoon.

At least that's when we found her. When we left for church that morning, she was alive.

Aunt Fannie lived with us in one of the upstairs bedrooms, and Mama looked after her, day and night. She was too sick to take care of herself, and had been that way for years.

I was helping Mama carry the dinner tray upstairs. Aunt Fannie always ate before the rest of us did on Sunday, and if I helped, Mama usually let her give me a cookie or a piece of cake from the tray.

I noticed something different right away when we walked into the room, but Mama didn't. She went straight to the windows and opened them, just like she always did, and the wind billowed the white lace curtains like sails.

Aunt Fannie was all propped up on her pillows, and tucked in with a white quilt that had pink roses embroidered on it in every square. Her face was powdered—she always did that; she said she could go through the whole week just plain, but the least she could do was look pretty on the Lord's day—and there was just a little touch of pink on her cheeks.

She held a Bible in one hand loosely. The wind came in the room and lifted the filmy wisp of gray hair that had fallen on her cheek, pushing it back on her head and making it tremble, just for a moment.

She looked like she was asleep. I knew she wasn't. I knew because I couldn't hear her breathing.

Mama tried to wake her up several times. I didn't say anything. Then she told me to get Papa.

We buried her Tuesday morning, in the grave I had watched Mr. Beauchamps dig. The site was littered with wreaths and sprays of bright-petaled flowers, with weeping, long-faced adults dressed in black, most of them carrying Bibles; and with frightened children—Bobby and his friends included—who either clung to their parents singly, or stood together in groups of three or four, trying to understand what had happened.

I knew they were all seeing an illusion I couldn't see. The flowers, somber clothes, the prayers couldn't hide the clumps of uncut grass, the color and smell of the earth in the grave, the impressions left on the gravesides from the pickax or shovel, the black stone Mr. Beauchamps had tossed up on the canvas after digging around it and cursing for half an hour, the way the wind danced through the oak trees, inviting me to climb them. Or the way Aunt Fannie smiled when she died.

But more than all those things, I wondered how Mr. Beauchamps had known to dig her grave. I tried to spot him all the way through her funeral, even up to the point where it was my turn to throw a handful of dirt on Aunt Fannie's casket. He was nowhere to be seen. The granite angel was the only witness of the weekend's events; she stood silent, reigning over the proceedings, her eyes fixed on a point off on the horizon.

I stopped at the Evans Cemetery every day for two weeks after that, but I still couldn't find him. Where could he be, I wondered. How did he know?

I knew he had to have been there while I was gone: when I went to look for him Wednesday, after the funeral, the flowers were gone, and the canvas; the grave was filled up and the sod put back in place. There was a brand spanking new granite headstone to mark her grave, half as tall as I was. The front of it was polished shiny, and I could see my own faint image in it.

Mama had green eyes, and when she would watch me, I was sure she could see what I was thinking. I wasn't afraid of being watched, exactly—sometimes she would keep at it for weeks at a time, though it never would bring enough trouble to warrant Papa spanking me—but when she got that look and I knew she was watching, I knew I had to be good, or at least be careful.

And she watched me after the funeral.

Now, Mama would never say much to me while she was watching. Nothing out of the ordinary, that is; she would still say things like, "Timothy, sit up straight," or "Timothy, pick your things up when you're through with them." Sometimes I would get a clue why she was watching me from what she didn't say.

But I never knew all the reasons for all the times she would watch. There would be times, after a bout of watching, when she would make up her mind about what she was thinking, and then tell me about it. But just as often, she would stop as quietly as she started, and never say what I did to bring it on, or why she stopped, or what she saw.

After Aunt Fannie's funeral was one of the times she decided to talk. I was in the kitchen at breakfast one morning, when Papa had left for the store but before Bobby was gone.

I knew something was up when I saw her making only one sack lunch instead of two for Bobby and me. I felt all queasy inside when she came over and put it on the table next to Bobby; I hunched over my cereal and pretended I hadn't seen, and that nothing out of the ordinary was happening.

"Timothy," she said, and I had to look up at her, "stay put for a while after you finish. I want to talk to you." She smiled at me—a quick, toothless twitch almost, which was supposed to let me know that everything was all right—but it didn't help.

"Yes, ma'am."

She walked back to the counter and began cleaning up, washing the knives, screwing the top on the peanut butter jar, packing up the bread, brushing the crumbs toward the sink. Her window was open, and from where I sat I could see the tops of the sweet peas in her garden out back; but no wind came blowing in the kitchen to flap the yellow checkered curtains, or stir the leaves on the two tiny plants she had growing in the pots on the sill.

Bobby stared at me over his cereal bowl, the spoon briefly frozen in his mouth—he had black curly hair and freckles, and people said he looked just like Papa when Papa was small; I was blond, and Mama had light brown hair, straight as rain when she didn't have it pinned up, so I guess I must have looked like her by default, though people didn't say that—and he applied himself to finishing quickly, not looking at me again until he stuck out his tongue at me as he grabbed his lunch and ran out back. The spring on the screen twanged as the door slammed shut behind him.

Mama came back to the table, took away our empty bowls and spoons, and washed them, untied and hung up her apron on its hook by the refrigerator, poured herself a cup of coffee, and then sat down in Bobby's chair.

"Timothy, you've been spending time down at the graveyard—haven't you?" She said it all casual-like, but her green eyes swung up at me, even though her head was tilted down at her coffee cup.

"Yes, ma'am."

Mama looked down again; carefully grasping her cup by its handle with her right hand, thumb on top, she slowly turned the saucer underneath with her left. "You know what your papa would do if he found out, don't you?"

"Yes, ma'am."

Her lips formed a thin, straight line across the bottom of her face, and she stopped turning the saucer. "Your Aunt Fannie loved *you* very much too." She glanced at me, almost like she was afraid I would say something, then took a deep breath and went on. "You know, you were such a colicky baby, and so fussy, your Aunt Fannie was over here quite a bit after you were born. She said she felt like it was her duty, her being your godmother and all."

Mama was silent for a moment. She hesitated briefly, then lifted the cup to her lips and sipped, setting it back with slow, graceful determination, still not looking at me. "Your papa was having hard times at the store, so we couldn't afford hired help like we could with Bobby. Least, that's what he said; I could never tell the difference between the hard times and the good times there, just by going in and looking. I don't suppose that made it any less true, though."

She looked at me now, and smiled her twitchy smile. "There were times I used to wonder if there wasn't anything more to raising babies than feeding you, and washing your dirty diapers, and cleaning you up. And I used to wonder if you were ever going to be anything but hungry, or in pain, or just crabby. That's why your Aunt Fannie was such a godsend." Mama leaned back in her chair. "You used to fuss so, and cry and cry and cry, and there was nothing anybody could do for you until Fannie came over. She knew lots of ways to quiet you, her raising a family that had been and gone already; but your favorite was her music box. She'd bring that little thing with her, and open it up and you'd be just all smiles and wonder. Not that it worked when anybody else played it, mind you. We tried that." Mama chuckled. "You were just too smart for that, I guess."

She sat forward and drank her coffee again. "But you got better, and I got better, and business got better for your papa, and Fannie got worse. That's the truth of it." Mama started to turn the saucer around again, sighed, and stopped, still holding it, though. "They read your Aunt Fannie's will last week," she said, staring at her hands. "She left money for you and Bobby to go to college, when the time comes. Not that we couldn't have sent you, of course; it'll just be easier now. We should be grateful for that."

"Yes, ma'am," I said, my voice a whisper.

That startled Mama; I don't think she expected me to say anything. She studied me for a second, and then got up and went to her apron, digging her hand in its pocket as she brought it back to the table with her. "She willed me her gold locket," she said, pulling it out and putting it on the table in front of me. It spun when Mama put it down; I could see the delicate rose engraved on the front as it slowed. "Go ahead and open it," Mama said over her shoulder as she hung the apron up again. "Your papa said I could go down to the store and pick a chain for it later in the week."

There were pictures of me and Bobby and Papa on the inside. "It's pretty," I said.

"Yes, it is, isn't it?" Mama answered, sitting down again, this time putting a small wooden box in front of me, and setting three fat brass rollers on end next to it. The box was made of dark walnut, with nicks and dents worn smooth by age and polish; across the lid were inlaid two black stripes with red diamonds. Mama opened it, and delicious music came pouring out. I recognized Brahms's *Lullaby* right away. "Fannie left this for you," Mama said. "Your papa didn't think you should have it until you were older; he said you might break it. You'll be careful, won't you?"

"Yes, ma'am."

"Take it then, and keep it safe," she said. She showed me how to change the brass rollers so I could play four different songs. Their names were engraved on their insides: Beethoven's *Für Elise*, Bach's *Sarabande*, Mozart's *Minute Waltz*, and the lullaby by Brahms. We both listened to the Bach piece play all the way through, the somber minor chords twinkling so you could hear all the notes in a row.

Then it was over.

"Timothy," Mama said as I went upstairs to put the music box away. "I want you to keep away from Evans Cemetery for a while."

I leaned over the banister and looked at her, her figure a dim, hazy silhouette framed against the sunlit kitchen doorway. "Yes, ma'am."

"Just for a while," she said. "You can go back and visit your Aunt Fannie after the summer is over. It's just that there will be other people going to visit her now, and I'd rather they didn't find you there."

"Yes, ma'am."

She smiled. "Maybe you and I can go together and take flowers to her grave sometime. Would you like that?"

"Yes, ma'am."

We never went.

I gave up waiting for Mr. Beauchamps. But I still wasn't getting along too well with Bobby and the rest of the gang, so instead of hanging out at the cemetery, I would spend time over at the old Robinson house. I was safe there; the rest of the kids thought it was haunted.

It sat off by itself, on a hill along the road to Mariana Marsh, and there was a big dead gray tree in front of it with all the bark stripped off. None of the windows had any glass. Someone had tried to board them up a long time ago. But they had since been opened by brave adventurers like myself.

It might have been painted white or yellow once. Most of the paint had peeled or worn off over the years, and the wood underneath was the same color as the tree in front—gray. There were still patches of nondescript color that clung tenaciously to the outside, in a futile attempt to defy the elements. The roof over the front porch sagged, and would probably fall off soon. The outside steps were gone.

My favorite spot was up on the second floor, by the bay windows that faced south, toward town and Robinson's Woods. I made it my room. On clear mornings I could see Mama hanging laundry out behind our house, or watch the cars drive into town and park in front of Papa's store.

Every time I was there, I would clean up the new collection of dead branches and litter that had blown in through the open windows. I fixed up an old rocking chair I found in the basement of the house, replacing the tattered upholstery with a burlap bag that said "50 Lbs Net, Parkinson's Cabbage, Produce of U.S.A." I hid Aunt Fannie's music box in the window seat, and I could sit and rock and listen to it play while I looked out at town or over the woods. Or I could just read.

It was Mr. Beauchamps who found me, two months after the funeral, and it was in the Robinson house. There was a light rain outside, and I was in my rocker, listening to the music box play Mozart's waltz, thinking about having to go back to school again in a month and a half. The song ended, and I reached for the music box to start it over again.

"That was real pretty, Timothy."

I turned around and looked, real quick, but I already knew it was him from the voice. He had his own rocker, put together out of a dozen pieces of twisted cane, painted red. He smiled at me, rocking back and forth.

I wasn't going to let him know he scared me. "Hello, Mr. Beauchamps."

"Where did you get that music box?"

"From Aunt Fannie. She willed it to me."

"I see." He stopped rocking, and dug his hand into one of his overall pockets. "Here. Try this."

He tossed something at me, which I caught, examined long enough to realize it was identical to the other brass cylinders that had come with the box, and then fitted it into the machine. It was labeled Chopin's *Nocturne*. I turned the key as far as it would go, and then started it playing.

I could hear Mr. Beauchamps humming softly with the melody.

"How did you know Aunt Fannie was going to die?" I asked without looking at him.

He stopped humming. "We're all going to die," he said huskily. "I told you that before."

"But how did you know when?"

He sighed wearily. "I just knew I had to dig the grave—that's all there was to it."

I turned around and looked at him. "Do you know when everybody's going to die?"

He chuckled and relaxed, and his rocking chair started to squeak in time with the music. "Not everybody," he said, after listening for several beats. "Strictly speaking, I'm just limited to the people in Evans. They managed to die without anybody knowing before I came, and will probably continue to do so after I'm gone."

"But how did you know to dig their graves?"

"I just knew." He chuckled again. "Take tomorrow, for instance."

"Somebody's going to die tomorrow?"

"Now, I didn't say that. I'm just saying I got a grave to dig over in the Quarters Cemetery. I want you to meet me there and help."

"So somebody's going to die over in Quarters! Who's it going to be?"

"I ain't saying."

"It's old Mammy Walker, isn't it? She's been sick for months."

"Nope."

"Sam DeLuth?"

"Nope."

"Will Atkins?"

"Nope."

I thought for a moment. "Jackson Hardich?"

Mr. Beauchamps looked startled for a second, long enough to stop his chair. "I told you—I ain't saying." He fell back to rocking.

"It *is* Jackson—isn't it?" Everybody in Evans knew that Jackson Hardich was going to take on more trouble than he could handle one day. He was always picking fights out in the Quarters after dark, and there were several times recently when Sheriff Tucker had to be called to settle things down.

"Maybe yes and maybe no," Mr. Beauchamps said. "Whoever it is, it don't change the fact that there's a grave that's got to be dug." He leaned forward and squinted at me. "You going to be there tomorrow?"

I looked outside at the rain and then back at Mr. Beauchamps. "I can't come if it's going to be raining."

"Oh, then there's no problem. Tomorrow will be a fine day."

"If it is, I'll be there."

"Good."

There was a hot white flash and a thunderclap that made my chest rumble from being so close, and when my ears stopped ringing, I turned to ask Mr. Beauchamps more about Jackson Hardich, but he was gone, along with his rocking chair. I remember smiling to myself, rocking back and forth vigorously, watching the rain come down harder, listening to the music. It had been fairly easy to trick Mr. Beauchamps into revealing who the grave was for. Now that I knew who the dead man was, I could go see him before he died.

It took all day to dig the grave, the same as before. And it was a Saturday, the same as before. But the Quarters Cemetery wasn't as nice as the Evans Cemetery. The grave markers were smaller, most of them made out of wood, many of them cracked and gray and slowly falling over. There were fewer flowers, fewer trees, and the work was harder. I had to help Mr. Beauchamps pull up half a dozen huge stones before we were through; my hands were rubbed raw in spots from it.

It wasn't a bad day, though. We had our lunch together and fed biscuit crumbs to a family of meadowlarks who sang for us later. As a surprise, Mr. Beauchamps brought harmonicas for both of us; once I got through his "brief demonstration of the proper technique for the mouth organ," I was even able to keep up with him on a couple of the songs we had only sung last time. He said I was a quick learner, and taught me to play Chopin's *Nocturne*, just like my music box, though nowhere near as fancy, and with none of the right harmonies.

When we finished the digging, Mr. Beauchamps stood in the cool afternoon shadows that spilled into the bottom of the grave. He smiled. "This is good work, Timothy," he said. "Good, honest work. You should be proud of it." He grunted as he climbed out on his pickax, laboriously settling himself into a sitting position with his feet still dangling in Jackson's grave. "You go home now and eat a good dinner," he said. Then he leaned over and poked at me with his finger. "Take yourself a hot bath, too. Hot, mind you." And he tapped his nose. "And you soak in it. We wouldn't want you to be stiff and sore like some old man before your time."

I left him while he was still laughing about that. But I didn't go home. Instead I headed for Potter's Drugstore, on the edge of the Quarters, to spy on Jackson Hardich.

He worked there for Mr. Potter most days, and on Saturdays he and his friends would meet there before taking off for the evening's festivities. Potter's was also the scene of the last two fights Jackson got into.

When I got there, Sheriff Tucker's squad car and an ambulance were there before me, pulled up crooked against the curb, their lights flashing, red and amber spots dancing up and down the outsides of the dingy frame houses huddled together on Sultana Street, the power lines off in the distance winking with an orange glow.

I hid by the gas station garage across the street, behind a pile of old tires. Potter's was closed, but there were lights on in the barbershop next door. A small crowd had begun to gather— mostly older black men, dressed in dark gray suits and hats, standing around the way people did at Aunt Fannie's funeral— when Sheriff Tucker came out of the alley behind Potter's and told everybody to get on home. Right behind him came two ambulance attendants carrying a litter with a white sheet-wrapped body on it. Whoever it was, it was plain to see he was dead. But I had to know who.

That was when I became aware I wasn't the only one hiding behind the garage.

I couldn't see his face. All I could tell was he was black, he was watching the attendants put the body into the ambulance, and there was a dark stain spreading high up on his left shirt sleeve, almost by his shoulder.

"You killed him—didn't you?"

"Who's that?" He whirled around, holding a knife in his right hand, his face all shiny with sweat. It was Ronnie Johnson. He couldn't see me.

"You killed Jackson Hardich."

"No!"

"You knifed him."

"No! It ain't true!"

"He made you fight him, and you stabbed him in the middle of it. I know it."

Ronnie began to move toward me, crouched. "You can't say that. You don't know nothing. Who's back there?"

"You're going to die for it too!"

Ronnie stood straight up. "No! He ain't dead!"

"He is!"

"You stop right where you are, boy!" It was Sheriff Tucker. He'd spotted Ronnie from across the street.

Ronnie took off down Sultana Street, running as fast as he could. The sheriff was right behind him.

They found him guilty. I knew that before anyone else did. Mr. Beauchamps dug Ronnie Johnson's grave while the jury was still deliberating.

As I got older, I got better at guessing whose grave we would be digging. And by the time I was in high school, I could get a sense of when Mr. Beauchamps was about to show up as well as who it was we'd have to go gravedigging for. He paid me for my help when I was in high school; he said I was doing my share of a man's work.

Bobby went off to Raleigh for college, and came back with a degree in business and a wife. Her name was Mary Sue Alders— Mary Sue Evans after she married Bobby. They got themselves a house in town, and Bobby started helping Papa with the business, supervising the clerks and keeping the inventory.

I was a loner all through high school, and the kids were happy to leave me to myself. I would watch the people in Evans, waiting; when I felt the time was right, I would go out to the old Robinson house and meet Mr. Beauchamps.

There came a time, though, when I was a senior, a month away from graduating, when he showed up at school to find me. I was out behind the gymnasium, skipping pebbles across the lagoon. He stepped out suddenly from behind one of the willow trees.

"Hello, Timothy."

I looked around to see if any of the other kids were in sight. "What are you doing here?"

He walked down to the shore, his big mud-crusted boots making the gravel crunch, stooped, picked up a stone, tossed it at the lagoon, and watched it skim the distance to the far shore. He looked pleased with himself. "Fancy that," he said, "and at my age too." He looked down at me where I was sitting. "I'll need your help tomorrow, Timothy."

I stood up, beat the dust out of my jeans, and then looked him square in the eyes. "Who's it going to be this time?"

He chuckled. "You won't guess it. I can guarantee that."

"Well, then tell me the cemetery."

"Evans. Over by the oak trees."

"Evans. That means it's somebody white." I thought for a moment. "Couldn't be. Old Mrs. Forester is the sickest one of the lot, and even she's doing better, according to Doc Morrison."

"Ain't Mrs. Forester—you're right about that."

"All right. You just wait and see. I'll have it figured out by tomorrow morning when we start."

He took his engineer's hat off and held it over his heart, like the flag was passing by, and sticking out his jaw defiantly, said, "You won't neither, Timothy Evans. I know it."

I stayed awake past midnight, going through the phone book, trying to figure out who it could be. I made lists and tore them all up. I even called the two motels in town, to see if there were any elderly visitors I had somehow not heard about. In the end, I decided to give up graciously, and wait and see who was going to die, just like any other normal person.

The next morning, Mr. Beauchamps knew I hadn't figured it out, but he didn't say anything. He was more cheerful than usual, though.

It was a good gravedigging day: the sky was a clear, bright, cloudless blue; it was warm, but not so warm as to be uncomfortable; there was the tiniest of breezes that played with the grass tops as it came blowing across the cemetery to cool us off. Mr. Beauchamps let me do most of the work. He said if I had it in me, I ought to do it—like singing a song, building a house, or dancing.

I did the best job I could, but that didn't hurry the finish of it. Mr. Beauchamps inspected the entire grave very thoroughly when we were through. He was pleased with it, and paid me twenty dollars extra—my fair share, he said. So I headed home to start the vigil that would let me know who was going to die.

Mary Sue was waiting for me when I got in. She was the only one there. She sat down and told me that Mama and Papa had been in a serious automobile accident, and that Bobby was with them now over at the Long County Hospital. She said it didn't look good for either of them.

I went numb. I should have known, I told myself. I should have tried to stop them from going out. I should have warned them. I should have prevented it somehow.

I don't remember Mary Sue driving me to the hospital. I don't remember trying to find my parents in the emergency room. I don't remember Doc Morrison trying to calm me down. I don't remember being dragged away by the orderlies to the waiting room. Mary Sue told me about it later.

I do remember the waiting room. It was ugly. The furniture was white wrought iron with cushions, and you could see the shiny metal spots where other people had worn away the paint with worry, waiting.

Bobby and Mary Sue and I had cups of coffee from a machine all night, and we hardly said to word to one another. Bobby must have smoked four packs of cigarettes. Mary Sue sat next to him with her arm around him.

It wasn't fair—knowing that one of them was going to go for sure, and not knowing which. I didn't want to choose which one I'd rather have alive, but I couldn't stop myself from choosing, over and over again. When morning came, we found out it was Mama that had survived, although she was paralyzed from the waist down. Papa had died in the operating room.

We buried him Monday morning. Bobby made me go to the funeral. I hadn't wanted to.

We buried a man I realized I never really knew—my father. As we lowered the casket into the grave I had dug, I wondered who he was, how he met my mama, whether he loved her right away when they met or whether it took time to get to know her, whether he was always good at business, whether he had ever sat up all night waiting for someone to die, whether he loved me.

I felt like a stranger to the whole world. I had spent years watching it, waiting for people to fall down like targets in a shooting gallery. And now, here I was, somehow back in it, and all the names and faces I had known were distant, mysterious and cold.

Mary Sue did her best to help. She and Bobby moved back into our house, and we put Mama up in Aunt Fannie's old room. Mary Sue and I took care of Mama—keeping her company more than anything else. We took her on walks. We went with her to the show. We sat with her in the garden, on the porch, in her room. I think she used to hate being crippled. Most of all, I think she missed Papa.

I dug up stacks of photographs Papa had taken and then hidden away in the attic, and Mama and I would spend evenings pasting them into newly bought albums.

Most of them were family picnics and Fourth of July gatherings, the lot of us scattered across the backyard, eating huge chunks of pink watermelon, lying on the grass or sitting in lawn chairs with various aunts and uncles and grandparents, before they all died.

I found a picture of myself in diapers, sitting on Grandma Larkins's lap, a blanket draped over my head while I drooled all over myself, white socks barely staying on my feet because they were too big to fit.

And there were pictures of Bobby and me. We had climbed trees together, peered around corners together, taken baths and swum in swimming pools together. There was one where we stood arm in arm, looking doubtfully at two live turkeys Papa had bought for Thanksgiving one year.

But the best pictures were of Mama. She was pretty, in a simple, open-air way. That was how Papa must have seen her. She didn't smile in most of the photographs, but rather appeared to be thoughtful, moody, elusive, quietly untamed. One photograph Papa took of her I remember particularly: she was in the kitchen, and she must have just gotten up, because her hair was mussed and she was wearing her robe that had tiny white flowers embroidered in it near the top; she stood next to an old, scarred butcher-block table with a baby bottle on it, holding her hands together, and behind her I could see an old black telephone and a couple of cartons of empty cola bottles on the floor next to the refrigerator. But she looked so regal, so stately, like she owned the world. Her mouth curled in a little smile.

Mama would tell me stories about every single picture as we put it in an album. The only drawback to this was that Papa had always been the photographer and never the subject. I only heard about him. I never saw what he was like. I could see that it was painful for Mama to talk about him, now that he was gone.

I still dug graves for Mr. Beauchamps. But my purpose was different. I waited to know when we would start to dig Mama's grave.

We never talked about the accident, or Papa's death. He never brought the subject up, and neither did I. All we ever talked about was the proper digging of graves, and he remained just as cheerful as he had ever been.

Mama and I were together by ourselves one night. I think she arranged for it to be that way.

"Timothy," she said, "you and I have to have a little talk."

"About what?"

"I think it's about time you should be getting to college."

I looked at her. She seemed a tiny woman now, and so

old—even compared to the pictures Papa had taken just before their accident. "There's plenty of time for that," I said.

"There isn't!" she snapped, like she always did when she didn't want to hear any more about it. She regretted it right away, though. "I think it's wonderful," she said, "your staying here to take care of me and all, and it's meant a lot to me. I can't say it hasn't. But you're nearly a grown man, Timothy. You've got to start living your own life, finding out what it is that you want to do, and doing it. Why, it's not right for you to keep from putting yourself to good use. You've got intelligence. You've got talents. You've got money. With those three things, there's nothing you can't do."

"But—"

"I don't want to hear any buts!" She glared at me for a few seconds, and then looked down at her hands. "Oh, I thought so careful 'bout what I wanted to say, and it isn't coming out right." She started to cry. When I tried to comfort her, she waved me away, and pulled out one of those tiny rose-embroidered old-lady handkerchiefs and dabbed at her eyes with it.

She sniffed. "I'm sorry."

"That's all right, Mama."

She tried to smile at me, which prompted another, shorter crying spell, only this time she let me hold her hand. Neither one of us said anything for a couple of minutes. Then she pulled her hand away and started fidgeting with her handkerchief.

"I had a dream," she began, not looking at me. "And in that dream, there was an old colored man, dressed in a white tuxedo with a white top hat, who came to me. He said, 'Hello, Mrs. Evans. I've come to take you for a little walk.' I started to tell him I couldn't walk, when I found myself walking already, and since there wasn't much else to say, I didn't say anything.

"He seemed like such a nice man, and he brought me to the edge of a huge plowed field. 'I'll tell you a secret, Mrs. Evans,' he said. 'That isn't a field at all. It's angels' wings.' I wanted to tell him that was a bunch of nonsense, but I looked and saw feathers, growing up out of the ground.

"Oh, Timothy, they were so beautiful! They were all different colors, like they were made out of rainbows, and they grew huge right in front of me, without hardly any time passing at all. So I turned to the man and said, 'Mister, I do believe I'd like to go out there and lie down in those feathers.' And he smiled at me—such a nice smile—and said, 'Why, of course you would. That's why we came here.'

"Then he helped me out into the field, and I found a spot I particularly liked, and sat down, and wrapped myself in feathers. They were soft and cozy. It was wonderful."

Mama took my hand and looked at me again. "When I turned around to thank the man, he wasn't there. Neither was anything else. The whole earth had kind of unfolded like, and I found myself riding on the wings of the biggest angel I ever imagined, tucked in just like a little baby, safe and sound and warm and secure. She smiled when she saw me looking at her."

Mama let go of my hand and started carefully folding her handkerchief. "That's all I remember."

"That was very pretty, Mama."

"No, it's not! Least, not in the way you're thinking. That dream meant something."

I swallowed because my mouth was dry, and asked her what.

She didn't answer me at first. She just sat there, folding and unfolding her handkerchief. The sound of crickets chirping came in through the open window. "I'm going to die, Son."

"No—"

"I am!" She waited for me to say something else, and when I didn't, she went on. "Maybe tomorrow, maybe years from now. But it's a fact. It's going to happen. And it's not your place to sit beside me while I'm going about it. That's all I'm saying."

"Maybe you're right."

"I'm right."

"Yes, ma'am."

We sat together and listened to the sounds the night was making. After an hour, a chill began to creep into the house, and I bade her good night and went to bed.

Mr. Beauchamps was waiting for me in his red rocker when I got to the Robinson house the next day. "Morning, Timothy," he said. "I'm going to need you tomorrow."

"I know." I pulled the music box out of its hiding place in the window seat and let it play. Mr. Beauchamps started to play along with it on his harmonica.

"It's Mama's grave—isn't it?"

"I never tell who I'm digging for," he said, picking up the melody again when he finished talking.

I let the tune run out. "What if we don't dig it?"

"We have to dig it," he said.

"Well, what if we don't?"

He stopped rocking. "Timothy Evans, I swear to you, I won't never pass up a grave that needs digging."

"Oh."

"You going to be there?"

I looked at him. "Yeah, I'll be there."

"I thought you would." He started rocking again, and played a new song on his harmonica. The notes lingered in the air long after he disappeared.

I met him in the morning, just like always. It was a cold day, and the oaks waved their fire-colored autumn leaves at us, mocking. We still had no problem working up a sweat as we dug, though.

Mr. Beauchamps was more given to humming than to conversation. He hardly said a word to me all day, or I to him. For lunch, we sat huddled over his picnic basket like a couple of scavengers; the wind was too brisk to lay out the tablecloth and take our time.

Still, even with a short meal, it was a long day of hard work that sank into tones of gray as the afternoon wore on. The sky was black, colorless and unrelieved. The dirt stuck to itself, almost like clay, and it was hard to break up.

We finished. I climbed out first, and Mr. Beauchamps went on his usual inspection tour. Then he walked over to the pickax, stood on it, and started to pull himself out.

I swung the shovel for all I was worth. It sliced into his skull as if it were slicing into a piece of clay, sounding much the same, and then stuck there. I tugged on it—once, twice, and a third time before it came loose, and Mr. Beauchamps tumbled back into the grave. As he lay there, blood pooling around his head in a red halo, he slowly smiled.

I shivered. The chill of the day penetrated me all at once, turning my insides to ice, squeezing all the breath out of me, choking me. I dropped to my knees, then to my hands, and let the shovel slip from my grasp into the open grave.

Slowly, quietly, tiny clods of dirt, on their own, began rolling down the graveside pile of earth. They trickled over the edge of the grave in twos and threes at first, sounding like summer hail as they hit bottom, or bounced off Mr. Beauchamps's body. They gathered numbers and strength and speed rapidly, forming a brown waterfall that covered him, and filled the air with growing thunder, until the heavens roared with it, and the ground shook with it, and I thought I would burst. I pressed my hands to my head and rocked back on my heels, dizzy.

Then there was quiet. Abruptly. I opened my eyes to see the pieces of sod slowly crawl off the canvas, like big green caterpillars, moving back to the spots where they belonged, settling in and weaving their edges together where we had cut them. A cold wind came up, whipping through the trees behind me and cutting through the wings of Great-Great-Grandpa Evans's stone angel, who stood a little ways off, aloof and praying.

I folded up the canvas, collected the two-by-fours, threw them into the wheelbarrow, hid them all in among the oak trees, and left.

Doc Morrison's car was parked outside our house when I got home, a silhouette in the gray shades of evening against our whitewashed front porch. I waited for him to come out and drive away before I went in.

I found Bobby and Mary Sue at the kitchen table, drinking coffee, Bobby's cigarette in the ashtray in front of him sending a long plume of smoke straight up until it curled away two feet over their heads. The fluorescent light made their faces pale, and Mary Sue looked like she'd been crying. They both stood up when I walked in, helplessly rooted in place for a moment. Then Mary Sue darted to the stove and poured me a cup of coffee.

"What happened?" I asked, cradling the coffee's warmth in my hands, trying to rid myself of the chill that had followed me inside. I left my jacket on.

Bobby realized he was staring at me; he sat down, reached for his cigarette with one hand, and rested his forehead in the other.

"Your mother had a stroke," Mary Sue said, sitting down again and putting her arm around Bobby's shoulder.

I wanted to shiver—out of hope, out of fear, hardly daring to give in to one, lest the other should overcome me. Still holding the cup, I pulled a chair out with my foot and sat down, not bothering to scoot up to the table. "Is she going to be all right?"

Bobby took a final drag on his cigarette, sucked the smoke in deep, and then blew it out in a cloud of frustration. "She's paralyzed," he said. "Doc Morrison says by all rights she should have died."

Nobody spoke for a moment. We didn't look at each other either. "Then she's alive," I said, trying to hide my smile.

"She can't move," Bobby said. "She can't feed herself, she can't sit up, she can't move her arms or her hands, she can't talk. She's alive, all right, if you can call it that." He left the room. Mary Sue and I watched him go, watched the kitchen door swing slowly shut, listened to his footsteps pad down the hall and up the stairs to their bedroom. Mary Sue crushed out his still-burning cigarette.

"The doctor says it's still too early to tell the extent of the damage," she said. "Your mother could get better. She might recover the use of her arms, at least partially. He said she might learn to talk again. He wasn't sure her condition would be permanent. He'll call for a specialist Monday morning. We're supposed to bring her to the hospital then—"

"If she survives, you mean. He's waiting for her to die."

Mary Sue stared at the palms of her hands. "Yes," she said. "That seems to be just about the size of it." She looked up at me. "I'm sorry, Timothy. If you'd been here when the doctor came and heard what he'd said, maybe you'd think differently. As it is, just right now, she might as well stay home. There's nothing they can do for her at the hospital."

"Until Monday?"

"Until Monday."

"Well, she's not going to die," I said, the sweat trickling down under my arms, beading on my forehead.

"You don't know that, Timothy—"

"I do."

"But you can't—"

"I *know*," I said, staring her full in the face. Her eyes were brown, like Bobby's. It was something I had never noticed before. "She won't die." I dropped my gaze and sipped at my coffee. The table seemed miles away.

Mary Sue sighed, sat back, and ran her fingers through her hair. "All right then. You know. More than me, more than your brother, more than the doctor. More than anybody. She won't die." She stood up, and her chair scraped across the floor the way Bobby's did. "I wish I wanted you to be right." With that she left.

I was so excited I could hardly contain myself. Mama was alive! She had made it! She would get better. We would bring her doctors, nurses, medicine—whatever she needed. It was only a matter of time before she got better. That was all. I drained my coffee cup and headed upstairs.

Mama's room was warm, and filled with a pale rosy glow from the nightlight—a frosted white hurricane lamp with pink flowers painted on it. Mama was asleep, so I contented myself with standing next to her bed, jacket draped over one shoulder, and watching her breathe. I had to stand still and observe carefully to do it. But the faint indications were there.

As I moved to leave and close the door behind me, I thought I noticed movement in the shadows on the far side of the bed. I froze. "No," I whispered at the darkness. "I won't do it." I flipped on the light switch, half expecting to see Mr. Beauchamps. But there was nothing. Only Mama's thin, wasted form, captured by the bedsheets and the quilt. Her eyes came open, staring at the ceiling first, then turning her head, slowly, searching for me, finding me. I turned out the light and knelt by her bed, my head close to hers.

"I will not dig your grave, Mama," I told her. "I won't do it."

But she stared at me, her green eyes pleading, unmoving. I took her limp hand in mine. "I won't. We don't know what can happen, Mama. We'll take you to the hospital Monday, and there'll be doctors, and special equipment, and medicine. We'll fix you, Mama. We'll make you better, and you'll talk and write and maybe even walk again. Who knows? But you're not going to die, Mama—we've got that on our side."

There wasn't anything else I could say, or any way Mama could answer, so I tucked her in again, and went to bed. I dreamed about her green eyes staring, and about the cold all night.

In the morning I woke to find Mr. Beauchamps's pickax and shovel in my room, propped against the wall next to my bed. They were wet with dew. I wiped them off with my bed sheets, so they wouldn't rust, and put them away in the garage.

Long County Hospital did what it could for Mama, reluctantly. For the two months she was there, I visited her during the days, sometimes with Bobby, sometimes with Mary Sue, most often by myself.

I would read to her—newspapers, poetry I knew she liked, Bible passages. We'd prop her up so she could see what I was reading, and follow along with me. She wouldn't, though. On good days, her green eyes would watch me wherever I went in the room; on bad days, she would just stare at nothing.

It was the same routine after we brought her home, once Doc Morrison and the hospital made it clear there was nothing that could be done for Mama, even if they had wanted to. We put her back in Aunt Fannie's room, hired a live-in nurse, bought a whirlpool bath, rented all sorts of fancy monitoring equipment—anything the experts asked for. Christmas came and went.

And the dance with Mr. Beauchamps's digging tools began to be an odd diversion, a game that wouldn't stop.

I was frightened of them at first, not sure if something worse was waiting to happen. No matter where I hid them, they would show up in my room mornings, always in the same spot, damp, but no dirt, no rust.

The novelty of it took over after the fear wore off. It was like having my own rabbit in a hat. I would hide them further and further away, or make it harder, to see if the trick would still work. I started in the garage at first; locked, chained, bolted, encased in cement out back. From there I went to the graveyards. And the Robinson house. The marsh. Long City, when I had the excuse to go.

I nearly got in trouble when I left them at the store—Bo Potter bought the pickax, and it vanished from his shed during the night. Bobby replaced it without saying anything, and I couldn't figure why. I couldn't ask, either. That was another game: discovery, hoping and fearing Mary Sue, Bobby, or Althea—Mama's nurse, Mammy Walker's girl who trained for medicine instead of midwifing, like Mammy—would find out. I tried to imagine what they would do if they knew.

Once the specialists started coming to our house to see Mama, after the first of the year, I let the pickax and shovel stay in my room on hooks. The playing got weary, tedious, losing its edge with each new prospect for Mama's recovery.

They all seemed cut from the same mold, the specialists—gray-suited, bald, bespectacled; embarrassed smiles on all their faces. They came to us from New York, Washington, Chicago, Los Angeles, more out of curiosity to see Mama like she was some kind of freak than because they thought she could be helped. They examined her, consulted, and we waited. She didn't get any better.

I kept reading to her anyway. I didn't feel it was as much a matter of hope as it was a matter of time.

Bobby and Mary Sue adjusted rather quickly to Mama being home. They would help me with the reading, and Mary Sue and Althea worked as a team to take care of Mama—giving her baths, preparing her food, keeping records. Bobby took me with him to the store to teach me the business, which was fine as far as I was concerned; I was through with gravedigging, and willing to help out running things.

The situation lasted until February, when Bobby said he was tired of all the gloom and doom hanging over our heads, and he and Mary Sue started going out on the weekends. I stayed home with Mama.

Which was why Mary Sue asked me to help with a surprise birthday party for Bobby—she said she thought it would do us all some good to have regular people over at the house. I was hesitant at first, but she kept at it until I agreed to help.

My part in the plan was to take Bobby over to the county seat—to file some tax papers, ostensibly—and stall him while we were there. We weren't supposed to get home until eight o'clock. I called over to Jameson's Garage in Long City ahead of time and let them know what was going on, so when the car wouldn't start from the distributor cap being jimmied, they wouldn't give me away. They timed it just right, holding back from fixing the car until seven-thirty. None of them could tell me how the shovel and the pickax got in the back seat; they acted like it was somebody else's joke.

I raced home. After the first five minutes at eighty miles an hour, Bobby stopped asking me why. He just buckled the seat belts and wedged himself in the corner against the door and the seat, one arm over the top of the front seat, the other braced against the dash.

We first heard the sirens when we passed the Evans city limits. I screeched the car to a stop outside the circle of fire trucks, and it was plain to see the firemen were fighting a losing battle against the burning house. Our burning house.

Bobby tried to run inside, but that wasn't what held my attention. Rather, it was the bank of ambulances parked along the drive, one or two of them pulling away as we pulled up. There were burnt and charred bodies being loaded up and down the line, and moans filling the air above the roar of the fire and spitting of the hoses. I began opening the back doors of the ambulances nearest me, reeling in the sweet stench of cooked flesh that boiled out every time. They were all alive.

I found her in the fifth car. Mama had been burned beyond recognition, except for a single, lidless green eye that turned toward me.

I slammed the door shut, screaming, stumbling away. A pair of attendants carrying a squirming body on a litter ran past me. The world began to spin, and I could feel the heat from the fire reach for me, even as I heard the sound of the explosion.

I knew what I had to do. I grabbed the pickax and the shovel and ran for Evans Cemetery, as fast as I could, the moon lighting my way as I rushed across the open fields, trying to leave behind me the sounds of the fire, the smell of burning people.

I found the wheelbarrow where I left it, rolled it to the first spot, measured out a rectangle with my two-by-fours, and started digging. I wept until I couldn't see through my swollen eyelids, cursed and screamed until I was hoarse, swung the pickax at the defenseless earth with a vengeance until I was barely able to lift it, and the moon glared down at me like Mama's eye, lighting everything I did. When I finished the grave, I sat for a minute at the bottom, panting.

It was still night.

I picked up my boards and laid out the dimensions of the next grave. It went so much slower than the first, and now I began to regret killing Mr. Beauchamps, not out of guilt, but because I could have used his help.

The digging became painful; even in the moonlight I could see the bruises and cuts on my hands. My feet hurt. My back ached from the strain. I thought of Mr. Beauchamps digging graves even after he reached ninety, going slow and steady, and that gave me hope to go on.

I finally finished the second grave. I was barely able to crawl out. As I lay there, exhausted, I suddenly realized I had been listening to music. -

It took me a minute to recognize the tune: Chopin's *Nocturne*, played on the silvery, tinkling tones of Aunt Fannie's music box.

And then I realized it was still night, and I was still looking at a scene illuminated by moonlight. I rolled over.

He was sitting on the shoulder of the old stone angel, dressed in a white tuxedo instead of his blue and white striped overalls, and his engineer's hat was replaced by a white silk top hat. "Hello, Timothy," he said. The music box sat in his lap, its lid open.

"Hello, Mr. Beauchamps," I croaked back.

"Save your strength," he said, pushing off from his perch and slowly floating to the ground. "You've got a lot of work ahead of you tonight."

"The moon—"

"Never you mind about the moon! I'm doing my part, and you do yours—there are lots of graves to dig before morning gets here. You can rest a little before you get started on the next one, though."

So I rested to Chopin. And dug to Mozart, Beethoven, and Brahms. Grave after grave, until the pain, the remorse, the revulsion drained away; and there was nothing left but the sound of the shovel, the shadows dancing with the moonlight that poured down from the sky, the crisp, brittle notes of the music box, and the gentle encouragement of Mr. Beauchamps. The sun came up as I finished digging the twenty-seventh grave.

There is no one left to get close to anymore. Except for Mr. Beauchamps. In addition to bringing me lunch when I'm working, he always comes by on special occasions—the anniversary of our meeting, my birthday, his birthday, the day I passed his gravedigging total of 743—and that was well over a decade ago.

I am ninety-six years old now, and have buried 915 people—my brother, my sister-in-law, my cousin, my nieces and nephews, the sheriff, the doctor, the black folk who lived down in the Quarters, the white folk who used to work for the Evans family business; people I never knew, or met, or even heard of. As I dug every one of their graves, I wondered who they all were, where they came from, and I was glad to give them their deaths, to help them step into the next Kingdom. But I am tired. I have been tired since the night I dug twenty-seven graves.

When there's a nice day and I don't have to go digging, I put flowers on Mama's grave, or on Mr. Beauchamps's. He was the first black man ever to be buried in Evans Cemetery, even if no one else knows about it.

And I keep hoping the next grave I dig will be my own.

All Vows

by
Esther M. Friesner

Esther M. Friesner's first sale was to Isaac Asimov's Science
Fiction Magazine *in 1982; she's subsequently become a regular
contributor, as well as selling frequently to* The Magazine of
Fantasy and Science Fiction, Amazing, Pulphouse, *and elsewhere.
Since 1982 she's also become one of the most prolific of modern
fantasists, with thirteen novels in print, and has established herself
as one of the funniest writers to enter the field in some while. Her
many novels include* Mustapha and His Wise Dog, Elf Defense,
Druid's Blood, Sphinxes Wild, Here Be Demons, Demon Blues,
Hooray for Hellywood, Broadway Banshee, Ragnarok and Roll,
and The Water King's Daughter. *She's reported to be at work on
her first hard science fiction novel. She lives with her family in
Madison, Connecticut.*

*In the poignant story that follows, a sharp change of pace from
her usual funny stuff, and a finalist for the Nebula Award last year,
she offers us a haunting and powerful look at the hardships that
sometimes must be faced if you want to live up to your promises,
no matter* what *obstacles may be in the way . . .*

* * *

I'm cold. I wish it'd stop raining. Granny Teeth never comes when
it rains, and I like her, even if Sammy don't.

"What you want any ol' gook ghost-lady to come hanging
'round bothering us?" he asks. Then he smiles at me. I think
maybe he likes her, too. Some. Even if the only reason why he
likes her's 'cause she keeps me quiet. That's important, keeping
quiet, for a kid.

When we're warm, when we're places out of the rain, that's
when she comes. Other people don't see her, and Sammy . . . I
dunno if he sees her or if he just says he does, for me. Times
Sammy gets enough money together to buy the two of us a couple
of hamburgers at McDonald's, that's funny, then. We go in, see,

and Granny Teeth, she comes in after. Sammy says what we want and puts down the money, all crinkly and dirty like it gets. Times we go in, ain't hardly nobody there 'cept us and the people behind the counter. They act like they're half asleep most times, seeing nothing, almost. Sometimes Sammy's gotta shout and shout to get our order heard, and even then . . .

While the girl's got her back to us—getting our burgers, I guess—Sammy talks to me. He don't say boo to Granny Teeth, though. Could be he don't see her; could be it's a game. I dunno. Sammy, he plays games with me. Anyway, this game he turns away from the counter and Granny Teeth shuffles around him real careful, then she just floats up over the counter and down behind it. Ghosts can do that. Ain't no place ghosts can't go. Sammy, he don't look, but I see what she does. She grabs us a bag, stuffs it full of burgers, fries, two chocolate shakes, what we wanted, shoves it over the counter at us and takes our money real fast. "Have a nice day!" she says, and her teeth flash gray and gold.

One time I looked back. She swapped our money for her own. I know, even if I never seen her do it. I saw the girl back of the counter pick up what should've been Sammy's money, only all it was was a bunch of brown, dry, dead leaves. Granny Teeth was just standing there, watching the girl, looking all upset. Maybe 'cause the girl's gawping at them leaves, I dunno. Sammy says gooks got fifteen thousand different ways you can insult 'em, and something mean to do back at you for every one of them insults. I hope the girl didn't get in no trouble with Granny Teeth, insulting her dead leaf money. I guess when you're a ghost, money don't matter. I wish Uncle John knew that.

I wish Sammy'd buy me a Happy Meal sometime. I never had one of them. But I don't like asking Sammy for more than he gives me straight out, on account of he'd give me what I asked for and go without himself. So I don't ask. Already he give me more than Uncle John ever did, and I never give him even my last name.

I give that to Granny Teeth, though. I give her my name; hers, too. Sammy tells me, "Corey, thing about these gooks is, see, that they got some names no way a kid like you could pronounce. What are you—six?—seven?"

I won't tell. You tell *one* thing, you start telling all of 'em. Anything you say maybe gets back to someone else. Maybe the police, and then I know what *that* means: They'd take me back.

I'm not going back. I'm going to Washington, D.C., with Sammy, and Granny Teeth, and after we get there and see what Sammy says he's got to see, then I'll try to get him to let me stay with him forever.

If he says no, I'll run away again. I can. I got to. If you can't go back, you got to run away.

It's safe to tell Granny Teeth, though, seeing as how she's a ghost. I talk to her; Sammy don't. You got to name what you talk to, else it's not real. She has these gold teeth, see? Two gold teeth right where a vampire's got fangs, only she ain't no vampire. I call her Granny Teeth, and she smiles.

It's raining now. Seems sometimes like it's been raining forever, the black over me, and the wet, and the cold. We found us a place to sleep 'long by an old road that used to be a pretty important highway. Used to be, people'd stop here. Lotta things used to be. Sammy, he's got us a fire burning in this old oil drum was a trash barrel, but there ain't nowheres near anything like a solid roof over our heads; just only trees. Picnic tables, too; most too bust up to lie under so it'd do any good, though.

Sammy looks up into the rain. He got brown hair color of the dirt back home and green eyes pale as a peeled twig. He smiles up to heaven and his teeth run shining with the falling water.

"This it, Lord?" He's laughing when he talks, so easy with his god. "*This* the thanks a man earns from you for trying to keep a promise?" He taps his wrist like he's got a watch there. He ain't got a wristwatch since I know him, since that night I come on him out of the trees and there he was, like he's waiting for me.

"You can't tell me You don't know what day it is, Lord," he says. "And that means You know what day's coming. When I heard that last blast, I got on the road right away, but ten days isn't all that much when you're going so far on foot. Now listen: I don't have all that much money; I never did. Anybody wants to tell you any lies about how us Jews got all the money in the world, you send them around to have a word with Sammy Nachman. I'll set 'em straight, You bet. If I had the bread, I'd be sitting in some nice, warm Amtrak train, drinking a cold beer. But it's all on foot, all the way, and the kid—" He looks at me and I don't know what to do with the good feeling it gives me "—the kid can't march as fast as me. So whaddaya say, Lord? You do Your part, I'll do mine. Ease up on the rain, okay? Save it for spring."

I look up at the same spot in the sky I see Sammy do. Nothing but clouds, nothing but rain. I never knowed the Jews to pray like he does, out loud, talking so anyone can understand. I hope his god don't mind English. I thought it was against the rules or something for a praying Jew to talk like that to his god. We need Sammy's god to listen to him now. I'd ask mine, only Jesus don't listen to all the lies a dumbass little kid makes up to tell. Jesus hates liars; he burns 'em in Hell. Anybody knows that. I didn't need Uncle John to tell me something I knew. I don't take off Jesus no more; just only Sammy.

Granny Teeth got her a god? A ghost-god? I wonder. She comes back, I'll ask.

Sammy asked real good. The rain stopped that night, while we lay wrapped up in our old green blankets on the ground by the picnic tables. I brushed the hair out of my eyes, first up. It's pretty cold, and the little bit of grass I see's got frost. Sammy says he could always sleep through anything, even in 'Nam. Home, I got used to waking the minute I hear any noise. Nothing sneaks up on you that way. It's safer.

So I wake now; and the first thing I see is Granny Teeth's feet next to my face. She's sitting on one of them bust-up tables. Ghosts don't mind splinters or the cold. Her toes are curled up, brown and round like a row of acorns. She goes barefoot—what's a ghost got to worry over about where she steps, anyhow?—and her toenails are thick and yellow and gray.

"'Morning, Granny Teeth," I say. I'm glad she's back.

"Good morning, Corey." I like how she bows her head to me—not much, only a little. It makes me feel grown up and worth something. "Does it go well with you and this man?" she asks.

"Could be better." I smile to let her know I'm joking. Ghosts, they're monster kin. It don't do to get 'em mad. I remember how

Granny Teeth looked the time I told her just a bit about Uncle John and how it was. I thought her eyes'd take fire, burn me right up then and there.

"Better? How? You are hungry?" She's wearing an old brown robe, loose, but she's got a cracked blue plastic pockabook hanging off her neck. It snicks open and she roots through it. "You need money, you and Sammy?"

Money? From Granny Teeth? Ghost money. Dead leaves. She scrabbles in that old pockabook of hers, I can hear 'em rustling. I don't laugh, because of what I said about ghosts getting mad. I don't laugh, but I know how it makes me feel full of bubbles inside, holding in the laughter. It feels good, holding in laughter, knowing laughter's all that's in there to hold.

"We be okay, Granny Teeth," I tell her. I know how to talk respectful. I got taught that much, didn't I? Hard taught. "You keep your money." *Your dried-up old dead leaf ghost money.* "Thanks anyhow."

I smile, 'cause it just tickles so to think I'm please-and-thanking this ol' gook-lady ghost for offering us them leaves she totes 'round and swaps for the real dollars we plunk down every time Sammy and me buy food. I smile big—can't help but—and that feels good, too. More right-feeling things are coming into my life these days. I'm some surprised I recognize them after this long.

Granny Teeth clicks that cracked blue pockabook shut; her lips, too. She don't smile. Her whole face folds in at the mouth, all the wrinkles running like fishnets, like roads crisscrossing good brown country earth. "Sammy is a good man," she says, "but he does not know."

"Know what?" I ask. She shakes her head.

"You do not know either, Corey. You are too young to know."

"'Bout what? The war? I know all 'bout that," I say, proud. "Soldiers an' bombs an' fire-fights an' the jungle—bugs big as cats, rats big as dogs, I know it. Sammy told me."

Granny Teeth sighs. "Sammy is a good man," she says again. "But he can never teach you what he refuses to see for himself. He can not tell you what he will not let *himself* know." And she sits so still it's like I could reach out and scoop a piece of stillness off her, hold it in my hand. Then, any time the hollering started up, and the hitting, I could just uncup my hands, let the silence and the stillness fly high, fly free, soar up to Heaven and drip down over me, wrap me safe in the blanket of the rain.

Sudden I 'magine that was I to come close, lean in, put up my arms to her long, skinny ones like I used to do with my daddy and lay my head against the hard bones bottoming her neck, could be I'd smell the earth smell. New-turned earth, wet with the deep-running water of melted snow. Spring earth, gulping down the seed, pushing up the flowers.

My daddy once give me a little red plastic shovel, let me plant yellow tufty flowers by the big tree out behind the house come spring. After he went and let that tractor roll over on him, stupid like he done, and Uncle John come, I didn't get no more time to do more'n smell the springtime earth. No red plastic shovel any more. No yellow tufty flowers.

What'm I doing? I was only dreaming 'bout doing that, putting my arms 'round Granny Teeth, and here I *go*, catch myself doing it for real. I yelp loud and push back from her, squirming out of her arms, shaking bad. Oh Jesus, touch a ghost like that, it's cold. *Cold!* Her robe's like fuzzy brown worms all over—I *felt* them, I *did*. Worms that crawl in your skull, eat out your eyeballs when you die. Oh Jesus, I didn't mean what I said before 'bout you. Jesus, You gotta help me now, don't got no one else but You, like my daddy always did used to say. You don't burn up liars when they're only little children, You couldn't do something half so heartless, no, and anyway, no matter what Uncle John says, don't believe him, they was *his* lies, all! Jesus Lord, I'm scared, and Sammy's sleeping, and maybe his god won't pay me no mind 'cause I'm no Jew. Oh Jesus, *cold!*

"Corey!" Granny Teeth stares at me. I see by her eyes how sharp I hurt her, shouting like that, shoving her away. Lord, it wasn't *my* fault, I swear. One minute I'm just thinking 'bout how nice it'd be, smelling home earth, next I'm in her arms. . . .

Magic. Yeah, that's what. Ghosts can do magic, can't they? Witch you any old way they can?

See, I said so. Not my fault at *all*. I don't lie. I don't care what *he* said, or the way that tired-eyed skinny lady with the clipboard looked at me that time she come 'round to ask all those questions. I don't ever lie.

I don't know I'm still shaking 'til Granny Teeth lays one hand on my arm and I feel my flesh twitch and shudder in her grasp. Her face is flat and calm, like the surface of a pond. Almost I dream I'm seeing her eyes through a depth of brown, weed-scummed water. She's got kind eyes. She's not even some mad at me. Not like the *waste-my-time* clipboard lady at all.

"Corey . . ." Hearing my name soft-spoke that way makes the shakes stop. She takes away her hand from my arm. "I did not mean to frighten you. I am only here to help you and Sammy. It is difficult. There are too many walls, but I must try. It is a debt. A vow I made. Do you understand vows, child?"

I nod. Not that I *do* understand or anything, not really. Vows are for when you get married. Who'd marry a ghost, birth a bunch of ghost babies? Debts are what bills mean—too many bills, not enough money; too many mouths, not enough work got in return to make feeding 'em worth a man's while. But only live folks got debts to pay and money to pay 'em. What's she mean to do? Count out stacks of dead leaves into Sammy's hand?

Granny Teeth got the gentlest smile I ever see, even if it does always look half sad. "You are a good boy, Corey." Her hand's cool, full of the spring-earth smell cupped in the palm. "You will help me pay out what I owe Sammy, and there will be enough left to repay all that is owed you, too."

Owed me? What's owed me? 'Cept the farm, and the earth, and I'm not going back for *that*. Uncle John wanted it so bad, let him keep it. Maybe my daddy'd should've left it to *him*, like he was always saying after he drunk too much. Sometimes when he didn't drink a drop. I don't want nobody owing me *nothing*. Just let me alone.

The longer Granny Teeth looks at me, the stiffer her smile gets until there's no softness left at all. Little ghosts get under my skin just looking at her. Stern, she says, "To bury such treasure! This is sin. It shall be repaid! Oh yes, this debt too." Then she's gone.

Well! Sure enough, now I *do* know what ol' Granny Teeth

meant with all her talk of debts and help and the like. Treasure! Why, sure, I heard the tales, the old ghost stories telling how the dead lead the living to riches hid deep in the walls of abandoned houses, buried at the roots of old trees.

But when it's light and I wake up Sammy to tell him what Granny Teeth's promised us, he just laughs.

"Treasure, Corey? *Her?* Tell me some ol' gook ghost got any money hidden? Sure, maybe a coupla dozen coins buried back in 'Nam, but *here?* Sorry, Champ. No way you and me're gonna go back to 'Nam to dig up that kinda treasure."

He don't say no more about it and I don't say nothing too. I think maybe Granny Teeth's gonna come looking after us, all her talk of paying, but that's the last I see of her for nights and nights.

Sammy and me, we press on. Nights, it gets lonesome. Sammy and me, we make fire, steal fire, borrow fire anyplace we can. When we take another man's fire, Sammy pays with his stories 'bout 'Nam. If they'll hear 'em. Sometimes the men we meet got too many 'Nam stories of their own and don't even want what they got to start with. Then we move on.

Finally the night comes when the dark runs out and all the sky's a light we can't ignore. No more shadow-walking. ("Folks see a raggy man like me with a kid like you, they'll ask questions, and I got no time for answers. Let's try to get there on the quiet, Corey.") There ain't no more shadows. Lights everywhere, every street, every road, and the sky ahead's holding a white dusting of light that makes the shapes of buildings burn black and shiny against my eyes.

City light. Washington, D.C., city lights. Sammy says we're almost there.

We walk in over the hard roads. Nighttime and no rain. Sometimes, beside the highways, there's trees. Days, we sleep there. I like the feel of the bark against my back, the roots twisting down deep into the earth like they're looking for something they lost. I put my ear to the trunk and dream I can hear the old tree's heartwood singing.

Soon there's big buildings, harder roads, and more houses than trees. Sammy says we're in the city itself now. We pass houses where the light inside's all warm and gold. I put out my hands to catch the sweet spill of it, like it was magic that could warm me. Oh, it's cold out here! I stare at the windows, slabs of shining light thick enough to be tombstones, holding back the warm, keeping it away from me. I can't hardly recall how it used to feel, being on the right side of windows, and a roof above, and someone to give me a way to keep warm without a fire to sear my skin.

I look at my arm. The old marks' still there. Little round red blisters all up and down the inside of both my arms from the cigarettes. Some come fat, some come thin. Uncle John rolled his own. *Be a man, Corey! Christ knows, you eat enough for a man!*

I can still smell the soured beer hot on his breath. The sizzle of my own skin clogs my ears so much, sometimes I miss hearing anything else. So, when I try, why can't I remember more than the sweet spring earth smells, and the little red shovel, and the tufty yellow flowers by my eyes? Where's my mama's face? Where's my daddy's arms to keep me safe, the way he promised when she died? But all I got to wrap 'round me in the dark is Sammy's old green blanket, and that smells burnt some too.

Comes the night we don't got to steal fire no more. There's steam grates to lie on, and that feels nice. The other folk, the ones who tell us to shove over, we got their spot and they'll fight us for it maybe, Sammy knows what to say to 'em:

"Look, I got a kid here." And they kinda blink their eyes and tilt their heads like sorry old birds to stare at me. But they move over and they let us rest.

This is the night we'll go there. Where's there? I don't know. Only Sammy said it like it was the most important thing in the world, *there*. He puts all the weight of his heart behind a word, you know it's important, even if you don't know nothing else, nor need to be asking.

"Soon as it's dark, Corey," he says. "We're gonna go there. I'm gonna sleep some now, you stand guard, okay? Sentry duty. You can sleep tonight, while I do what I came here to do."

"I don't wanna sleep then," I tell him. "I wanna help you do it."

He smiles at me, and when he reaches out his hand to touch my cheek I don't flinch back. Funny. His hand's hard, got a bitter, sad smell to it, but under the shell there's a kindness makes it softer than anything in my memories. "You don't even know what I'm here to do," he says.

"I don't care," I tell him.

"Yeah, I guess you don't." His smile gets some brighter, and it's so sweet to feel a hand on me that don't got any pain behind it. "Okay, then. But I bet you're gonna be all confused. See, there's a vow I've got to keep—"

"A vow! You getting married, Sammy?" It's the first I hear of it, and my stomach goes to knots.

"Marri—? Nah, not *that* kind of vow, kid!" He laughs, and I can share it with him. "A vow's a *promise*, is all. Just let me do what I gotta, you keep quiet. If you get bored waiting, find something to do with yourself, no questions until after, then I'll explain, deal?"

"Deal." I nod. I'm good at keeping quiet. And a vow's a promise; now I know.

"Okay," he says again, curling up like a fat ol' caterpillar in his green blanket. "Wake me when it's sundown."

While he sleeps, I watch the people. They don't see us. We're camping on a steam grate up against one of the big buildings here. There's plenty of bushes for cover. Sammy told me all 'bout how that's important, cover. There's all kindsa ways a man can hide, he said, and sometimes knowing when to hide will save you. I knew that already; I just wasn't so good at it. I sit real still on guard over Sammy. I find this big branch and I pretend we're in 'Nam together, and I got a gun in my hands. Nobody better try to mess with me now. He tries, I'll shoot him dead.

I watch the feet of the people passing by, see 'em through the roots and low branches of the bushes. It's boring all right, but I stay true to my promise. My *vow*. Now I got me a vow to keep too, like Granny Teeth, like Sammy. I start off pretending that I'm all there is to stand between him and them who'd stop him from keeping his vow, and I end by believing it's truly so. Like a little nothing kid like me could really do anything to keep off danger! Like I got any kinda power in me at all, that's *so* funny! That's so funny, I forget to laugh.

Then she's there. One minute I'm watching these feet going by, counting the high heels and the polished fancy shoes and the cool high-tops, and then being surprised 'cause there's this one pair of scruffy ol' blue bedroom slippers hustling past, and then all of a sudden the scruffy blue slippers turn the corner of the bushes and come right on in, and it's Granny Teeth herself.

Why's she want to come here like this, in daylight? I thought ghosts don't like the day. Maybe that's just evil ghosts as fear the light. I don't know too much, I guess.

"Corey, does it go well with you and this man?" she asks, like always.

"We're doin' good, Granny Teeth," I tell her. "We're almost there. Tonight's when we're gonna do it."

Granny Teeth nods. "His vow. He told my daughter of it many times. I often saw them sitting together, speaking. She told me he was a man who carried the burden of many ghosts, although he was guilty of none of their blood. To carry a ghost's weight is a heavy thing, child. No wise man does it willingly. It is done when it can not be helped, for guilt. But sometimes it is done for love."

"Sammy love your daughter?" I ask. Could be he *is* getting married. My stomach hurts around that.

She shakes her head this time. "His promise was made to *all* my family, not just to her alone. No one believed him but me. We were his friends; he told us he would be our shield. That vow was kept. When the soldiers left our village but came back later, running, frightened, all the eyes of the jungle burning cold into their backs, acting as if they did not remember who we were, friend or foe, he was the only one who stood between us and them—them, his own people!—so that we could flee their fear, the fear that killed first without asking, without thought, without—"

Granny Teeth sighs away the rest. "He did not love my daughter as you would think, child. But yes, he did love her."

I'm confused. "How come you say, no, he didn't love her, then, yes, he did?"

She squats down flatfooted so's we're eye to eye, and the shiny black of her eyes holds me so still I 'most forget to breathe.

"Because, Corey, in this world there are as many loves as ghosts, and as many vows as loves." Then she's gone.

When it starts to get dark, I wake Sammy. I'd been thinking on what Granny Teeth said and I still couldn't make heads or tails of it, so I decide it wasn't worth more trouble. Still, I have to ask:

"Sammy, what's this vow of yours you're gonna keep?"

He just says, "You'll see," and he stows his blanket and picks up his pack and takes my hand warm in his.

It wasn't far we had to go. Just a couple city blocks, and into some trees and out again. The moon wasn't up yet that I could see. There's this long stretch of flat ground, and a big lawn all crisp with frosted grass. Sammy says, "Sure did get cold early this year." I been feeling cold so long, it don't make much difference to me, but it seems like it matters to him, so I agree.

There's some signs. There's a pretty domed building near our end of the lawn, lit up white. There's this metal thing like a one-legged table, like the place where the preacher stands up in church and rests his Bible when he gives the sermon. Sammy goes over to it, and I see how weird it is, because instead of being a place you can rest a book on top of, there's this big fat book *underneath* the glassy top, see, and Sammy has to reach under to turn the pages. The book's chained down. Why'd anyone want to chain a book?

I guess Sammy was right 'bout me getting bored. I watch him turn the pages awhile, but he goes so *slow*. I look around some more. There's some people strolling in the dusk, but they walk right by us 'cause we're so raggedy-looking. Sammy says being poor's next best to being invisible. I look back at Sammy and I see there's some drops of wet starred out on the glass. I hope it don't start to rain again for real until we're done.

Sammy stands up straight, holding on to the edges of the glassed-in book like he's gonna preach a text. He even cries out, "Oh Lord!" like he's moved by the Spirit. But I remember he's a Jew, and I don't think they do it like that. His hands look mighty white, especially where they're grabbing hold. You can almost see the metal edges and the glass cutting through. I feel my whole chest get tight with fear so's it starts a black burning. I'm afraid.

When he lets go, I can draw breath again. He don't say 'nother word to me, just jerks his head so I know I'm to follow. We walk to this statue of three soldiers. That's where he lays down his pack and takes out a funny little thing, like a ladies' pockabook, almost, only it's flatter and smaller and it don't got a strap. It's white with blue stripes, 'cept it's so dirty the white part's just a guess. Sammy unzips it and takes out a book and a shawl.

He puts the shawl on his head. It's clean enough so's you can see it really is white and blue; got all these fringes at the bottom, but not all the way across. He surely does look funny with that thing draped over his head. "I lost my *yarmulke* a long time ago," he says to me, and smiles when he realizes I don't know what the hell he's talkin' about. "Never mind, Corey." The book's a clean blue and he kisses it.

There is a place in the earth and you go down into it slow. I follow Sammy, but it's like he don't see me no more. There's a sliver of black, shiny stone rising at our feet like a wave, and the farther down we go into the earth, the higher up the black stone rises. Sammy looks straight ahead, like he don't know the black wall's rising at his left hand. I follow him, and there's a scary tingling in my bones.

I look down at the gray walk at my feet because I don't want to see the wall. I tell myself *It's rock! It's just rock, what's to be afraid of? Don't be so stupid, Corey!* 'til I sound like Uncle John, so I stop. There's things on the ground propped up against the wall, bright things with some color to them besides black and gray. I see a flag, folded up so just the star part shows, all wrapped in plastic. I see fake flowers bound in little wreaths, bobbing stiff on wire stems. I see real flowers, touched with frost, lying on the stone. There's a wind that comes up and sighs down into the earth behind me, tugging at the little scraps of paper weighted down. One blows away, and something in me makes it important that I run and catch it and put it back by the wall. I can read the words, "We will always love you." Someone once said that to me.

I look up. The wall's taller now. I can just about see over the top to where the grass is growing. I can read the names in the wall, but they're just a lot of names to me. I look to where Sammy's gone

ahead, deeper into the earth, his white fringey shawl blowing on
the wind like a ghost. I wonder if he's going to go on forever, when
he stops.

"*Yit-ga-dal ve-yit-ka-dash she-mei ra-ba*—" Sammy's voice
climbs the wind and the wall and the night like a ladder of angels.
"*Be-al-ma di-ve-ra chi-re-u-tei*—" All the words he sings, they
must be the right way for a Jew to pray, 'cause I don't understand
a one. "*Ve-yam-lich mal-chu-tei be-cha-yei-chon*—" It's his *voice*
I understand. I can feel it straining for the sky, crying out, tugging
at the one tip of God's sleeve that trails down out of Heaven.
Daddy! he's crying. *Daddy, why'd you ever go away and leave me
here alone? Oh Daddy, Mama, help me, save me, I need you, don't
leave me! Mama, I'm so frightened! Daddy, I'm so cold!*

He's touching the wall down there. I shiver in my skin. Cold,
too *cold,* the black shiny stone. Even up here, where I can still see
over the top, I'm scared to get too near.

But that's Sammy down there. And now he's done with all his
wailing prayer. He's looking up here, smiling for me, stretching
out his hand. I look over the top of the wall at the grass, all
cold-killed and withered. If I look hard, I think I see what's left of
living flowers. I look back at Sammy, and then I run into his arms.

"Just one more prayer, Corey," he says to me. He still looks
funny under that white shawl. "Just the one I promised them I'd
say tonight. Tomorrow I'll see if maybe we can't find a syna-
gogue'll let me in to say the rest of it, ask God to forgive us for all
the bad things we've done. That's what this is all about, kid, no big
mystery. My people have a special day for telling God we're sorry,
that's all. I bet you understand about that, huh? Saying you're
sorry, being told it's all right."

I understand. All except the part where you get told it's all right.
I understand saying I'm sorry without knowing what I done,
getting told sorry ain't enough. Getting *worse* than told, even
while I'm screaming out I'm sorry, I'm sorry, I'm sorry. . . .

"But see," Sammy's saying. "See, when there's people you care
about, people you've loved, and they can't stand up for themselves
tonight, you've got to stand up for them. Anyhow, I promised
them I would, back in 'Nam. This is a good night to keep

promises. It's not just my sins I'm carrying tonight, but theirs. That's what we believe, that no man stands alone before God, that all of us carry our sins and our salvation."

He laughs. "Listen to me! Bugging a kid your age with words like *salvation*, when you probably don't know what I'm talking about."

I look at him very steady. "Jesus is my salvation," I say.

Sammy hugs me tight. "Good for you, kid. Good for you."

Then he's on his feet again and the words are pouring out. The singing's different, sadder than before: pleading, but not like a whipped dog's eyes beg you not to hit him any more. More like knowing you've hurt the one person you love best in all the world and you want to make it be all right again. Like all the pain for what you've done wrong is pain you've given away.

"Kol ni-dre ve-e-so-re, va-cha-ro-me, v'-ko-no-me. . . ." It's just Sammy and the wall. And the song. And maybe God.

I turn away. We're deep into the earth now, the wall's above my head. There's light behind us, cutting all the names so deep it's like the letters are a blacker black than the wall that's frozen 'round them. If I bring my nose up close to the stone, I can see that the black ain't all black. There's little flecks of light caught there, gold and silver, like it snowed stars.

Black. Black and shiny over me. Black and shiny against my eyes, against my mouth, covering me, making me fight for air, fight for each last, burning breath. Black like the names are cut black, black without the shimmer or speck of a star to light my eyes. Black letters in the wall, black burning my eyes with what they say, black that's wrapping me all 'round so that I can't escape it ever, black and sharp as truth or waking:

SAMUEL NACHMAN

And out of the blackness in the words that spell out what's truly so, Granny Teeth's reaching up to take my hands. . . .

She don't talk, just leads me up the rising path. I feel the black wall falling away from me, and I smell the good smell of fresh-turned earth.

There's a man looking down at me. I'm scared, but Granny Teeth's got her hands on my shoulders and she pushes me up forward to meet him, up into the light. He's the same man I seen riding 'round town with Sheriff Randolph; deputy somebody, but I don't know his name.

Why's he looking at me like that? Why's he look and say, "Dear God," and all the color leaves his face?

I hear a voice I never want to hear no more. I hear Uncle John, shouting like he always does, shouting and stomping around and hollering, "I don't give a damn what kinda warrant you got, you get the hell off my land before I—"

Then he sees me, too, and all the color that left the deputy's face seems to want to flood into his. I try to pull back, but Granny Teeth won't let me. Maybe she won't let Uncle John hurt me no more neither. I try to face him and be brave.

But it's so hard, having to look at Uncle John again, seeing the deputy's face go hard as stone, watching him turn and crack Uncle John across the jaw like Uncle John once did to me. Uncle John falls down and puts his hands on his face. Jesus, don't let him lay the blame for this on me too!

Granny Teeth's whispering in my ear so soft I can hear the gold in her mouth go *tappa-tap*. "This day all vows are fulfilled," she tells me. "This day all debts are paid." And she makes me go stand beside the deputy, over Uncle John, and beside Sheriff Randolph, who's just come out of our house. He don't look too strong either, for such a big man.

Deputy says, "Under the oak tree. Just like she told us. He had him wrapped up in a plastic garbage bag. Like he was trash. Just like that poor little boy wasn't nothing but trash!" Then: "He tripped," meaning Uncle John. I ain't gonna be the one to call it a lie. He's smiling like he's done something good, even if he got no real joy from it.

But Sheriff Randolph says, "You know the woman who called to tell us 'bout—" He don't say what, just jerks his head. I turn in spite of Granny Teeth holding me still and see he's nodding at our old oak. Someone's been messing 'round, digging up by the roots. The smell of home earth blankets me moist and cool.

"Yeah, from New York, that old Vietnamese lady, Mrs. Tran," the deputy says. "I couldn't hardly understand her."

"I don't wonder." The sheriff takes off his hat, wipes his forehead with the back of his hand. "I just called back to tell her what we found. I got her daughter on the line. Mrs. Tran's been six months comatose in the hospital."

"Yeah, but today—"

"Last night she died."

Who died? Who they mean died? I turn around real sharp, but all I see in front of me's the wall. I put out my hands to hold it back, but it rears up above my head and crashes over onto me. I cry out when I feel the blackness fall across my face again, because now I know, I really *know* what's been lies and what's so, and why the blackness won't ever let me go.

"Corey . . ."

In the dark, a voice. He's there. Sammy's there beyond the wall, reaching out his hands to me. And Granny Teeth, she's with him, holding out the edges of dead Sammy's white shawl like they was wings. First I just stare; I'm afraid of ghosts. Then I take me a deep breath and throw myself heart first against the wall, shatter it, plunge through the cold black surface to meet them. The black closes around me, but it's kept away by the circle of their arms. And wings; all around us, wings: Sammy's wings, Granny Teeth's wings, wings of glory, wings of prayer, shining white wings like the sword of God to cut away the blackness and wrap me in the warmth and the love and the light forever.